DID I KILL MY HUSBAND?

BOOKS BY AJ CAMPBELL

My Perfect Marriage

Leave Well Alone

Don't Come Looking

Search No Further

The Phone Call

The Wrong Key

Her Missing Husband

DID I KILL MY HUSBAND?

AJ CAMPBELL

bookouture

Published by Bookouture in 2024

An imprint of Storyfire Ltd.
Carmelite House
50 Victoria Embankment
London EC4Y 0DZ

www.bookouture.com

ISBN: 978-1-83525-103-4
eBook ISBN: 978-1-83525-102-7

For my sons, Billy, Edward and Josh. I am so proud of you.
Carpe Diem.

ONE

'What do you think is wrong with Michael, then?' Ted asks as he finishes his pint of lager shandy.

Christina fiddles with a branded beer mat, lifting the edge and peeling away a layer. 'I wish I knew.'

Ted covertly glances around the crowded pub before leaning across the table and whispering, 'I know a man who knows a man who could make him just disappear.' He clicks his thick fingers. 'Just like that. Problem solved.'

The dusty chandelier above the table projects a glow over his feigned evil face.

Christina slaps her brother's shoulder. Their laughter blends in with the chatter and jovial atmosphere of the pub. 'You wicked man, you.'

Ted raises his arms and readjusts his black baseball cap. The sleeves of his Iron Maiden T-shirt ride up. He's a handsome guy, a sturdy unit, muscular from his work as a builder. It's hard to believe they are twins. They have such different builds. 'Just saying.'

Picking up her handbag, Christina fishes out her car keys. 'I should get going. I told Michael and the kids I'd be back by ten. I'm half an hour late already.'

Ted grabs her arm. 'Remember what I said?'

She frowns at him.

'Life's too short to be unhappy.'

She gives him a closed-lip smile.

'I love you, sis.'

She kisses his cheek. 'I love you, too.'

After hugging her brother goodnight, Christina pushes open the heavy door of the pub. It's raining hard, the howling wind blowing her thick mass of curly hair wild. Making a mad dash for her Range Rover parked in the far corner of the car park, she curses for forgetting to bring her umbrella. But then again, the wind would have mangled it in a heartbeat.

She grasps the steering wheel with white-knuckled intensity, the beat of the wipers ineffectually slashing at the rain-battered windscreen, as she hurtles through the familiar winding country roads. Slowing to twenty miles per hour, she negotiates the treacherous surface water on the road notorious for accidents and a hairpin bend before picking up speed again to thirty. She is desperate to get home. This is not a night to be out.

The reality of her circumstances hits her. Talking about it openly with her brother has somehow given the gravity of the situation more weight. She fears that despite Ted's reassurances, there is something more terminal going on with her husband. Sadness overcomes her as she thinks of the marriage vows they exchanged. Thoughts battle for space in her mind with her brother's parting words, 'Life's too short to be unhappy.'

Her momentary lapse in concentration is met by an almighty jolt.

A resounding thud reverberating through the car comes out of left field.

Quite literally.

The deafening sound makes her gasp in panic. She slams her foot on the brake in an emergency stop.

Time pauses.

What the hell was that?

TWO

The world around her stops.

The monotone noise of the flashing indicators sounds like a drumbeat.

Christina rams on the hazard lights and sharply turns to look in the rear windscreen, her eyes wide in horror. The weather is far too bad for her to see anything.

She jabs her finger on the control button of her Apple CarPlay, currently blaring out Fleetwood Mac's 'Go Your Own Way'.

And the music stops.

The sound of incessant rain thunders on the roof of the car.

Wipers scrape the windscreen.

Panicking, she opens the car door and starts to get out. A gust of wind slams it against her, catching her foot. She tries again, pushing the door hard against the force of the relentless and violent wind.

Managing to get out, she walks to the rear of the car. Rain whips across her body, throwing her off balance. The tail lights of the car illuminate the road.

But there's nothing there.

Spinning around, she takes in the darkness, just about working out where she is along the country lane flanked by open farmland and a scattering of dwellings that leads to her house. She must have just passed the local pub, The Black Horse.

The harshness of the wind makes her eyes water. She must have hit an animal, and it has fled in fear. She hit a deer once. When she first moved to the area with her ex-husband. It was dusk, but it came out of nowhere too quickly for her to react. It made the same terrible noise. She couldn't believe her eyes when it jumped up and ran off, bouncing across the fields as if nothing had happened. The incident stayed with her for months. She felt terrible about it.

Taking several paces along the road, she stops. She peers around.

But there's nothing to be seen through the sheets of relentless rain.

She hurries back to the car, drenched and shaking. With trembling hands, she grabs her phone and finds the torch, going back to have another look behind her car. She still can't see anything. She needs to call the police. Just to make sure.

But when she gets back in the car she notices five missed calls from Abi on her phone.

Has something happened?

She calls her daughter's number. There's no answer.

She panics.

It could take the police ages to turn up. Her daughter needs her. Returning the phone to the cradle on the dashboard, she slowly begins the short distance home.

The rain persistently thrashes the windscreen. She can hardly see. The incident has unnerved her. She grips the steering wheel tighter as the car slides, aquaplaning on the surface water. She needs to get home quickly.

THREE

When she pulls up to her beautiful Georgian home – Ivy Brook – the house is in darkness. She groans with dread. Ben's car isn't on the drive. Where has he gone? She clenches her teeth. He said he was staying in tonight. How she despises Adam, her ex-husband, for buying their son a car. What would happen if Ben had been the one to hit an animal in these weather conditions? He doesn't have the experience to control the car.

Stopping at the edge of the grass verge in front of the house, she slips out of her coat and lifts it to cover her head before dashing inside. Boy, is she relieved to be home.

Silence greets her. A noiseless existence she usually welcomes, but tonight, there's something eerie about it.

The heavy quiet is broken when her faithful Irish Wolfhound regally saunters along the wooden floor towards her, his tail offering the lightest of wags. She bends down to greet him, his charcoal grey wiry fur tickling her face. 'Hello, gorgeous one. I missed you.'

She hugs the dog, riddled with guilt as he reminds her that she might have injured another animal. As she stands up, shivering from the weather that has seeped through to her core, Wilf returns to his bed that snuggles in the gap beneath the stairs.

Where's Abi? She needs to see her daughter. Kicking off her trainers, she discards her handbag in the small room to the right of the front door that she uses as a study and hangs her coat up to dry. She checks her phone. There's nothing from Ben. Damn him. He could have at least told her where he was going. And how many times has she told him to keep in contact when he is out in the car? She doesn't want to disturb him with a call, in case he is driving, so she drops him a text, asking him where he is.

At the end of the dark hallway, the familiar dim light from the TV on standby beams through the gap in the lounge door. A sight she is used to, but that doesn't make it OK. At least Michael has turned off the Christmas tree lights. They only put up the tree at the weekend. A family tradition that stems from her daughter's illness, the decorations always go up mid-November.

Christina pauses, leaning her head on the doorframe. Drops of water drip down her face.

How have they come to this? Him in there, her upstairs, their eyes meeting at the ring of the morning alarm, or the breakfast bar on the days he never even makes it to bed.

She pops her head around the door. The sour smell of alcohol hangs in the air. A bottle of bourbon sits on the coffee table beside an empty glass. She stares at the back of the sofa on which Michael is lying, under the navy blanket she bought him a couple of Christmases ago because he feels the cold on nights like these.

Christina sighs. It's nearly two years since the incident at work rocked their lives. She has tried so hard with him since. One divorce already under her belt is gut-wrenching enough. She doesn't want to face another. But Michael has changed. He was gentle and loving before and then, almost overnight, he turned as cold as the weather.

From the day they met, Michael had his career mapped out like a route planner. He'd been hankering after the deputy head position since he joined St Christopher's school. It was the stepping stone to him becoming headteacher. A goal he was on track to achieve. When the previous deputy head handed in her notice, it was generally considered by Michael's colleagues that the position would be his. Everyone at St Christopher's loves Michael, teachers, pupils and parents alike.

Then one girl ruined everything for him, and the Board of Governors passed him over for another candidate. Although Anne-Marie – the headteacher and a close friend of Christina's – reassured Michael it didn't come into it, Christina believes the board didn't want a candidate taking the role with the kind of scandal behind them that Michael carried, guilty or not guilty. St Christopher's reputation cannot be tainted in any way. Period.

It's what's still eating away at him. Even after all this time.

Christina hates what it has done. It changed him. But she can't blame him.

You work so hard your whole life, and then overnight, one person ruins it all.

FOUR

Christina runs up the wide, dark staircase and heads straight for her daughter's room.

She opens the door. The plug-in nightlight emits a soft glow. Her daughter is wrapped in her duvet like an animal in hibernation. Christina hates it when she does that, fearful she will suffocate. She walks over to the bed and slides the duvet off her daughter's head.

Abi sits upright. 'Mum, where've you been? I've been trying to call you.'

'Sorry, darling. The weather has been atrocious. Are you OK?'

Abi had complained of a headache when she came out of school. Christina panicked, that deep-rooted panic that always rears its ugly self whenever Abi complains of any ailment. As it has done for years.

Christina's not alone. The fear is real, people reassure her on one of the Facebook support groups, Young Warriors, that she belongs to. One of the more upbeat networks for the parents of childhood cancer survivors. She had to drop out of many others she joined after Abi was diagnosed. They were too depressing. Christina is a woman who is all about looking for the positive in any situation. She firmly believes this is what got her and her family through her daughter's lengthy illness.

She had considered cancelling meeting her brother this evening. She gave Abi a couple of Panadol and told her she would stay at home with her, but as feisty as always, her daughter was adamant she was OK and Christina should still go out.

'I'm fine,' Abi says.

'No more headaches?'

'No.'

'Where did Ben go?'

'To see Cal.'

'OK. Now, get some sleep.'

Abi wriggles her body back under the duvet. 'Love you, Mum.'

'Love you more.' Christina tucks her in and gently kisses her forehead. 'See you in the morning.'

Rain thrashes at the hallway window. Grabbing a towel from the airing cupboard, she jumps into a hot shower. Steam fills the room as thoughts of her conversation with Ted fill her head.

Her brother's right. She and Michael can't carry on like this. However, whenever she tries to talk to him, he clams up. Blames his job. A teacher's work is never done, he tells her.

When she turns off the shower, she pauses. A noise is coming from downstairs. She opens the bathroom door. Someone is walking about down there. It must be Michael. Hopefully, he is coming to bed. She dries herself and slips into her silk pyjamas and winter dressing gown.

When she leaves the bathroom, she breathes a sigh of relief to see Ben walking into his bedroom. 'Where've you been?' she calls out, but he has his EarPods in. Damn things. She follows him into his bedroom where he has collapsed onto his unmade bed and is typing on his phone.

A streak of moonlight beaming through the gaps in the curtains spans the room to his troubled face. The teenage years haven't been kind to her son. When she and Adam split up, he became angry with life. An anger that intensified when she remarried and manifested itself into an unyielding hatred for his stepfather despite Michael's endless efforts to bond with him. And the whole drama with Michael at school affected Ben badly, as well. He and Michael barely speak now. How she aches for the days her son was a sunnier person. A nicer person. He was such a joy to be around. That person is still in there somewhere, buried below the defiance of adolescence. She just needs to be patient. That person will blossom again someday.

She walks over to him, turns on the bedside light and signals for him to remove one of his EarPods. 'Where've you been?' she asks, seating herself on the end of his bed.

He removes the chunk of white plastic wedged in his ear. Are his hands shaking, or is that her imagination? He glances over at the window, a troubled look on his face. 'I went over to Cal's.'

'I thought you were staying in to do your homework.'

'I finished it before I went out.'

'Listen, Ben.' She perches on the side of the bed. 'If the weather is still bad in the morning, I'll take you to school.'

'What're you on about? I can drive.'

'You only passed your test two weeks ago. It scares the hell out of me you driving in this bad weather.'

'Leave it, Mum. You're stressing about nothing. You said yourself I'm a good driver.'

It's true. He is careful in the car. But he doesn't have the experience of driving in this weather. 'I'll never stop stressing about you.' She points at his phone. 'Put that thing away now. You've got school in the morning.'

'Yeah. All right.' He returns to the screen of his phone, resuming his stony silence.

She leaves him be and towel dries her corkscrew curls, the winter chill negating the heat from the shower. It's almost midnight. She's usually in bed way before this. Collapsing under the duvet, she ensures her seven o'clock alarm is set.

Ted has left a voice message. He is worried about her and wants to know she has arrived home safely.

She drops him a text. Yes, she's home and in bed... alone.

Switching out the light, she burrows herself under the covers. It's cold, and no matter how much she cocoons her body into the duvet, she can't get warm. She thinks of Michael downstairs. He should be beside her, taking the chill off.

Eventually, she falls into a fitful sleep, disturbed by dreams of the animal she hit earlier. Middle-of-the-night angst sets in as she jolts awake. What if a deer is lying injured? Or what if it was a dog? Oh, no. What has she done? She tries to wipe the thoughts from her mind. There's nothing she can do about it now. She'll detour and check in the morning on the way to school. She tries to go back to sleep, but although the rain has eased, the wind is still raging outside, hammering against the windows as if it's trying to break in.

She tosses and turns as her thoughts grow darker. What if Abi's headache was something more serious than an everyday headache? That's how it all started. The years of misery, countless evenings spent eating microwave meals on hospital wards, watching her beautiful girl's tenacious fight to hear the word *remission*. 'My head hurts, Mum,' she said. 'Real bad. I can't see properly.' Christina imagines Abi back then, standing at the end of the bed, holding her head in her hands like a ball she wanted to throw.

She is finally just dropping off when a banging sound from downstairs disturbs her.

Wilf barks. It must be Michael coming to bed. She checks

her phone. It's three o'clock. That's about right. He often wanders up around this time. She'll hear the toilet flush in a minute and the crash of the toilet lid.

She waits for the sound.

It doesn't come.

A tapping noise makes her sit up straight. She listens intently. Wilf barks again, followed by a throaty growl. Is someone knocking at the front door?

She jumps out of bed, wincing at how cold it is. It reminds her of early-morning feed time when the kids were babies and the nights when Abi was sick, and she used to set the alarm for the middle of the night to check on her. Grabbing her dressing gown, she ties it around her waist as she trundles downstairs.

Passing the lounge, she thrusts open the door. The smell of bourbon hits her. 'Michael, get up. Someone's at the door.' Hasn't he heard Wilf barking?

She hurries to the front door, tugging Wilf aside to peer through the peephole. Her stomach sinks.

Two police officers are standing on her doorstep.

FIVE

'Mrs Blake?' the officer asks, his voice without emotion.

Christina nods, her stomach in her throat. It's Ted. Something has happened to her brother. She's sure that's what the police officers are here to tell her. It's one of her worst nightmares. Ted has always been her tower of strength when her world is falling apart.

It's still blowing a gale outside. She opens the door wider, beckoning the man and woman inside, rescuing them from the deluge.

The male officer flashes a badge and introduces himself and his colleague, PCs White and Abbas, respectively. He reaches out to allow Wilf to smell the back of his hand and then strokes his fur.

The dog sits, calmness personified. Unlike Christina, who is panicking, her anxiety stealing her manners.

The officers stand on the coir doormat that has *WELCOME* imprinted on it in block capitals. Ironic, really. Police officers knocking on her door in the middle of the night are not welcome here. The look on their faces tells her they are only there to deliver news she doesn't want to hear.

'Shall we go somewhere we can talk?' PC Abbas smiles, a small, kind smile. One tinted with sympathy that makes Christina nod in the direction of the kitchen, the heart of the house, and lead the officers along the hallway.

'Michael, can you come here, please?' Christina shouts, her voice hoarse from nerves. She turns to the officers. 'My husband will be here in a minute. He fell asleep in the lounge.'

PC White and PC Abbas glance at each other.

PC Abbas tells her to sit down.

Christina refuses, her hands clenching the marble worktop. The bright light above is too much at this time of night. How many times has she asked Michael to change it for a lower wattage bulb?

'I'm sorry to break this news to you, Mrs Blake,' the PC says, bringing Christina back to the moment. 'Your husband has been involved in a serious accident.' The officer's voice is soft as if he has tried to wrap his words in cotton wool to soften the blow.

Her husband? Is he confused? Did he mean to say her brother? 'That can't be right.'

The PC continues. 'I'm afraid it is. He was hit by a car sometime late last night, just up the road by The Black Horse pub.'

That doesn't make sense. Christina is confused. Michael was asleep in the lounge when she got home last night. Wasn't he?

Christina's legs turn weak. She leans against the worktop, her body heavy as the recognition of what she has done takes hold.

She fears the answer to the question before she asks it, but she can't stop herself from seeking the dreadful clarification. With a trembling voice, she spits it out. 'By whom?'

'That we're yet to ascertain. We believe this to be a hit-and-run case. Detectives are on to it. The attending paramedics did all they could, but he has sustained significant injuries. A motorcyclist found him. They saw him lying in the middle of the road.'

Christina runs her hands through her mass of corkscrew curls. 'Is... is he go... is he going to be all right?' Her mind races with the unthinkable as adrenalin courses through her veins. Her husband. Significant injuries.

She wills herself to keep calm.

'We don't have any more details. I'm so sorry.' The female officer hands a piece of paper to Christina with digits scribbled on it. 'The paramedics have taken him to the Royal Alexandra hospital. That's their number. We can give you a lift there.'

Distress takes an all-consuming hold. She leans over the worktop, as a guttural wail from deep within her alarms both the police officers.

'Can we call someone for you?' PC Abbas asks.

Her thoughts are a haze of confusion. 'I need to see him.'

'As I said, we can take you,' PC Abbas says.

'I'll call my brother.' Christina is visibly shaking. 'He can drop me off and come back to look after my children.'

A voice sounds through the radio attached to PC White's shoulder. He turns away, speaking into it.

'You're in shock, Mrs Blake. It's probably best if we take you,' PC Abbas says. 'Can I make you some tea?'

'No. No, thank you.' No tea, and certainly no lift to the hospital.

Christina wants the officers gone. She needs to get to the hospital to see her husband. But she doesn't want to endure a car ride with these strangers. In fact, she doesn't want them here a moment longer. 'It's fine. Thank you for the offer, though.'

'Our team will find out what happened, Mrs Blake,' PC White says. 'While we're here, do you know why your husband was out walking in such atrocious weather late last night?'

She shakes her head. Think. Think. The truth. 'I have no idea. Will he be in A&E? Where will I find him?'

'My guess is they would've taken him straight to the ICU,' PC Abbas says. 'I think it's best that we drive you to the hospital,' she repeats.

Christina stares at the floor. 'I'll be fine, honestly. My brother will do it. He can be here in ten minutes. You go. My daughter and son are here if I need them.'

PC White speaks into the radio attached to his shoulder again. The two officers nod at each other. 'If you're sure you don't need a lift to the hospital, or any more help, we'll make a move,' PC White says. 'What with the weather, we have several emergencies to attend to tonight.'

Christina fakes a smile for her unwanted guests and sees them to the front door, hoping to hell they don't look at her car. When she closes the door, she rushes to her study that overlooks the driveway. She trips over her handbag she chucked in there when she arrived home last night. Cursing, she goes to the side of the window, cautiously peering out, holding her breath.

Only once they get into their patrol vehicle, reverse and indicate as they leave the driveway does she let out a big sigh of relief. She rushes to the lounge and stares at the vacant sofa in disbelief. How could she have thought he was there?

She dashes upstairs as fast as she can. Abi is standing at her bedroom door, her burgundy and white checked pyjamas hanging off her skinny frame. 'What's happened, Mum?' she asks, a picture of confusion painted over her face in shades of a green-grey.

'Michael's been in an accident.' Christina fights for breath. 'Someone ran him over last night.'

Abi's mouth opens. 'Who?'

Christina's voice falters. 'I don't know. They didn't stop.' She inwardly curses for the lie she has just told her daughter.

'A hit-and-run?'

Christina nods. 'It sounds like it.'

Abi's hand shoots to cover her mouth. 'That's horrific. What monster would do such a thing?'

A blazing heat of shame rises up Christina's neck, as a creeping sense of dread envelopes her.

It wasn't a deer she hit last night.

It was Michael.

SIX

Why didn't she just come clean with the police?

It was an accident, after all.

But she'd been drinking. Only one glass of wine, but it had been a large glass. Even though she had only ordered a small one. Ted told her the barman must have misheard him. She only intended on drinking half, but she had got carried away as she began telling Ted about how bad things had got with Michael. She had only grabbed a sandwich for dinner as the kids usually go out with their dad on a Wednesday, however he had cancelled last minute because of the weather. And Michael had been working late and said he'd eaten a big meal in the school canteen at lunchtime, so she hadn't bothered to cook. She might have been over the limit. Would the police have been able to tell, if they had breathalysed her?

A monster, that's what she is. A monster and a liar!

'Mum, are you OK?' Abi asks.

'Where did Michael go last night?' she asks her daughter. She needs to make sense of this. Why was her husband out on that road at eleven o'clock at night? *Significant injuries.* The remorse is overwhelming.

'I don't know,' Abi says. 'He came up here and said he was popping out.'

'Out where?'

Abi raises her voice. It's so unlike her. 'I told you, Mum. I don't know. He said he wouldn't be long.'

'Didn't you realise he didn't come home?' The panic in her voice is alarming her daughter. She needs to calm down.

'No. Didn't you?'

Christina shakes her head. 'I thought he was asleep on the sofa. What time did he come up here to tell you he was going out?'

Abi shrugs. 'I dunno.'

'Think, Abi. What time?'

'I can't remember exactly. Eightish, maybe. Nine, perhaps. I don't know.'

He must have walked to the pub. That's the only place Christina can think he would have gone. Now and again, Michael strolls the fifteen minutes or so up to The Black Horse for a pint. It's too difficult to get anywhere else on foot without a car in their rural location.

Christina nods her head sideways in the direction of Ben's room. 'Michael told me he was staying in with you two. He had some essays to mark,' she says. 'And he was going to help Ben with some homework.'

'Well, he didn't,' Abi says.

'Did someone pick him up?'

'I don't know, Mum. What's with all the questions?'

She can't face her daughter at the moment. 'I'm going to call Uncle Ted to stay with you while I go to the hospital.'

'Mum, we're old enough to stay on our own.'

Her daughter is right. Christina knows she is overprotective; Abi is fourteen and Ben is seventeen, but she still doesn't like leaving them home alone. 'Go and get a few more hours of sleep.'

Abi protests, but Christina is already halfway down the stairs. 'Go to bed, darling,' she demands. 'I don't want to disturb your brother.'

She must get to the hospital.

She needs to see her husband.

Finding her phone, she calls Ted. It goes to voicemail twice. He eventually picks up on the third ring, yawning. 'What the bleeding time do you call this?'

'I need your help.'

Christina briefs her brother on the cruel direction her life has taken since they hugged goodbye last night. But she can't face sharing her fear about her involvement in her husband's accident.

The shuffling sound of him sitting up in bed reverberates down the phone. 'Is he OK?'

'I don't know. I need to get to the hospital. Can you come over?'

'I'll be right there.'

Christina changes into jeans and a hoodie. Her pulse is racing, adrenaline speeding through her. She doesn't know what to do for the best. Calm down. That's what she needs to do. She'll get nowhere in such a state.

Finding the piece of paper the PC gave her, she calls the number. It rings and rings. She gives up and googles the hospital and finds the number for the ICU. That's where he'll be, the police officer said.

Her husband is in the ICU.

And it's all her fault.

When there's no answer, she gives up and goes downstairs to wait for Ted. She puts on her trainers, and paces the kitchen, willing her brother to hurry up as she tries to fight the nausea swirling in the pit of her stomach.

Five minutes pass, the longest of her life, before headlights appear at the window and Ted's blue work van pulls up beside her Range Rover.

She rushes outside, meeting her brother on the shingle drive as he jumps out of his vehicle. The wind is still wild, blowing her curly hair into an untamed mess. Her voice is fraught with torment as she relays everything she couldn't face telling him on the phone, or voice to the police.

The truth about last night.

That she had an accident on the way home. That the animal she thought she hit wasn't an animal at all.

That she might have hit her own husband.

SEVEN

Ted looks at her in horror, shaking his head in disbelief. 'Why didn't you just tell the police the truth?'

'I freaked out.' The wind clips her words. 'I was scared I might have been over the limit. I didn't see him. I just heard a thud. I thought it was a deer. I got out and checked but there was nothing there.' She holds her head in her hands. 'I shouldn't have finished that glass of wine.'

'Chrissy, it was one glass of wine. You wouldn't have been over the limit.'

'Now I think about it rationally, I know. But I just totally panicked at the time. What do I do?'

'Did you tell the police you were out last night?'

Christina thinks. 'No. They didn't ask.'

Ted holds onto his baseball cap as the wind tries to whip it off his head. 'This isn't good.'

'He's going to be all right, isn't he?' It's a stupid question to ask. How can her brother possibly know? Her words are coated with desperation. 'I don't know what to do.'

'Move your car into the carport for a start,' Ted orders. 'There must be some damage. What's it even doing out here?'

'It was pouring when I got home. I wanted to get inside as quickly as possible.'

Ted walks over to her Range Rover and shines the torchlight from his phone around the front of the car.

'Hell, look at that.' Ted points to the edge of the bumper, guiding the light towards the dent so he can examine the evidence more closely. 'I suppose it hasn't caused massive damage, though you can see where you hit him.'

'I don't know what to do.' She hopelessly clings to his arm.

He squints, shaking his head in disbelief. 'You should've just told the police what actually happened.' He nods to the carport. 'Put it in there. We need to get it fixed as soon as. Unless you want to find yourself facing a prison sentence, that is.'

'Prison?'

'You left the scene of an accident. And you lied to the police. Those are pretty serious crimes, Chrissy. They'd probably throw driving without due care at you as well, and endangering life.'

She scrunches up handfuls of her curly hair. 'I can't believe this has happened.'

'That's if he lives. If he dies, then they'd probably charge you with causing death by dangerous driving.' Ted never has been one to mince his words, yet this is too much.

She covers her ears. 'Stop it. Stop it. I've been so bloody stupid.'

'I'm sorry, Chrissy. Look, I'll sort the car after I've taken you to the hospital.'

A gush of wind knocks her off balance. She drops her hands to her sides.

He catches her. 'Let's get inside.'

'This is a disaster,' she says, succumbing to him pulling her to the front door.

Once in the kitchen, Ted leans against the worktop. It's

hard to believe they are twins. They've always jested that if they'd been born nine months apart, they would've questioned their mother's fidelity. It was only a joke, of course. Their parents' relationship was as solid as the massive diamond their dad placed on their mum's finger the day he proposed, which is why Christina and Ted have always wondered how they've made such a mess of their own relationships. At least Ted has never married.

'You really need to put Michael to one side for a moment, sis. Steel yourself. You've got two options. You can confess and face the consequences. It won't look good. You'd be in lots of trouble.'

'Will I really go to prison?'

The corners of his mouth drop. 'I'm sorry, sis. You know I'd never lie to you, but I think you'd be in deep trouble. If you confess now, say you were in shock, they may be more lenient. I don't know. Or you can keep quiet. Say nothing, and hope nobody saw you. Is it possible anyone was around? What about the motorcyclist who found him. Could he have seen you?'

'No. The weather was awful, and it was pitch black. I'd have seen a motorcyclist.' Is there a chance someone witnessed what she did? It was pitch black. How could she know for sure? 'What if *he* saw me?'

'I doubt it. Unless he was looking over his shoulder.'

'What about the dent in the car?'

'I know a guy up on the industrial estate who would do it for me. No questions asked. Owes me a favour.' He raises his eyebrows. 'A very big favour. I guess it comes down to whether your conscience can live with it.'

'I can't believe what I've done.' She laces her shaking hands behind her head. 'What would *you* do?'

His eyes bulge as he releases a long breath. 'I don't mean to make you feel worse, but I think I would've owned up from the start.'

'I thought I'd hit an animal. I did get out to look. Honestly, I did. There was nothing there. I must've knocked him into the verge.' She scrunches up her face and drops it into her hands. 'This is a nightmare.' She lifts her head, running her hands down her cheeks. 'I can't think about this right now. I need to get to the hospital. I need to know how he is.'

'I agree.'

'Can you drop the kids at school?' she asks. 'I don't want Ben driving in this weather.'

He nods. 'Do you want me to come into the hospital with you? You don't know what state he's going to be in.'

'I'd rather you were here with the kids.'

'Chrissy. I can't let you drive. I'll drop you off.'

Christina reluctantly agrees. 'Let me go and tell Abi.'

'Give me your keys. I'll get the dent sorted out. If that's the path you want to go down.'

It has to be the right path, doesn't it? If she was sent to prison, what would happen to the kids? She couldn't bear being parted from them. And Michael's going to need looking after.

Then it suddenly dawns on her.

What if Michael dies?

That would make her a killer.

EIGHT

She's faced with more signs of the reality of her situation as Ted drives them to the hospital. A police sign and cordons have closed the whole of Ivy Road.

Christina groans. 'The police are all over this.'

'I guess so. They must be trying to carry out forensic investigations, collecting evidence.'

'What kind of evidence?'

'I don't know. Tyre marks on the road.'

Christina looks at him in horror. 'Will they be able to tell the make of the tyres? Won't that lead them to my car?'

Ted shakes his head. 'I very much doubt they'll get far. Something about the weather to be thankful for. The rain would've washed away the kind of evidence they're looking for.'

Christina recoils into the seat.

After a minor detour, Ted rejoins the familiar route to the hospital. The van rattles along, leaving the country lanes for the main road leading into town.

It's still dark, yet Christina knows the way as well as her own reflection. How many times has she taken this journey with Abi over the years? And now she is on another journey where she can't contain her anxiety.

Ted turns into the hospital car park. 'I'll come in with you.'

'No, please. Just get home for the kids.' She opens the van door. 'I'll get a cab back.'

He reaches for her hand and squeezes it. 'Just call me if you need me, and I'll be right here. Let me know how he is as soon as you can.'

Taking the rotating doors to the main concourse, Christina follows the signs for the ICU along the eerily quiet corridor to the lift.

Anxiety surges through her as she stands outside the double doors to the foreboding intensive care unit. After pressing the call button on the intercom, she gels her hands.

An eternity passes before a crackling sound gives way to a woman's flat voice. 'Can I help you?'

'I'm here to see my husband, Michael.' Christina clears her throat. 'Michael Blake.'

The grey doors buzz. As she pulls one open, the sterile smell of antiseptic immediately hits her. She commences the walk familiar to every airless ward, along fluorescent-lit, narrow corridors dodging busy nurses and doctors moving in different directions. Various pieces of equipment, trolleys and spare beds line the walls. A walk she has experienced many times along the rocky journey with her daughter.

The weight of dread anchors each step as she approaches the reception desk, trying to block out the sounds of beeping machines and wheezing ventilators, the disconcerting sounds of uncertainty. 'I'm looking for Michael Blake,' she says to the heavy-set nurse slouched behind a computer screen tapping on a keyboard. 'The police told me he was admitted here.'

The nurse pushes her chair away from the desk. 'Come with me.' She guides Christina to a side room and tells her someone will be in to see her in a minute.

It's an agonising ten-minute wait before a harassed doctor turns up trying to conceal the need to yawn. He repeats the words of the police officers earlier. 'Your husband has suffered significant injuries.' He is matter of fact, sparing no punches. Clearing his throat, he explains the extent of the trauma that has been inflicted on her husband. A bruised spine, cracked ribs and a fractured ankle, but it's the head injuries they are most concerned about. Michael is in a coma.

'A coma?' Christina cries.

'A medically induced one. It allows us to alleviate the swelling so the brain can rest.' The doctor continues talking. She can't concentrate on what he is saying.

A coma.

Her husband is in a coma.

'I'll take you to see him but please prepare yourself. All the machines can be quite daunting at first. And there're wounds to his face.'

The doctor guides Christina to B Bay to the right of the reception desk.

Emotions tear through her as she grabs the edge of the blue curtain on a track pulled around the large bed. A female nurse with a mop of wild grey hair leans over the patient, straightening the sheets. A male nurse records the readings from a beeping monitor onto a chart.

Is that really Michael?

A plethora of wires and tubes connect his broken body to machines intermittently beeping. She gasps. One is helping him to breathe. His face is barely recognisable with the amount of swelling. His eyes are closed. The skin below his left eye is puffed up like a sausage, and abrasions and stitches cover the area above, right up to his hairline.

Every beep from the machines surrounding the bed warns of the danger he faces.

Two tears fall down Christina's face. Remnants of blood

run through his hair, and his lips are bruised deep red like the colour of beetroot. Death feels like a hair's breadth away.

The male nurse leaves the bay, and the female nurse breaks Christina's trance-like state. 'Are you Michael's partner?'

Christina's nods. 'I'm his wife.' She slowly approaches the bed. 'How is he?'

The nurse smiles warmly. 'I'm sure if he was awake, he'd say he's seen better days.'

How can she be so calm?

The nurse whips off her plastic apron and removes her nylon gloves, throwing them in the bin. The lid closes with a clang, piercing through Christina's frail state of mind. The nurse leaves the vital pieces of equipment monitoring and sustaining Michael's existence and asks, 'Can I get you anything?'

Christina shakes her head, trying to swallow the ball of guilt trapped in her throat. But she can't. It's too damn big.

It's all her fault.

She did this to her husband.

NINE

Another doctor arrives, a much younger one.

Christina has lost all track of time. It is now light outside. She still can't get over seeing her husband in such a terrible state.

The doctor asks questions. So many questions.

Christina answers them the best she can.

The next twenty-four hours are vital.

What if he lives but never makes a full recovery? It will destroy him. And her. He is an English teacher, and the school's football and rugby coach. What if he won't be able to run up and down the football pitch and the rugby field again? And what about his Sunday morning bike rides with the local cycling club? What if he won't be able to ride a bike ever again? Will he even survive? The doctor doesn't make any guarantees.

The questions continue.

No, her husband doesn't have any medical conditions they should know about. He had his appendix out when he was six years old. No, no other surgeries that she's aware of. No, he's not taking any medications. Yes, he does have an allergy. He's allergic to cow's milk. An intolerance that makes his lips swell like he has had Botox injected into them and gives him an itchy angry rash over his neck and chest.

Heart problems? No, he doesn't have any heart problems.

'I'm asking because your husband has extremely high blood pressure,' the doctor says. 'Which could be a result of his injuries.'

'He's never had high blood pressure as far as I know. When will he wake up?' Deep concern raises the pitch of her voice. The same as it does every time Abi complains of a headache, a sore throat, or any ailment.

The authoritative male voice responds. 'Your husband has suffered severe injuries. We'll be monitoring him closely in the coming hours. Our priority at the moment, as in the initial stages of any such significant injuries, is to keep him stable.' The doctor's final words fill her with anguish, leaving her lightheaded.

Her phone rings. It's Sophia.

She doesn't want to speak to her sister at the moment. She declines the call. A minute later, her phone beeps. Sophia has left a voicemail. Christina listens to it. Ted has already updated her about Michael. Sophia says she will come up to the hospital. All Christina needs to do is call her and tell her when. It gives Christina a level of comfort. She doesn't want to be with anyone. Nonetheless, she doesn't want to be alone. Other than her brother, her sister is the only person who she could deal with at the moment. She texts her.

No visitors allowed atm. Will update you when I know more. X

A text pings straight back.

How's Michael? Please tell me he's OK. X

Not great. They have put him in a coma. X

A coma? WTF? Is he going to be all right?X

I hope so. Will tell you more when I can. X

'Is he going to be OK?' Christina asks the new nurse, Glenda, joining the day shift.

'We need to give it time. It's early days. Everyone is different. Some bodies bounce back quickly. For others, it takes longer.' Glenda touches Michael's forearm. 'He took a fair bump to the head.'

Christina is confused. That doesn't sound right. 'Did the car hit his head?'

'No, I believe they think he hit it when he fell to the ground. But youth is on his side. And he's fit and healthy. We'll know more in the coming days.'

Christina is frightened. Being responsible for running someone over is unthinkable. Make that person your husband – who is struggling for his life right in front of you – well, it's off the scale. She is more scared than she's ever been in her life. Well, nearly. She casts her mind back to when Abi's illness was at its worst, when she felt as if she'd been ripped from a beach and flung into the ocean by a huge wave.

Grim thoughts whirl around her mind.

What if Michael doesn't make it?

Her husband dead.

What then?

What is he thinking? Can he think? Does he know it was her who ran him down? Surely not? Christina stifles a sob.

'How long have you been married?' Glenda asks, her voice comforting and friendly. She's a large lady with a reassuring smile, her eyes a soft brown colour that matches her beautiful silky skin.

'Just over five years,' Christina replies. 'It's gone in a flash.'

'Life has a habit of doing that. Children?'

'We don't have any together, but I have two children from my first marriage. A boy and a girl.'

'Snap,' Glenda says, her eyes lighting up at the mention of her children. 'My daughter is fourteen, and my son is seventeen.'

Christina manages a weak smile. 'Snap.'

'Teenagers, eh? My son is a saint, but my daughter.' The nurse exhales a large breath and pulls a face of horror. 'That young lady sure keeps me awake at night. Everyone warned me girls are harder than boys at this age.'

'It's the opposite for me. My daughter's an angel. My son is the difficult one.'

'In what way?'

'His mood swings are dreadful. And I've caught him lying about his whereabouts a few times, which, despite being frustrating, really hurts. It doesn't help that my ex-husband spoils him rotten. He bought him a car. He passed his test two weeks ago, so now he's out and about. He's a good driver, but it scares the life out of me.'

'That's a difficult one. My friend is in the same boat. He'll come good in the end. Have faith.' The nurse nods at Michael 'Where did you two meet?'

'He's a teacher at St Christopher's school.'

'Ah, we have a clever one here, then.' She gently taps the side of the mattress. 'What does he teach?'

'English and sport.'

'A busy man.' Glenda touches Michael's hand. 'A busy, clever man. We need to get you out of here pronto, sir. Back to your loving wife.' Glenda smiles at Christina, a smile that reaches the kindness in her eyes.

It makes Christina want to cry.

If only this woman trying to nurse her husband back to health knew the truth.

TEN

Christina stares out of the large window, gripping Michael's cold hand like his life depends on it. If only that was the case.

She fiddles with the love heart pendant around her neck that he bought for her when they first met, as her mind wanders back to better times. When she could never imagine anything like this happening.

Anne-Marie was the one who persuaded Christina to come and work at the school after Adam had done the dirty on her. 'We have a part-time position going in the finance department. It's only three days a week, but it'll get you out of the house,' Anne-Marie had said.

Christina was initially reluctant. It had been a long time since she had worked. She gave up her career in the city when Ben was born, and then Abi's cancer prevented her from returning to the banking job she had loved so much. But her friend had convinced her she needed to start rebuilding her life again. So, she had given in.

And the attraction between her and Michael was instant, the chemistry explosive. Two compounds that were destined to be together.

Everything about the dishy teacher blew her mind: his tall, muscular stature, tidy beard and crew cut, and gorgeous brown eyes that made his face constantly smile, not to mention his kindness that shone around the school like all the polished sporting trophies on display in his study.

A week into her new job, Michael caught her as she was leaving one day. 'I hear you used to play hockey for England.'

His magnetism attracted her like a moth to the brightest flame. A warmth rose up her neck. She felt like a smitten teenager again. She tripped over her words as she told him, yes, he was right. In her late teens, she had played for England, until a broken leg that needed pinning and the subsequent complications prevented her from playing at that level again.

'I want to set up an after-school hockey team. We've got some good players out there. Would you be up for running it? Two afternoons a week, I thought. We could fit it in with the days you work.' He'd done his homework.

She was good too, and getting the girls' team to The Schools Championships is still one of her proudest moments. And, of course, it had given them more excuses to spend time together.

The rest is history. The way she felt about him in those days was like nothing she'd ever felt. Beyond the feelings she'd even ever had for her ex-husband.

'Did you hear me?' Glenda asks. 'I'm really sorry; you need to leave now. There are strict visiting times on this ward. Go home and get some rest. I'll give you a number you can call at any time for an update.'

The sounds of the hospital return, the incessant beeping and alarms singing their songs. Christina stares at her husband. 'I'm scared to leave him.'

'You must pace yourself. We'll take good care of him.' The nurse dismisses her from the bay with a flick of her gloved hand. She glances at the pink fob watch on her uniform. 'The main café should be open now. They do great coffee. Grab one for the way home. We'll see you later.'

Christina gently kisses Michael's cheek. 'I love you, darling. Please get better soon.'

ELEVEN

Christina has been here a few hours now, and the hospital is a different place from when she arrived. As if it has woken up and is getting on with its day. Porters push patients along the corridors on trolleys, and people wearing lanyards fly around, tending to their business.

She heads down to the café, calling Abi on her phone, as she descends the stairs.

Abi answers straight away. Ted is just dropping her and Ben at school.

Christina gives an update, sparing her daughter the details for now as she tries to pump her words with optimism.

'That's awful, Mum.'

'I know. Can I speak to your brother, please?'

Abi passes the phone to Ben.

He grunts, complaining about Ted not allowing him to drive to school.

'It was me who insisted. The roads are dreadful.'

'I need to learn to drive in all conditions. You've said so yourself.'

She could murder her ex for buying him that car. The

brand new Peugeot is the worry of her life. 'Let's not argue about it now. Michael's not in a good way.'

Ben mutters something about her utter unfairness.

'I need to ask you a question. What time did you go out last night?'

There's a pause. 'Why?' he asks.

She grits her teeth. This is not a time for his awkwardness. 'I want to know what time Michael left. Was he still there when you went out?'

'I dunno.'

'Didn't you say goodbye?' This is a stupid question. Ben barely talks to Michael these days.

It's strange how everyone at school loves Michael, yet Ben has never accepted him. Michael is the most popular teacher in the whole school. Christina has always put it down to her and Ben being so close. Until she met Michael, that is, and the jealousy Ben felt when Michael moved into the family home only six months after Christina met him.

She breaks the silence. 'I'll see you later. Tell your uncle to call me when he's dropped you off.'

She slips out of the exit door next to the café as she hangs up, relieved to feel the morning air on her face. She shivers. What was she thinking, leaving home without a coat? She wasn't, that's the problem. At least the rain has stopped, and the wind has died down, but it's bitterly cold. Walking to the side of the building, she huddles in a corner and waits for her brother's call.

'How is he?' Ted asks.

She reels off Michael's injuries. 'They've put him in a coma.'

'Hell, no! Why?'

'To protect his brain until it heals and the swelling goes down. What if he never recovers, Ted?' The words catch in her throat.

'Don't be silly. He'll be OK. You'll see.'

'What if he can never ride his bike again? Or he's left with a brain injury? You hear these horror stories all the time.'

'You're not thinking rationally,' Ted says. 'Where's your positive spirit, sis?' Lost in her guilt, she goes to say, but he continues. 'He'll be up and riding that bike again in no time. Your car's getting sorted by the way. I dropped it at my mate's place before the kids got up. I thought it best to do it while it was still dark.'

That's it, then. This is the route she is going down.

'Didn't the kids ask where it was?'

'They were too engrossed in their phones.'

Christina lowers her voice. 'What if the police come back and ask me where it is?'

'Why would they do that?'

'What if they suspect it was me?'

'You're being paranoid.'

'I'm not. How long will it take to fix it?'

'My mate said it's not serious. He'll try his best to do it by the end of the day.'

'Isn't he curious?'

'We go way back. No questions asked. It'll be fine. Trust me. I can't pick the kids up after school, I'm afraid. I'm meeting a guy about a big job. Do you want me to ask Sophia?'

'I'll pick them up.' Christina ends the call, feeling sick.

She returns inside and queues behind yawning theatre staff dressed in green scrubs and nurses wrapped in coats, grabbing a coffee for their journey home. The smell of heated breakfast sandwiches churns her stomach even more.

When it's her turn, Christina orders a black coffee. It's all she can face. Searching the busy seating area, she finds an empty table and plonks herself in a white plastic chair. She sips her coffee and searches for Anne-Marie's mobile number. Her friend answers straight away. Christina explains what has happened.

'Oh, poor Michael. This is awful,' Anne-Marie says. 'But he's a strong man, Christina. I know he'll pull through.'

'I hope so.'

'I'm so sorry you're having to go through this. Is there anything I can do for you?'

'Can you get Michael's work covered, please?' Christina says.

'You don't even need to ask.'

'He was taking the year eight boys to a match against Edge Hill School on Saturday. That'll need covering too.'

'I'll sort everything. Don't you worry about a thing.'

'And can you organise for someone to run hockey practice? I can do some work from home, but I doubt I'll be in school for a while.'

'I won't hear of you doing work of any kind until Michael is better. Don't you worry about a thing.' Anne-Marie offers her condolences. 'Everyone is going to be so upset. Please send him our love. And look after yourself. Keep me posted. And if there's anything I can do, call me. Anytime. I'm here for you.'

Christina sips her coffee, fighting tears.

She doesn't deserve people's kindness.

TWELVE

In the taxi on the way home, the driver tries to engage Christina in conversation.

Not in the mood for small talk, she grunts a yes and shuts her eyes. She shudders. All she can see is Michael's smashed-up face.

The house is cold when she arrives home. She should be in school today, so the heating has turned off.

Wilf greets her, wagging his tail. Squatting, she buries her head in the comfort of his welcome, but he's eager to get outside. Usually, she walks him for half an hour before work.

Her phone rings. It's her sister trying to get hold of her again. She answers the call.

'What the hell's happened?' Sophia asks, her voice full of concern. 'Are you OK? How's Michael? I'm coming over.' The quick-fire questions are a mark of how worried her sister is.

'Give me half an hour. I need to take Wilf for a walk. He hasn't been out yet.'

Christina switches on the heating and grabs the dog's lead. A brisk walk will help clear her head.

Another police sign has joined the one reporting Ivy Road is closed. This one is asking for witnesses to the accident that took place last night.

She crosses the road and takes the footpath that loops one of the nearby fields. The word echoes in her head as she briskly circles the field.

Witnesses.

Coldness runs through her veins.

What if someone saw her?

They couldn't have. There was no one around. Was there? Could she have been mistaken? She wills herself not to add that worry to the growing list of problems she has on her overflowing plate. Of course no one saw what happened. No cars passed her and no one would've been out walking in that terrible weather. Which is one of the reasons why she can't understand what the hell Michael was up to.

Her phone beeps. News has spread fast. Several texts fill the screen from well-wishers, mainly staff from school, saying how sorry they are to hear the dreadful news about Michael and offering their help.

She reads them all, still unable to believe what has happened.

Arriving home, she spots her sister's head of bright copper hair walking along the path to the front door.

Sophia hugs her. 'This is awful. Just awful.' She follows Christina into the house and removes her coat. Sophia looks pale, and her eczema has returned. The condition that plagued her during childhood only comes in times of stress now. It doesn't distract from her attractiveness, though. She is one of the most stunning women Christina has ever met.

'Where's Lily?' Christina asks.

'I left her with Nancy.' Nancy is Sophia's mother-in-law.

'Sebastian's got a funeral today. He said he can go to the hospital later if you want him to.'

Sophia's husband, Sebastian, owns an undertaker's that he took over after his dad passed. Christina has never understood how anyone could be drawn into the profession, however it seems to suit Sebastian's staid character.

'Shame,' Christina says, leading her sister into the kitchen. 'I could've done with a Lily hug.' If there's one person in life that makes Christina smile, it's her spirited niece. 'We need to play it by ear with visitors. Only two are allowed on the ward at a time.'

'I'll make some coffee,' Sophia says. 'You sit down and walk me through what has happened.'

Christina slides her weary body onto one of the breakfast bar stools. Closing her eyes momentarily, she takes a deep breath. She doesn't want to break down in front of her sister. She has always been the strong one. Ever since they were young, she has always protected Sophia, especially when her sister got teased at school because of her eczema.

Gathering her strength, Christina briefs her sister on the nightmare she is living as Sophia prepares two cups of coffee. But she only mentions part of the truth.

She is close to her sister but doesn't share the same relationship with her as she does with her brother. It's the twin thing. There are some things about Christina only Ted will ever know.

'He is going to be OK, isn't he?' Sophia asks, clearly concerned by the time Christina has finished talking. She hands Christina a cup of coffee and slides onto the stool beside her.

'I hope so.'

'It's horrendous.' Sophia's eyes glass over. She and her husband, Sebastian, have always had a good relationship with Michael. From the beginning, Sophia said Michael was a better match for Christina than Adam ever was. 'Drive off and leave him for dead. Who would do such a heartless thing?'

'I don't know.' How many times is she going to hear people ask her that question?

'Don't worry. They'll catch who did this.' Sophia's voice breaks. 'We'll make sure of it.' Sophia shuffles her stool closer to Christina and tries to hug her.

Christina draws away. Her guilt rejects Sophia's comforting arms. Her phone rings, saving her from the awkward moment. Not recognising the number, she lets it go to voicemail before picking up the message. The sip of coffee turns bitter in her mouth.

It's the police.

A detective called Cyril Macintosh, who is leading the case of her husband's accident. She winces as his message tells her he wants to come and see her some time today. He has questions to ask. Please could she call him back with a suitable time.

What if he asks to see her car? Would he?

This isn't good. She is riddled with guilt. She should have just come clean last night.

'Who was it?' Sophia asks.

'Just someone from school leaving a message,' Christina lies.

She needs to speak to Ted. 'I must get going.' She hops off the stool. 'I need to get myself organised for the coming days.'

'What can I do for you?' Sophia gets up. 'There must be something. I'll come to the hospital with you, of course, but how about I cook some meals to bring over?' Sophia is a doer – always has been. Ever since they were kids, she'd be the one making crafts or running errands for their mum while Christina and Ted preferred to play outside. She looks as if she's going to cry. 'Or I can do the school runs.'

'There's nothing at the moment,' Christina says. 'I just need to get myself together.'

'You're in a daze. I'll come with you to the hospital.'

'There's no point.'

'Yes there is. I want to support you. Look at you. You're shaking like a leaf.'

Christina clasps her hands tightly together. She knows her sister means well, still she'd rather be alone. She needs to find a way to process what she has done. 'There are strict visiting times. I'll call you with any update.'

Sophia hesitates. 'OK. Please make sure you do. I'll worry otherwise. We all will. What about Sunday?'

'Sunday?' Christina asks. She can't even think about today, let alone the weekend.

'Lily's birthday party.'

'Oh, no. The cake.' Christina had promised to make her niece's first birthday cake.

'Listen. Forget it. I'll sort it,' Sophia says. 'You've got enough to worry about.'

'I'll buy one.'

'No you won't. I'll sort it.'

Christina clenches her jaw. She wanted to be the one to get her niece's first birthday cake. 'I insist on buying one. And I'll still come and see her on Sunday.'

'Listen, Chrissy. Think about it. Michael has got to be our priority at the moment. I'll sort the cake.'

Christina eventually relents. At this moment, she just wants to be alone.

With Sophia gone, Christina calls Ted. 'The police want to come around. A bloody detective. I can't believe it. They have more questions. I need my car back.'

'Calm down. I'm sorting it.'

'They want to come around today.'

'I said, calm down. It's not a big job. I told you. The guy's going to have it done by the end of the day.'

'I need to call the police back with a time for them to come around.'

'Stall them. I'm just finishing a job, and I'll chase my mate.'

'How will you get it to me? I'm going back to the hospital soon and then picking the kids up from school. Then I'll go back again when I've fed them.'

'My mate will give me a lift, or I'll sort something out. Stop stressing. Stall the guy. I'll get the car back to you before seven. That should be plenty of time.'

'I don't want to speak to them.'

'You've got to.'

'I'm scared I'm going to put my foot in it. You know what I can be like.'

Ted snorts affectionately. 'Yes, I do.' It's a characteristic of hers he finds endearing.

The unease convulsing her stomach is overwhelming. She's utterly stressed out. But her overriding thoughts remain with Michael. She would willingly go into the police station right now and confess if she had some sort of guarantee that he was going to be all right.

As if sensing this, Ted tries to lead her thoughts in a different direction. 'Have you found out what he was up to last night, yet? Abi told me she reckons he went out about eight or nine.'

'I guess he went to the pub.'

'Is that normal?' Ted asks.

'Not when he's got work the next day, no,' she says, slowly, her brain trying to catch up. 'And especially not for that long.'

So, what *was* her husband up to?

THIRTEEN

Christina contacts the detective once she has calmed down enough.

Cyril Macintosh seems like a straight-talking guy, friendly, but that doesn't put her at ease.

She arranges for him to come over that evening.

Feeling the need to tidy before his visit, she pulls open the heavy curtains in the lounge. In the daylight, she understands how she thought Michael was in the room when she arrived home last night. She had mistakenly thought he was lying beneath the navy blue blanket spread across the sofa, like he usually does.

The bottle of bourbon on the table clearly visible from the lounge door last night catches her attention. More reason to assume he had been there, lying on the sofa. She picks up the empty glass beside the bottle. A residue of reddish-brown liquid lies at the bottom of the glass, and the side of it is sticky. She slides her finger around the rim.

That's why Michael didn't take the car when he went out. He'd already been drinking.

Christina shivers. It's cold in here. The door to the conservatory is ajar. She closes it and tidies the sofa, neatly folding the blanket and draping it over the arm. She continues wrestling with her innermost thoughts. What if Michael dies? Thoughts of him in the ICU on a ventilator return. She'll never see him lying under this blanket again. And it would be all her fault. Her chest tightens. No, that can't happen. He has to live. Think positively. He's going to be OK. Michael will be home soon.

The rest of the morning passes in a blur of anxiety and guilt while she tries to organise her life to cope with the coming days. She sends an email to the Head of Resources team at St Christopher's. He won't be expecting such a comprehensive update, not in the circumstances, but Christina is a dedicated member of staff with a strong work ethic. She details outstanding issues and where she was up to with certain projects, so he can delegate important items to other team members.

After making a sandwich that she barely touches, she jumps in Michael's Volvo and drives back to the hospital. She doesn't like this car. She can't put her finger on why, but ever since he bought it last year, she feels queasy every time she rides in it. Michael says it's all in her head. There's something about the smell in here, a sickly-sweet waft that makes her woozy.

With a heavy heart, she hurries to the ward where Glenda, the nurse on duty, updates her on Michael's situation. Not that there's anything new to report other than they have put a cast on Michael's ankle.

'How long will he have to have that on for?' Christina asks.

'Four to six weeks.'

Christina grimaces. Michael won't be able to ride his bike. She ridicules her thoughts. That's the least of their worries. 'What happened to his belongings?' she asks. 'His wallet? His phone?'

'I'll ask for you. Usually the police would've taken them.' The nurse whips a pen out of her pocket along with a scrap piece of paper plastered with scribbles, and scrawls another note to herself.

Christina spends two hours by Michael's bed, gnawing the knuckle of her right forefinger. A bad habit she has no control over when she is stressed. It started the night she discovered her ex-husband had cheated, and grew so bad during the divorce, her finger got infected. Her phone regularly beeps with messages. Michael's school fan club asking how he is. What can they do to help?

It reminds her of when Abi was ill. Christina wanted help, however the only thing she truly desired, no one could give her. No one could make her daughter better, only the professionals.

To distract herself, she types out a standard answer that she copies and pastes in reply to every message.

Michael is stable. Thanks for asking. I'll be sending Anne-Marie regular updates. Best wishes, Christina.

With traffic so bad, Christina arrives late to collect the kids from school. They're waiting at the end of the tree-lined path, sitting on a low fence, hunched over their phones.

They wouldn't be at an educational establishment as exclusive as St Christopher's if it weren't for their dad paying the fees. It was part of the divorce settlement they remain there until they finish their schooling. That and the house and her car and everything valuable she owns.

Abi jumps up first and opens the car door. 'I've tried to call you.' She lunges for the front seat, eager to ride shotgun. 'I turned my phone on as soon as I got out of class, and there was nothing from you. I've been dead worried.'

Ben flings his backpack and games kit on the back seat with a grumble of frustration. 'If you'd let me drive, we could be home by now.' He jumps in behind his sister and slams the door.

'How's Michael?' Abi asks. 'Everyone is asking after him.'

'I'm sorry. I should've called you, but my phone's dead.' Christina turns around, indicating for Ben to remove his EarPods. He looks up, his face suddenly looking older than his seventeen years. His dark brown eyes stare at her blankly. Even though she says it herself, he is a good-looking lad. These past six months he has shot up and broadened. If it wasn't for his facial features still to mature, you could be forgiven for thinking he was a lot older.

'Take it out,' she says, pointing to her ear.

'What?' Ben says, removing an EarPod.

Christina relays Michael's injuries, looking from her son to her daughter. 'He's in a coma.'

'What? No way. That's dreadful,' says Abi.

'It's a medically induced one while they wait for the swelling in his brain to calm down.'

'That's awful,' says Ben. He reaches forward and squeezes her shoulder. 'I'm sorry, Mum.'

Christina sighs and pulls out of the school drive.

'This is real shit,' Abi says.

'Don't swear.'

They discuss Michael's injuries in detail. Abi yearns to be a doctor one day. Christina would've thought her daughter had seen enough hospitals and medical teams to last her forever. She explains the rationale of medically induced comas better than the doctors. 'Don't panic, Mum. Loads of people survive worse than this.'

'Why are you driving his car? Where's yours?' Abi asks.

'It wouldn't start.' Christina inwardly cringes. She hates lying, especially to her kids. Lies breed lies, she has always taught them. 'Ted's sorting it,' she adds before turning to her daughter. 'Any more headaches?'

'I had one this morning, but I got a tablet from the medical centre at lunchtime. I'm fine now.'

'Listen, Abi. You will tell me if you have another one, won't you?'

Abi rolls her eyes. 'Stop stressing, Mum.'

'You had a headache last night and another one today.'

Abi returns her attention to her phone.

Christina taps her daughter's knee to get her attention. 'I'm going to drop you home, get you something to eat and go back to the hospital.' Christina hates the thought of leaving Abi when she has been feeling unwell, but she can only be split in so many directions. 'You can have those salami pizzas in the freezer.'

'What about you?' Abi asks, forever the thoughtful kid.

'I'll grab a sandwich,' she lies. Christina's stomach is hollow, as if it has been sucked empty, but still she can't face food. 'The police are coming back later.'

'Why?'

Christina gulps. 'They want to ask some questions. To find out who did this.'

'I remember what time he went out now,' Abi says. 'I was thinking about it earlier. It was just after eight.'

Christina glances at her daughter before turning her attention back to the road. 'How do you know?'

'*Inside the Ambulance* had just started.' It's one of Abi's favourite programmes.

Christina makes a quick calculation. So Michael left the house forty minutes after her last night. The accident happened just before eleven o'clock. By her calculations, he must've spent almost three hours down the pub. That doesn't sound like him at all. He would never do that on a school night.

Something feels off about it.

Very off.

What the hell were you up to, Michael?

FOURTEEN

Arriving home, Ben heads straight upstairs.

Wilf follows Christina and Abi into the kitchen where Christina switches on the oven and puts her phone on charge.

Abi dumps her school bag on the worktop and pulls out her homework diary. 'He's going to be fine, Mum.'

Christina wishes she shared her daughter's conviction. 'It's odd he didn't say where he was going last night.'

'He might've done and I wasn't listening.' That's possible. When Abi gets engrossed in one of her medical programmes, she's in another zone. 'I'm off to start my homework.'

'Dinner will be ready in twenty minutes.'

Christina takes the pizzas out of the freezer. The sight of food heightens the nausea that hasn't left her since the police knocked on her door in the early hours of the morning. The slices of salami remind her of Michael's face, red and raw. She can't look at them. Busying herself, she tidies up until the oven reaches temperature. She slides the pizzas in and sets the timer.

Wilf shadows her into the lounge. Overcome with emotion, she drops onto the sofa, scrunching Michael's blanket and holding it to her face. 'I'm so sorry,' she whispers into the smell of his Lynx deodorant, vanilla and geranium.

Wilf whines, sensing her sorrow.

She drops the blanket on her lap as she notices the TV remote control stuffed down the side of the sofa. A habit that drives her nuts. The kids do it as well. Grabbing it, she realises it's not the remote control at all. It's Michael's iPhone. She's heard nothing from the nurse or police about Michael's belongings after she asked during her visit. No wonder.

Why didn't he take it with him last night? It doesn't make sense. She stares at the phone. Does it hold a clue as to where he went? She tries to switch it on but the battery is dead.

Her phone is using the only charger downstairs, so she runs up to Michael's study at the top of the house. She doesn't often come up here, where two attic rooms serve as a guest room and Michael's study. She has no reason to, other than when people stay over.

Michael's study is the smaller of the two rooms. It has a sloping ceiling and barely space for a bookcase, a desk and a filing cabinet. Books and trophies of Michael's sporting achievements throughout the years fill the bookcase. He was a prolific cyclist in his twenties, fractionally missing out on joining Team GB at the London 2012 Olympics Team Pursuit. Guilt stabs at her heart like a knife. He won't be cycling again anytime soon.

The smell of leather wafts from his jacket hanging on the back of the door. She runs her fingers along the sleeve, the leather smooth to her touch. She bought him this jacket the first Christmas they were together, six years ago. She shivers.

Searching for his phone charger, she lets out a low sigh to see a photo frame lying face down in the left-hand corner of his desk next to his computer. It holds a photo of the two of them cutting their wedding cake. She frowns. Did he turn it down? But why would he? Perhaps it fell. She stands it up.

She spots the lead to Michael's charger poking out from the

rear of the desk. Taking his phone out of her pocket, she plugs it in as Ben calls her from downstairs. 'Mum, where are you?'

Leaving the phone on charge, Christina runs downstairs to sort the kids. Not that they need much sorting. While they are eating, she grabs her phone and goes to her study to check her emails. She needs to answer a couple of work ones to help others who will be taking over the bulk of her work. Her phone beeps. It's a calendar reminder of her weekly buddy calls.

She belongs to a support group for parents whose children have recently been diagnosed with cancer. Every week, she has two half-hour Zoom calls, helping individual families by sharing the wealth of knowledge she has gained over the past ten years. The calls are tough, yet she knows how much they help these people. She still keeps in touch with Sandy – her and Adam's anchor of support in the rough tides of the first year of Abi's illness. She groans as a wave of guilt hits her. She won't be able to make the calls tonight. Emailing the group's main organiser, she apologises and explains her situation, temporarily withdrawing her help. Her husband has to be her priority.

Ben pops his head around the door. 'What's for pudding, Mum?'

'There's ice cream in the freezer.' Usually, she makes wholesome puddings: apple crumbles with oat-based topping, rice puddings and fruit pies. Something she started doing when Abi got ill to help her gain weight. However, tonight, junk food will have to suffice.

Before leaving for the hospital, she returns upstairs to Michael's study. She wants to look at what's on his phone. To see who he was in conversation with before he went out last night, because it seems very odd that he would've gone out for nearly three hours alone. He must've been meeting someone. Perhaps it was one of the guys from the cycling club he joins every Sunday morning.

She unplugs the iPhone and switches it on. The screen

lights up, asking for the passcode. They've always used their dates of birth. It's not very original, but at least they have a back-up by knowing each other's. She keys Michael's in. The screen flashes, telling her she got it wrong. She tries again. The same message appears on the screen.

Goosebumps appear on her arms as she tries for a third time. Slower this time.

Still no.

That's odd.

Why has Michael changed the passcode to his phone?

FIFTEEN

In the quietness of Michael's car, the changed passcode drums in her head as Christina pulls out of the driveway. She can't understand why he would've changed it.

The need to know tortures her as she drives along Ivy Road, which is now open. She can't help slowing down at the site of the accident. She shivers as it all comes back. The sickening thud as she hit something: Michael; getting out of the car in the torrential rain; searching in the darkness; the police turning up at her door.

A traffic jam delays her progress to the hospital. Too many roadworks and the dire weather conditions aren't helping. Michael's iPhone consumes her thoughts. But however hard she tries she can't answer the question: why would he have changed the passcode? It's something and nothing, but she wants to know. And why did he go out last night?

She can't concentrate. The fretfulness that has not let up since she was awoken early this morning refuses to leave her. Instead, it's worsening by the hour. A driver honks his horn at her for pulling out at a junction as he narrowly misses hitting her. Another one does the same when she veers into the wrong lane on a roundabout.

Sophia calls. 'Any news? Sebastian and I were thinking of going to see him this evening.'

It's not a good idea. Christina wants to protect her sister. She's never been able to deal with the sight of blood. 'Do you mind waiting? He's not yet awake.'

'Why not?'

'He's in a bad way, Sophia. I'm not sure if it's a good idea at the moment.'

'When will they wake him up?'

'They're not sure. It could be a couple of days. It could be weeks. It's too soon to say.'

'Perhaps we could go and visit him tomorrow?'

'Let's see, shall we? I think we're going to have to take it a day at a time.'

There's no change when she arrives at Michael's bed. The same wires rest on his body, the machines still flashing and beeping. She gently kisses his forehead, but there's no response.

A doctor drops by to give her an update. Not that there's anything new to report. Her husband's bloods are stable, and they're monitoring the swelling in his brain.

'Are people allowed to visit him?' Christina asks the nurse changing Michael's drip bag. 'My sister and brother-in-law want to come and see him.'

The nurse nods. 'As long as there's no more than two at a time. He had a visitor late this afternoon.'

Christina sits back in her chair. 'Who?'

The nurse shrugs. 'I don't know. I was just going on my break when they arrived. My colleague, Paul, mentioned it.'

'Were they male or female?'

'I don't know. I only saw the back of them quickly as I passed the bay.'

'What colour hair?'

'I'm sorry. They were wearing a baseball cap.'

'Can I ask the nurse? Paul.'

'He's left for the day. I'll ask him when I next see him.'

A horrible thought enters Christina's head. Jessica James, the girl who ruined everything for Michael, wears baseball caps. Christina saw her in town with her mum one day, shortly after the incident. She's put out. Surely she should say who sees her husband and who doesn't. But she doesn't have the energy to complain.

'Try talking to him. There's evidence to suggest he might be able to hear you.' The nurse's jolly face is a stark contrast to Christina's grave mood. 'Or at least sense that you're here.'

Christina doesn't know what to say to the unconscious man she has put in this position. The one she was discussing with her brother so depressingly only twenty hours ago. Not when she has so much on her mind. 'What do I talk about?'

'The kids. Your family. What do you all like doing together?' the nurse asks.

Christina thinks. What do they do other than eat the occasional dinner together some evenings, and work at the same school? They don't even drive to work together any more. He goes in much earlier than her. She works her schedule around the kids.

She holds her husband's cold hand as she tells him about the traffic and the weather, of all things. Her voice sounds fake. Talking to him is wholly uncomfortable. 'At least it's dry,' she says. *Unlike the night when I ran you down.* 'There's talk of snow for Christmas. That's a rarity in this part of the UK, isn't it?' *Maybe you won't get to see it.* 'The kids will be happy.'

He is so still, so unresponsive.

She racks her brains, thinking of something else to tell him, when all hell breaks loose.

SIXTEEN

An alarm sounds.

It's from the adjacent bay. A woman screams. The nurse seeing to Michael rushes from his bedside.

Christina blocks her ears. She can't bear to listen to the commotion that sounds like an inescapable road to death. It doesn't die down. Voices shout out frightening medical terms. Machines are wheeled towards the adjacent bay.

Her head spins.

For a moment, it was Michael's emergency.

It's suddenly stiflingly hot. It won't do anyone any good if she keels over while the medical staff are dealing with an emergency.

She stands and kisses her husband's broken face.

She needs to get out of here.

When she leaves the hospital, the weather is bitingly cold. It's a relief. She attempts to call Ted but has no signal. Climbing into Michael's car, she starts the engine. Suddenly she is shaking, not just from the drop in temperature but the fear. Michael's stillness had lulled her into a false sense of security. She'd forgotten, for a moment, that he was still in the ICU. He could still make a turn for the worse. Just like the guy in the neighbouring bed.

She eventually pulls out of the car park and checks her phone sitting in the cradle on the dashboard. Her thoughts turn to her Range Rover. What if Ted hasn't managed to return it yet? There's a signal now, so she calls her brother, swearing at his cheery voice telling his caller to leave a message.

Cutting the call, she pulls into a side road and tries another time, only to get his voicemail message again. 'Have you got my car back yet?' she says. 'Call me when you get this, please.'

She ends the call.

'Please, Ted, just phone me.' Her screaming voice echoes around the car. She needs to calm down, but she can't. 'Put my mind at ease. Tell me you've got my car back.' The thought of the detective arriving and asking after her car is too much to bear.

Why, oh why, did she go out last night?

Her heart weighs heavy as the realisation of her predicament takes full hold. She drops her head in her hands and takes a moment alone to deal with the guilt that has hit her as hard as a speeding lorry-load of bricks.

The journey home proves worse than the one there. The wind is cutting. She drives slowly, unable to calm her nerves. She can't have another accident.

Accident. That's all it was. She should've come clean. It's true. Once you lie, you can't stop. If only she'd just owned up last night. She glances at her phone again.

The weather is still causing chaos with the traffic. Christina thumps the steering wheel. She has to get home before the police show up. She waits in the queue of traffic, tapping the steering wheel while listening to the wind swirling around the car.

At six-fifty-five, she finally pulls into her driveway. The security lights on the side of the house and the carport flick on. She breathes a massive sigh of relief to see her Range Rover parked in the carport. The comfort quickly disappears as she realises Ben's car isn't on the drive.

Where has he gone? He is worrying her so much at the moment. He should be at home studying on a school night. His A levels are only a little over six months away, and he has coursework that is due in before the Christmas break.

Slotting Michael's Volvo beside her Range Rover, Christina gets out and finds the torch on her phone. She inspects the bar at the front of her car, surprised as the large breath she didn't realise she was holding escapes her shaking body.

Ted's mate has done an impressive job. As far as she can tell, the dent has miraculously disappeared.

She dashes inside. Wilf confronts her. She is late with his dinner, and he makes no bones about loading more guilt on her shoulder. With the faintest wag of his tail, he marches into the kitchen and sits beside his bowl, his head raised expectantly. Christina leans over and strokes his face. 'Want feeding, do you, Lord Muck?' Filling his bowl, she grins at her faithful dog, who, one could argue, has assumed an over-elevated position in the family food chain.

She runs upstairs to find Abi sitting at her desk, doing her homework, earphones on, oblivious to Christina's presence. She walks over and gently taps her shoulder. Abi startles and slides her earphones down her neck to sit on her shoulders. Taylor Swift blares out.

'How is he?' Abi asks solemnly.

'The same.'

'He's going to be all right, Mum.' She points to the screen of her laptop. 'Look. I've been doing more research. He's stable, you said.' She rattles off a list of statistics. 'Drug-induced comas are reversible, Mum. The chances of surviving them are high compared to natural comas. Hopefully, they'll wake him up soon,' her daughter says as if she's already the doctor she someday wants to be.

'How are *you*?' Christina asks.

'I'm fine.'

'Where's Ben gone?'

Abi shrugs. 'Haven't a clue. He said he was popping out and wouldn't be long. I said you wouldn't be happy.'

'I wish he'd let me know when he goes out. A simple text would do.'

'You can track on his car, you know. Dad told me. Then you'd know where he was all the time.'

'He would hate that.'

'Loads of people do it. It's easy. You just need to download an app.' Abi reverts to her screen.

'I'll have to look into it,' Christina says as she walks to the door. She doesn't want to invade her son's privacy. He would kick off. However, she can threaten it if he doesn't start letting her know where he's going. Perhaps his dad can have a word with him.

She rushes downstairs. The police will be here any minute. She switches on the kettle but changes her mind and steps to the fridge, pulling out a bottle of Pinot. Grabbing a glass from the cupboard, she fills it with wine and takes a generous gulp, trying to control her nerves as she prepares for the police to knock on her door. Her phone rings. She fishes it out of her bag.

It's Ted. 'How're things?' he asks.

She updates him on her visit to the hospital.

'I posted the keys through the letterbox. He's done a great job.'

'I've seen. How much do I owe you?'

'Nothing.'

'No way. You can't foot the bill for this.'

'I've sorted it. No arguments.'

'I owe you.'

'Don't be stupid. You're my sister. Let me know what the cops say.'

Car lights appear through the kitchen window. She walks over and peeps out. An unmarked car pulls up outside the house, activating the security lights. 'They've just arrived,' she tells her brother.

Two figures emerge from the vehicle. Are they the police? They don't have uniforms on like the two last night.

'At least I think it's the police. Catch you later.'

Christina gulps the last of her wine, places the glass in the dishwasher and rushes to the front door. She runs her hands through her hair, trying to tame her wild curls. She must compose herself.

Perhaps she should come clean – relay what actually happened last night. She restrains Wilf's collar in case he deems it appropriate to lunge at the visitors as she opens the door.

'DS Cyril Macintosh, we spoke earlier today,' the man says. He's of average height, medium build and has a rugged-looking face, like a hiker who has spent too many hours walking in bad weather. 'I'm leading the investigation into your husband's accident.' He gestures to his colleague. 'And this is DC Serena Cook.'

They are the police, then.

Christina steps backwards to let them in, hoping to heaven they can't hear her heart thumping in her chest.

Wilf inquisitively angles his head to study their visitors.

'Let him loose. We love dogs,' DC Cook says. She's a petite woman dressed in corduroys and a thick jumper. 'Don't we, Cyril?'

DS Macintosh nods, reaching to stroke Wilf's wiry coat. 'My Mum had an Irish Wolfhound. They're the best dogs.'

Christina doesn't have time for idle chatter. It will only prolong the agony of having them in her house. She guides them to the kitchen, pulls out two stools at the breakfast bar and offers them a drink. They decline, which silently pleases her.

'Before we start, how's your husband?' DS Macintosh asks. 'Has there been any improvement?'

'I've just come home from the hospital.' She briefs them on what she knows.

'I'm sorry to hear that.' The DS takes a deep breath. 'I know this must be a stressful time for you, so we'll try not to keep you for too long. We're just here to seek clarification on a few matters regarding your husband. We're trying to piece together his movements from last night as a number of things are not adding up.'

From Michael walking in a storm, to the unusual late night drinks at the pub and his phone passcode, Christina can't help but agree.

She just hopes that she's not part of the suspicion.

SEVENTEEN

Moving away from the officers, Christina leans her back against the white butler sink, the palms of her hands supporting her. She wills herself to suppress her emotions and speak concisely. It would help if her heart stopped pounding in her chest.

'What were your movements last night?' the DS asks, caressing the grey stubble on his chin. 'Were you in all evening?'

Are they onto her?

'No. Actually, I went out to see my brother.' Christina's attempt at acting cool is failing at the first hurdle. Her neck is flaring up as it does at any sign of stress or embarrassment. A quirk of hers that has always been a sense of amusement for her brother.

DS Macintosh's eyes flicker towards his colleague before returning to Christina. 'You didn't think to mention it to the officers last night?' he asks.

DC Cook writes in a small notebook.

Christina shrugs. Calm down, she tells herself. Getting stressed will only flame her cheeks even more. 'It was the middle of the night. They didn't ask. And I was kind of in shock.'

'I apologise.' The DS coughs. 'That was insensitive of me.'

'I'm sorry,' Christina says. 'I didn't think it was relevant.'

'So you went out to meet your brother. At what time was that?'

Christina hopes they can't detect the strained wobble in her voice that she knows is apparent – to her anyhow. 'Around seven-fifteen, seven-twenty.'

'Where did you go?'

'The Carpenter's Arms in Bradstock.'

'And you left Michael here with your children?'

Christina nods. 'That's what we agreed. When I came home, I thought he'd fallen asleep on the sofa.'

DS Macintosh repositions himself on the stool. 'Is that usual?'

'Sorry?' Christina says.

'Does he usually sleep on the sofa?'

'He gets bouts of insomnia. He stays downstairs some nights so as not to disturb me.' She pauses. Should she be offering up this information? She needs to tread carefully. One wrong step, and she's going to drop herself in deep water. 'Then he comes upstairs when he's ready.' That's a lie. Well, a part lie. He sometimes comes to bed. But not often any more.

DS Macintosh continues. 'We have video footage that shows him walking along the road at eight minutes past eight.'

Christina slowly nods her head. 'My daughter said he went out just after eight o'clock, so that makes sense.'

'Did he tell her where he was going?'

'No. He just said he was popping out and wouldn't be long.'

'Where do you think he went?'

'I'm guessing the pub,' she says.

The DS pauses. His lips twist to the side. 'We've conducted an initial house-to-house in the surrounding area, and video doorbell footage picked up Michael walking along Bridge End, as I said, at eight minutes past eight.'

Christina's frowns. Bridge End is the road almost opposite Ivy Brook. Now she *is* baffled. She'd assumed he had carried on left up Ivy Road to The Black Horse pub.

'Do you know why he would've been walking up Bridge End?' the DS asks. 'Where he was going?'

Christina thinks hard. She doesn't have a clue. 'I don't, sorry. I assumed he'd gone to the pub.'

A thought enters her head. Her jaw locks. Jessica James lives along a lane leading off the north end of Bridge End where her parents run another pub, The Farmer's Arms. Christina and Michael often used to take the kids there for a Sunday roast. Until the incident with Jessica at St Christopher's put a stop to that little family outing.

DS Macintosh strokes the stubble on his chin again. 'We've also discovered that Michael did go to the pub. However, not until later.'

Christina's frown deepens. What was he doing before that, then? 'Which pub?'

'The Black Horse. Someone dropped him off there at ten-thirty-six. Do you know who that could've been?'

She shakes her head, confused. She can't for the life of her think who that could've been.

DC Cook looks up from her notebook. 'Think about it. Sometimes answers don't come to us straight away.'

The conversation is getting uncomfortable. She wills herself to stay calm. They're not the only ones who want to know where Michael went last night.

'How do you know he was dropped off there at that time?' Christina asks.

'CCTV footage from The Black Horse, but we can't determine the make or model of the car. The same footage shows Michael entering the pub, and the landlord informs us he ordered a pint of beer, sat at a table in the corner and drank it quietly. Shortly afterwards, at ten-fifty-two, he is seen leaving.

From that, we estimate the accident happened between five and two minutes to eleven. Depending on how fast he was walking, of course. What time did you say you arrived home?'

Here we go. Keep it together, Christina. She shrugs her shoulders, biding her time. CCTV would've caught her at some point during her journey home. She chooses her words carefully. 'I'm not sure exactly. I left The Carpenter's Arms around ten-thirty. It's about a fifteen-minute drive home, so I guess around ten-forty-five.'

That's not exactly true. The ghastly weather delayed her journey. She had to keep slowing to take the bends and deal with the car aquaplaning on the surface water. 'It could've been later.'

'And you never saw him?' DC Cook asks.

She leans backwards, faking confusion at the DC's question. 'Of course not. I would've stopped to pick him up if I'd seen him.' Redness continues creeping up her face from her neck. She shouldn't have drunk that glass of wine. Alcohol is another culprit for turning her cheeks an unsightly shade of red.

'So the question is, where did he go between leaving here and ten-thirty-six?' DS Macintosh asks, although it's a statement rather than a question.

Christina's hand flies to her chest. 'I honestly don't know.'

'Could he have gone to a friend's house?' DC Cook suggests.

Christina is curious. Where the hell *did* he go? She clasps her hands together in her lap to stop herself from biting her knuckle. 'He doesn't have many friends around here. Apart from the guys he meets up with from the cycling club on Sundays, I guess.' She must remember to call Dermot, the guy who runs the club, and tell him Michael won't be there this Sunday. 'Most of his friends live up north. He moved down here for his job. He is a hundred per cent committed to his work and doesn't have much time for socialising.'

'How has his mood been lately?' DS Macintosh asks.

Does she tell the officers Michael has been depressed since the Jessica James incident, and the subsequent failing to gain the promotion he had dedicated his career to achieving? Yet what's the point in keeping quiet? If she doesn't tell them, they'll only find out from someone else. 'He hasn't been himself for a while.'

DC Macintosh fidgets on the stool as if he can't get himself comfortable. 'And why's that?'

'There was an incident at school with a female pupil, Jessica James. She told her best friend that something was going on between the two of them only for her friend to later call her out. Jessica admitted she had lied – made up the whole story. She had a crush on Michael and fabricated the incident because he had ignored her. It affected him badly. Really badly. As you can imagine.'

'Where does he teach, did you say?' DC Cook flicks her book.

'St Christopher's.'

The detectives exchange looks. 'Would you mind if we spoke to your children?' DC Cook asks.

'With you present, of course,' DS Macintosh adds.

'My son isn't in, but I'll go and fetch my daughter.'

Christina leaves the detectives and slowly walks to the stairs. What *was* her husband up to last night? Where *did* he go? She's as confused as the police. It's unlike Michael to go out on a weekday night unless it's a school event. And who the hell dropped him back at the pub?

When she returns with Abi, DS Macintosh questions her daughter about the last time she saw Michael. Abi is star-struck, as if famous actors are in the room. Christina has never seen Abi so transfixed. But it's not every day a couple of detectives turn up at your house and ask to speak to you. It's a big deal for her, but for completely different reasons.

Abi politely answers the detective's questions but doesn't add any information that Christina hasn't already told them.

DS Macintosh thanks Abi for her time and politely dismisses her. 'Something else confusing us is that Michael didn't have a phone on him,' DS Macintosh says.

'He left it here,' Christina says. 'I found it on the sofa.'

'Does he make a habit of going out without his phone?'

Christina shakes her head. 'I must say, I thought it strange.'

The detective frowns.

Is he thinking what she is thinking? Did he forget the phone, or did he not want to be tracked?

'Another strange occurrence,' the DS says. 'Have you looked at his phone?'

Christina pauses. Does she want to let on that Michael has changed the passcode? Will it look bad on her – that he changed his password and didn't tell her? Be reflective of a deteriorating marriage? 'No. I don't know his passcode.' She squirms at yet another lie, even if this one, at least, is small.

'Are you sure I can't get you a drink?' she asks, only to immediately regret it. She doesn't want them hanging about any longer than necessary.

To her relief, both detectives decline her offer. 'We're not stopping.' DS Macintosh stands and pushes his stool away from the breakfast bar. He fishes in his pocket and pulls out a business card. 'If you find out anything else that may help us with our inquiries, please do let us know.'

'Of course. And you me.' Christina takes the card. 'What happens now?' She needs to know what she's in for.

'We're hoping we can speak to your husband soon. When he's well enough, of course. He, hopefully, can answer our questions that will lead us to who did this.'

Is it her paranoia, or is that an expression of accusation plastered over DS Macintosh's rugged face he is directing her way?

'In the meantime, we'll continue with our inquiries. Learn

where your husband went last night and who he was with. We need to determine if this was in any way targeted or an accident where the driver panicked and drove off.'

He stares Christina directly in the eyes. 'Both are serious offences worthy of a custodial sentence.'

EIGHTEEN

'I'm sorry to hear about Michael.' Adam says, when he comes to collect Abi and Ben on Saturday morning.

Her ex is a such a good-looking guy: deep, expressive eyes, laddish stubble, and so tall at six foot three. But his beauty turned to ugliness the day she discovered he had cheated on her. If she had her way, she'd never have seen him again, but she doesn't want the kids to suffer because of their father's wrongdoing. She thought she'd done well in this regard, and it's a surprise that, for the first time, Ben doesn't want to spend the weekend with him.

She calls Ben's phone. 'Your dad's here. Come down, please.'

'What's up with him?' Adam asks.

'He's so moody at the moment.' Christina rolls her eyes. 'A typical teenager. Could you do me a favour, please? Have a word with him about letting me know where he's off to when he goes out in his car.'

'Of course I will. That's just not on.'

'It worries me sick.'

'Leave it with me.'

Ben appears, still in his pyjamas, hair on end, sleepy eyed.

'Come on, buddy. Your mum's busy with stuff,' Adam says. 'We've got a great weekend planned, and I've booked that restaurant you wanted to go to. The Japanese one.'

She glances at Adam. Where would they be now if he'd never cheated? He never wanted them to divorce. He begged and begged for her forgiveness, cried and cried for his silly mistake. But she knew there was no coming back from his infidelity, even if it was only a one-night stand. She now needs to find that strength again to get through the next drama playing out in her life.

After some persuasion, Ben agrees to go. Christina watches Adam's Porsche leave the drive with her children from the kitchen window. Normally, she hates the weekends they spend with their father. She enjoys time on her own, but that feeling of emptiness and the dull sound of an empty house for the whole weekend is depressing. And Adam spoils them rotten, overindulging them in things they don't need and unhealthy food that takes them a couple of days to work out of their systems. But she can't help the relief that they're off this weekend. It will be one less thing to think about.

She tries to keep occupied until it's time to go to the hospital, mindless activities, starting with the kids' bedrooms. A chore she always tackles when they go to their dad's for the weekend. In truth, it's a real effort today. In a trance, she quickly runs the hoover around Abi's room. Ben's room is not as easy. The floor is covered with crap she has to dump on the bed before she can contemplate hoovering.

Her phone keeps beeping with text messages – people asking if there's any news. Every message is a reminder of the unspeakable thing she has done. She'll answer them at the hospital. It'll give her something to do. She catches up on emails, but nothing can rid the fear of Michael dying hanging over her like a dark cloud that refuses to disappear.

The house is even emptier without him around. Not that they spend much time together any more. Even when the kids are away, he is either out at a sporting fixture for school or locked away in his study, marking pupils' work or planning lessons. And every Sunday morning, he joins the local cycling club for a lengthy bike ride.

That reminds her. She needs to call Dermot and let him know Michael won't be cycling tomorrow morning. She'll have to track him down via the club as she doesn't have his number. Or via Michael's Facebook page.

She heads to her study and fires up her computer. Clicking on Facebook, she opens her page and scrolls through her feed. August was the last time she posted when she took the kids on holiday to Wales. She stops at a picture of the three of them eating ice creams on Tenby beach. A post that brought in many comments about what a wonderful time it looked like they were having and what a fantastic photographer Michael was. She never bothered replying that a passer-by had taken the photo because Michael had been ill, so they had gone without him.

For the first time, the thought strikes her. Was he telling the truth? He'd been very cagey about it. Other than a slight cough – which, of course, he could've faked – he'd had no other symptoms. The night before, he'd come to bed and not slept on the sofa. She remembers because he'd packed his case before retiring for the night. The following morning he got up before the alarm went off, saying he felt like he had the flu and complaining about the cough he'd had all night. Not that she'd heard it.

She'd believed him. Why wouldn't she have?

'You're going to have to go without me. I'll stay here,' he said.

She was deeply disappointed. She had been looking forward to that holiday all summer, and so had the kids.

But now a sickly feeling makes her question if he did indeed stay at home. They had spoken every day, however a couple of times, she remembers not being able to get through to him. Calling back later, he said that he had been asleep.

Her stomach churns as she searches for Michael's Facebook page and can't find it. That's strange. Clicking on her friends, she types his name into the search bar. It returns *No Results*. She goes back to her feed and scrolls to find a post she would have tagged him in. She comes across a post from Easter last year when they went to Sophia and Sebastian's house for lunch. She would definitely have tagged Michael on that post. His account has been removed.

He must have deleted it.

Why would he have done that?

NINETEEN

DS Macintosh's call makes Christina jump.

Every second of the conversation with the detective makes her squirm.

He kindly asks after Michael and how she is bearing up. He doesn't have an update from his end yet wants to assure her he is doing everything he can to find the person who has done this to her husband.

She is not fully concentrating on what he is saying. She wants to get him off the phone so she can find out why Michael has deleted his Facebook account.

DS Macintosh ends the call. 'I'll keep you posted when I find out more.'

What was the point of that? He's making her nervous with his constant calls. Maybe that's the point.

She continues her search for Dermot Hall and finds who she is looking for straight away.

He posts regularly, mostly pictures related to cycling. Scrolling through his page, she studies the helmet-wearing selfies of him and other cyclists dressed in Lycra during their weekend rides. Happiness beams off the page like a ray of sunshine.

Frowning, she scrolls faster.

There are no photos of Michael with Dermot. She clicks on the photos section and examines them one by one. Michael is in none of them.

Dermot isn't a friend of hers, so Christina feels uncomfortable about messaging him. She sends him a friend request and re-examines the page in case she is wrong.

Squinting at the screen, she eventually finds a group photo of several cyclists with Michael in the background. But it's from March this year, eight months ago.

Before she can think too hard about that, a message flashes on the screen. Dermot has accepted her friend request. She sends him a message.

Hi Dermot. It's Christina here. Michael's wife from the cycling club. I'm not sure if you've heard. Michael's been involved in an accident. He's in the Royal Alexandra. So he won't be at the club for a while. I just wanted you to know. Best wishes, Christina.

She resumes scrutinising Dermot's page, pausing when her phone pings with a reply.

I'm so sorry. I didn't know. How dreadful. I tried to contact Michael a few weeks ago because we haven't seen him at the club for so long and we miss him. Please send him our regards. Is he allowed visitors? I'd love to see him. Take care, Dermot.

Christina stops reading, her stomach dropping. They haven't seen him at the club for so long? Where does Michael go every Sunday morning, then?

At least that's what he has told her.

So where has he been going?

She needs to speak to this guy. Holding her breath, she types another message.

Would you mind if I called you? Christina

Not at all. Any time. Dermot.

She presses the call button at the top right-hand corner of the screen.

Dermot answers straight away.

'Hi, Christina, I'm so sorry to hear about Michael. How're you bearing up?'

'As best as can be expected.' She briefs Dermot on what has happened.

'A coma? That's awful.'

'I'm praying he'll pull through. Can I ask you a question?'

'Fire away.'

'When did Michael stop joining your Sunday bike rides? The doctor asked me about the exercise he takes.' She winces. When did she get so good at lying? 'And I couldn't remember when he stopped cycling with you.'

'Now you're asking. Let me think.' There's a pause. 'I don't believe I've seen him all summer. I'll have to look at the log. I'll message you and let you know.'

'That'll be very helpful.' She considers inviting Dermot to come and see Michael when he is up for visitors but stops herself. What if Michael doesn't want to see him? She can't think of why he wouldn't. But there must be a reason why he stopped going to the club. It doesn't make sense. 'I'll keep you updated on when he can have visitors.'

'That'll be great. I expect a couple of the lads will want to come along, too. Take care of yourself, Christina. If there is anything I can do for you – anything at all – please let me know.'

She ends the call.

Michael hasn't been to the cycling club for over half a year at least.

So where has he been going?

TWENTY

Christina takes Michael's car to the hospital. She has been driving his Volvo since the accident. Every time she sits behind the wheel of her Range Rover, she is transported back to the moment she hit him and she can't function. Her car has turned into a friend she never wants to see again.

She drives carefully, conscious she is exhausted and on edge. How could Michael not have been to the cycling club for so long and she didn't know?

When she arrives at the hospital car park, she takes a few deep breaths, trying to prepare herself. The thought that Michael could die constantly plagues her.

Realising she has no change, she searches the glove compartment for the stash of coins Michael keeps around, just in case. There's a vending machine outside the ward where she can get something to eat later if she can face it.

She attempts to close the compartment door, but there's something sticking out of the bottom left-hand corner preventing her. What is that?

It feels like leather. She releases the seatbelt and leans her body closer. It's the finger of a black leather glove. She drops the door open and picks it up. Her stomach clenches. It's far too small to be Michael's. She lays it on her open hand. There's no mistaking. The glove belongs to a female. She searches through the compartment and finds a matching one. What is a pair of women's gloves doing in her husband's car?

She can't stop herself shaking as she makes her way to the ICU, wondering who the gloves could belong to. Does Michael have another woman? But it doesn't make sense.

Michael knows how devastated she was before. And she had made it clear, any signs of him cheating, and she would do the same she did to Adam – chuck him and his belongings out of the house without a second thought. Michael understood. She was the love of his life, he said, and vowed he would never cheat on her.

She believed him. She still does. However, things aren't adding up. A fleeting thought of Jessica James enters her mind, but she quickly dismisses it.

Reaching the ward, she finds Michael still unconscious. She squeezes his hand. It's cold. She whispers, 'Good afternoon,' in his ear. There's no response.

She's running out of things to say to him. It was inevitable. So she reads aloud all the messages well-wishers have sent, omitting the one from the drama teacher at St Christopher's whom Michael is close to.

I hope they find the bastard who did this to him.

She swallows the lump constantly in the back of her throat as she studies her husband. She needs him conscious. There are questions she needs answered. Her husband has become a mystery she has to solve.

An alarm sounds from one of the machines. It's deafening. The machine flashes red. Bodies appear like people darting off a crowded train onto a busy station platform.

A hand touches her shoulder.

Christina turns to see a nurse talking to her.

A melee of doctors and nurses frantically rush around, barking instructions to clear the way.

'Let's get you out of here,' the nurse says.

'What's happening?' Christina shrieks.

The nurse grabs her arm and pulls her up.

The machine is still alarming. His pulse has dropped dramatically.

'Michael?' she screams, watching helplessly as the nurse firmly leads her away.

'Let the experts deal with him. It's best for everyone if we give them the space they need,' the nurse says.

Morbid thoughts race through her mind. 'Is he going to die?' Christina cries.

This can't happen.

Her husband can't die.

TWENTY-ONE

Christina sleeps in fits and starts. Every time she closes her eyes, all she can see is the machine by Michael's bed flatlining as the nurse led her away yesterday, which forces them back open. And when she finally manages to fall asleep, every time she wakes up, it's with a heavy knowing that she's done something wrong. Something dreadfully, dreadfully wrong.

On Sunday morning, she washes her greasy hair, and throws on some clean clothes to shoot over to Sebastian and Sophia's house. She's not in the mood, but it's Lily's birthday. Facing a room full of strangers feels an unmanageable task, so she is taking a present and card beforehand.

She pulls up outside the 1930s semi-detached house on the tree-lined road. Stained-glass panelling encases the front door, and net curtains cover the bay windows. Sebastian's mother, Nancy, owns the house, and Sebastian and Sophia moved in with her five years ago after his father died. A temporary arrangement that turned permanent despite Sophia's insistence that they'll get their own place 'someday'.

Sophia answers the door holding Lily on her hip. The smell of freshly baked sausage rolls wafts in the air.

Christina smiles for the first time in what feels like days to see her niece. From the moment she was born, Lily has always managed to lift her when she has felt down. Her niece's presence in her life has evoked emotions Christina never knew she still had. From the moment she first set eyes on her fluffy wave of dark hair and wrinkly body, Christina has felt broody.

When they decided to get married, she and Michael agreed more children were not part of their future together. Michael had never wanted children. The kids at school were enough for him. And Ben and Abi were enough for her... until Lily came along. The desire to have another baby was so strong that in the summer she broached the subject with him. He wouldn't budge. Besides, at forty-five, she was too old. Not that it's unheard of to have a baby at her age.

Christina pecks Sophia's cheek and whisks Lily from her hip, savouring the smell of fabric softener as she takes the babbling bundle of perfection into her arms.

'How's my favourite niece?' she says, kissing Lily's forehead. The toddler gurgles in reply, smacking her hands on Christina's chest.

Stepping over the threshold, Christina shivers. There's something creepy about this house. Nancy has never got over losing her husband suddenly. After he died, she turned the house into a shrine to him. Every room, except for Sophia and Sebastian's bedroom, and Lily's, of course, is filled with photos of her deceased husband.

Christina follows Sophia into the kitchen-dining room, where every type of party food imaginable covers the extended dining table. Sophia loves entertaining and always goes full out on these occasions.

Ted is cutting the crusts off a pile of egg and cress sandwiches.

Christina hugs him. 'Where's Sebastian?' she asks.

'Playing golf as he always does at the weekends. And

Nancy's at church,' says Sophia. 'I dropped her off and Sebastian is picking her up on his way home. They should be back soon. Drink? I'm having wine.'

'Not for me. Make mine a cup of tea.' She turns her attention to Lily, squirming to get out of her arms. 'Aunty Christina's got a present for you.'

'Any news?' Sophia asks, throwing a tea bag into a cup.

'Nothing.' Christina bends down to release Lily onto the floor. 'There was a drama yesterday. It scared the hell out of me.'

'What happened?'

'I really thought I'd lost him.' Her voice wobbles. 'And it was just a faulty machine.'

Sophia's eyes well up. 'That's dreadful. How can important machines like that be faulty?'

'It was just one of those things.'

'What about the police?' Sophia asks.

'Nothing.'

'It doesn't make sense.' Sophia places her hands on her hips. 'I can't work it out. Surely someone must've seen something. Or found out where he went before the pub.'

Christina and Ted glance at each other. 'You'd have thought so.' Christina hates lying to her sister. But she doesn't want to tangle Sophia into her web of lies. 'The police have video doorbell footage of him walking up Bridge End just after eight o'clock. And someone dropped him off at The Black Horse just after ten-thirty.'

'I don't get it. They're in opposite directions.' Sophia hands Christina a mug of tea.

'Exactly. I don't get it, either.' Christina sips her tea, the warmth a comfort in the cold world she has found herself trapped in. 'I'm desperate to know where he went.'

Sophia pops a grape in her mouth and walks to the patio doors with her glass of wine. The sunlight glows on her head, giving her copper hair a golden glow. 'It all so weird,' she says, staring into the garden as she sips her wine. 'Where do you think he could've gone during that time?'

Christina shrugs. 'I just don't know.' She cups her cold hands around the mug, warming them. It's wrong. She *should* know. 'He told me he was staying at home with the kids.'

'Could he have gone to school?' Sophia asks.

'The police will check CCTV, I guess.' Christina changes the subject. She can see her sister getting upset and she doesn't want to ruin Lily's party. It's a day to be happy. 'I'll leave this here.' Christina takes Lily's present out of her bag and places it on the kitchen counter. 'I'm not staying long. I want to get to the hospital.'

'I understand,' Sophia says. 'Lily won't notice. Keep us posted on how he is, won't you?'

'He's going to be fine,' Christina says as convincingly as she can to comfort her sister. She doesn't need this.

Lily cries out. She must have crawled into the lounge. Sophia shoots after her before Christina can answer. 'Mummy's coming.'

Ted's phone buzzes. He lifts the screen and smiles.

'Who's that?' Christina asks.

'Someone I met a while ago,' he says, pocketing his phone. 'She's a client I've been helping.'

Christina laughs. 'Helping? In what regards?'

'Keep it clean, sis. I've installed a new bathroom for her.'

'What's her name?'

'Melanie. Mel for short.'

'Why haven't you told me about her?'

He shrugs. 'I wanted to see how it went.'

'You really like her, don't you? I can tell.'

He gives a coy smile.

'When can I meet her?'

He shrugs again, moving to the door, ensuring Sophia is

safely out of earshot. He lowers his voice and resumes sandwich duty. 'Any update from the police? Really?'

'Only what I just told you both. Listen, I'm thinking of handing myself in.'

Ted pauses, the knife sliced halfway through the crusts of a pile of sandwiches. 'It's a bit late for that, isn't it?'

'I don't think I can live with myself.'

'The police will want to know who fixed your car. How're we going to get around that one?'

Christina rapidly shakes her head. 'I don't know.'

'You can't involve me, Chrissy. I'd get banged up, too. Is that what you want – for us to both go to prison? Why are you driving Michael's car, by the way? I saw you pull up.'

'Every time I get in mine, I lose it.'

He steps over and cuddles her. 'You've got to pull yourself together.'

She can feel the knife against her back, the blade in her hair. 'I'm finding it so damn hard.'

'I know. It's not good, but falling apart won't help the situation.'

'Get this, too.' She draws away from him and relays her conversation with Dermot. 'He couldn't remember when he last saw Michael at the cycling club.'

Ted frowns. 'I drove past him a few months ago. He was on his bike.'

'Did you? When exactly?'

His eyes widen as he puffs out a large breath. 'I can't remember exactly when. It was a Sunday morning, though, because I remember thinking, he must be on his way to his cycling club. At least I think it was him. It's hard to tell sometimes. All these cyclists look the same to me when they've got helmets on.' He grabs her shoulders, the blade of the knife by her ear.

She leans her head away. 'Can you please put that knife down.'

He snorts. 'I'm sorry.' He places the knife on the counter. 'Listen! Get back into your car. It'll only raise suspicions if you keep driving around in Michael's. It'll get easier. You don't want to give them any reason to have you in for questioning.'

'That's what hits me, whenever I get in my car. I'm terrified that's what's going to happen.'

TWENTY-TWO

'Terrified?' Sophia bursts into the room, swinging a giggling Lily from side to side. 'What's happened? Have you had news?' She looks from Christina to Ted anxiously.

Christina fights a rising panic. What did Sophia overhear about that conversation? It's enough dragging Ted through her mess. 'No, nothing new. I'm just so terrified Michael's going to die.' What a silly thing to say when guests are soon to arrive.

Sophia's eyebrows pull together. 'Don't say that.' She swings her daughter faster. Lily's feet brush along the floor. 'It's not going to happen.' Her voice gets louder and louder. 'This was just a blip. You said so yourself. He's a fit and strong guy. And the sort of person who'll see this as a challenge. He'll pull through it and then—' She turns to a knock at the front door and sighs heavily. 'Don't say we have early guests. I'm not ready.' There's another knock. 'Bloody hell.'

Christina glances towards Ted as Sophia leaves the room. 'How much of that do you think she heard?' she mouths to Ted.

'For heaven's sake, Chrissy, stop being so paranoid.'

She can't help it. Ever since Wednesday night, she has been sick with fear that she's going to expose the truth about what she did that night. She's a straightforward person. But now her whole world has been rocked to its core, and she's struggling to cope. Absently, she picks up Sophia's glass of wine and takes a swig.

'What're you doing?' Ted says.

He's right. What is she doing? 'I don't—'

They turn to Nancy, a large lady who speaks her mind, entering the room with Sophia. Christina likes Nancy. They have always got on well, although she finds the woman's obsession with her dead husband a little disconcerting.

'I'm sorry to hear about Michael.' Nancy shakes her head. 'What a terrible thing to happen. I've been praying for him.' She tuts. 'There sure are some unscrupulous people in this world. Who would do such a thing?'

Christina inwardly winces. Unscrupulous. Another adjective to add to the growing list of words to describe herself. She replaces the glass of wine on the side. 'Where's Sebastian?' she asks to change the subject.

'Putting away his golf clubs in the garage,' Nancy says.

They chat about the party until Sebastian walks in. He's a reserved chap – sombre and dignified – but it suits his job as an undertaker.

Sebastian acknowledges Ted with a nod and addresses Christina. 'Any news from the police?' His fair eyebrows are raised in hope just the same as everyone who asks that question.

Christina shakes her head. 'Nothing.' She takes Lily from her sister, seeking a moment's solace in the comfort of her niece's infectious giggles. She holds her tighter as her family stand around, discussing the disturbing events.

'I'm surprised the police haven't found out more,' Sebastian says. 'I mean, come on, with all the CCTV around, you'd have thought they'd have something to go on.'

'It was bucketing down that night,' says Sophia. 'The weather has hounded their efforts, apparently.'

'I still can't believe who would do such a thing,' Nancy says.

Sophia stares at Christina, the corners of her mouth downturned. 'I hope they catch the bastard soon.' The venom in her tone is biting.

Christina leans against the fridge to steady herself. As she peers around the confined space of the kitchen, everyone seems to be looking at her, their eyes boring into her soul. What are they expecting her to say?

Breaking her trance, she makes her excuses. She needs to get out of here. It's claustrophobic. 'I have to get going. I don't want to be late for visiting hours. Here, take Lily.' She passes her niece to Sophia.

Ted steps in. 'Of course. You go.' His voice wavers. He is feeling the guilt as well.

How long can she continue this pretence with her family?

Something will give.

It has to.

TWENTY-THREE

It has taken two days, but Christina is finally behind the wheel of her car again. However, the disturbing thought won't leave her – the last time she drove this beast of a car, she ran her husband over.

Things are looking up. She had a call yesterday to say the swelling on Michael's brain had significantly reduced and the doctors were reversing the coma. He still wasn't awake when she visited, but the doctors weren't concerned. Everyone is different. They said it could take hours, days even for him to come around.

A doctor in front of her holds his pass over the buzzer when she gets to the ICU. She seizes her chance and trails him onto the ward. A crying woman passes her, barging her way through the doors. Despite the call from the doctor earlier, her sobs are a harsh warning of the gravity of the situation Michael is in.

Losing the doctor at the reception desk, Christina veers off to B Bay. When she gets there, she stops suddenly.

It's not Michael in the bed, but a young chap on a ventilator. His face is a pulp. She stares at him wide-eyed. His head is wrapped in bandages, and he is attached to as many machines as Michael was.

Panic, thick and suffocating, stuns her. She gasps. What has happened to Michael?

She imagines the worst. Visions of attending his funeral consume her – standing in the pouring rain throwing earth on his coffin and watching as Sebastian and his colleagues lower him into the ground.

There must be some mistake.

He can't die.

She can't have killed her husband.

Desperately, she dashes back to the reception desk. Her question is a shrill in the relative quietness. 'What's happened to Michael? Where's my husband?'

The three nurses sitting behind the reception desk simultaneously snap their attention from their screens. One of them, a forty-something woman as skinny as Abi, jumps up. 'Mrs Blake. Has no one been in contact?'

TWENTY-FOUR

'Michael has been moved. Someone should've informed you.'

'They didn't.' Christina's panic subsides. 'No one called. What's going on?'

'I'm so sorry. There must've been a mix-up. You should've received a call. He's been moved to Jarrad ward.' The nurse grabs a navy cardigan from the back of her chair. 'It's not far from here. I'll take you.'

As they leave the ICU, the nurse wraps her arms around her body and explains how some emergency cases came in overnight. 'There was a bad collision on the motorway. An eight-car pile-up. We had to admit four patients, so a couple had to be moved.'

'But he's still so ill.'

'Take it as good news. They wouldn't have moved your fella if they didn't think he was up to it.'

'Does this mean he's getting better?' Christina's voice breaks with relief and fear. Relief that he is still alive. Yet fear that now he is getting better he might expose what she did.

'It does, so please don't worry. It's still a high dependency ward, but not at the level of the ICU.' The nurse stops at a set of grey doors. 'Here you go.'

'Thank you.' Christina hesitates. 'Could I ask you something?'

'Fire away.'

'Michael had a visitor last week. On Thursday. I think a nurse called Paul was on duty. I want to know who that visitor was.'

'Paul's not on shift. I could ask him when I next see him and let you know.'

'Thank you. It's just strange that Michael had a visitor, and I don't know who it was.'

'I understand. Leave it with me.'

Jarrad ward has a different vibe to the ICU. The air is a concoction of the lingering waft of hospital dinners and antiseptic. It unsettles Christina's stomach.

A lively-faced nurse shows her to Michael's bed in a room with two other patients in various stages of recovery. But clearly none are as sick as those on the ICU.

The nurse's voice is as lively as her face. 'He came down to us around six o'clock this morning after a stable night.' She squeezes Christina's forearm. 'Please don't be alarmed. It's a step in the right direction. A step further to getting him home.'

They find Michael asleep. The swelling in his face has subsided significantly since Christina saw him yesterday. 'The move must've shattered him,' the nurse says. 'He was awake when I took his blood pressure earlier. Groggy, but awake.'

Christina sits beside the bed for a while, trying to talk to him as she stifles tears of sadness and shame. Why has he not woken up for her? Does it matter? He has been awake. Not in her presence, but it must mean he's making baby steps to recovery.

Ted was wrong, though. It's not easier to live with what she has done now that Michael's condition is improving. It's only getting harder.

This is her punishment.

The enormity of the situation overwhelms her. She's drowning in a river of guilt with no lifebuoy in sight. She leans over her husband, laying her head beside his, her nose almost touching his cheek. The steady beat of the monitor attached to pads on his chest is a stark contrast to the tumult troubling her mind. 'I'll bring your beard trimmer when I come tomorrow.' She runs her finger over the roughness of his chin. 'Tidy this up for you. I'll get some of that dry shampoo, too. Give your hair a wash.'

She continues talking to him. The ward is so hot, the smell of disinfectant and the continuous monotone sounds of the machines oppressive. She needs some air.

Standing, she picks up her bag, and kisses Michael's lips. They're so dry. Throwing her bag over her shoulder, she takes a mouth swab from the packet on the overbed table and dips it in the plastic pot of water. She dabs it on his cracked lips and swishes it around the inside of his mouth, suddenly stopping like a deer caught in headlights as his eyes open.

'Michael. You're awake!' She drops her bag to the floor. Emotion overcomes her. 'It's so good to see you.' She kisses him again, convincing herself he's going to be OK. He's going to live.

He stares at her. It's unnerving. It's as if he is looking into her soul watching the crime she committed on replay. The crime that put him in this bed.

She doesn't know whether to laugh or cry. He's awake. That's the important thing. He's going to be OK. The relief is overwhelming.

She hesitates before taking his hand. It's still so cold. 'Do you know why you're here?'

He nods, slowly, deliberately. 'Someone ran me over.' His

voice is gravelly, low and rough, as if he has smoked a thousand cigarettes.

'That's right.' She must restrain herself, fight the urge to ask all the questions on the tip of her tongue.

'Who?' he says, staring her out.

Fear trickles down her spine. Does he know it was her?

'We don't know, darling.' She grits her teeth, hating herself as she anticipates the necessary lies that are going to spill from her mouth over the coming days... weeks... months. 'They drove off. Did you see anything?'

His eyes glare at her.

TWENTY-FIVE

'I don't remember a thing,' he says.

'Nothing at all?'

He moves his head from side to side, slowly, as if it's painful.

'Do you not remember going out that night?' She tries to keep the mounting frustration from her voice. He has been through hell. She needs to give him time. But she can't help herself. Her inner turmoil won't let it go.

He squints, and keeps shaking his head, wincing. A nurse appears. She needs to do Michael's observations.

'I'll grab a coffee.' Christina kisses Michael's cheek. 'I'll be right back.'

Leaving the ward, a relieving stream of cool air hits her. She fishes in her bag for some change, buys a coffee from the vending machine and sits on a plastic chair in a row of three by the machine. She blows on the top of the coffee before drinking it, relishing the hit it gives her, despite its bitter taste. She needs to tread carefully with Michael, but there is so much she needs to know, it's going to prove difficult.

When she returns to him, he is sitting up in bed, sipping a beaker of water through a straw. He asks her questions. She answers them the best she can, before asking, 'What's the last thing you remember?'

There's a long pause.

She holds her breath, waiting for his reply.

'Being at work,' he says.

'You must remember going out?' She's pressing him too much. She can feel the desperation in her quivering voice. She needs to back off.

His reply is short and sharp. 'I don't.'

'Give it time, darling. It may all come back to you. The most important thing is you're here. You survived.' She briefs him on what has happened since the accident, before blurting out, 'I want to ask you about your phone.' She is pushing him too much too soon. But she has to know. 'You've changed the passcode.'

His glaring eyes continue staring her out.

'Why did you do that, darling?' she continues.

He shrugs.

'We've always used our dates of birth, so we've got back-up for each other. Why did you change yours?' A voice of reason is shouting at her to back off. And she can just hear Ted saying, 'Ease off, Chrissy.' But she can't.

'I don't remember doing it.'

Is that the truth?

'And why didn't you take your phone with you when you went out that night?'

The lines on his forehead deepen. 'Didn't I?'

'No, you left it in the lounge. I found it down the side of the sofa. I thought it was the remote control at first.'

'Makes no sense.' He shrugs. 'Must've forgotten. Can you bring it in?'

'I have it here.' She pulls it out of her bag. 'Perhaps you can get into it and we can see if you were chatting to anyone before you went out that night. To see if there are any clues of where you went.'

'Give it to me.' He snatches it from her.

Her line of questioning has obviously riled him. Nevertheless, his aggressiveness startles her. That was unnecessary. 'We need to know where you went, Michael. You said you would stay in with the kids and help Ben with a piece of homework he was stuck on, but you didn't. And Ben went out, so you left Abi on her own.'

'Did I?'

'Someone picked you up from Bridge End. You went somewhere with them, and two and a half hours later, they dropped you at The Black Horse.'

'That's strange.'

'Put yourself in my shoes. Or anybody's shoes. Wouldn't you want to know where I had been?'

'I don't know. I can't remember a thing.'

She clenches her jaw. Doesn't know or doesn't want to let on? 'You must remember something, Michael.'

'I'm sorry.' He appears confused. 'I simply don't remember a thing.'

She fakes a smile. 'OK.' She needs to back off.

He turns on the phone and stares at it. 'I can't remember the passcode.' He tosses it aside. Is he going to cry? 'I'll have to think about it,' he says, his voice high-pitched.

Have a think? Is that the truth? Or does he not want her around when he gets into the iPhone so he can delete any conversation he had before he went out? Sadness overcomes her. Never once did she doubt him before the accident. Is she being unfair?

She changes the subject, reserving further discussion for when he is stronger. What was she thinking? The poor guy has only just woken up. Her desperation got the better of her. She tells him about the dressing gown she bought Lily for her birthday and all the party food Sophia prepared. 'She was cooking sausage rolls when I got there. Homemade ones. You would've loved them.' Her voice wavers. 'I'll get the recipe and make you some when you get out of here.'

The lively-faced nurse pulls the blue curtain from around the bed. 'We need to take your husband for a scan.'

'I'll go for a walk.' Maybe she can eat something now he is awake. She kisses her husband. 'You're going to get better, darling. You're on the road to recovery. We can get through this. I'll see you soon.'

His eyes glisten with tears. He turns his head away.

TWENTY-SIX

Taking the lift to the ground floor, Christina sends a text to everyone telling them Michael is awake and she has spoken to him.

Messages flood in, sharing her relief.

She exits the hospital and circles the perimeter. It's bigger than she remembers. The cold winter breeze is refreshing. It goes some way to clearing her head for the fifteen minutes it takes for her to briskly walk around.

She should eat something. Hunger grumbles in her stomach for the first time since the accident. She has been, and still is, functioning on her nerves. Yet, as she peruses the items in the glass cabinet in the café, nothing takes her fancy. Usually, she has a sweet tooth, so she settles on a slice of rocky road. How fitting. Rocky road. It perfectly sums up the path her life has taken recently.

Finding a seat at a table at the edge of the café, she picks up a fork and stabs it into the lump of traybake. A piece breaks away and shoots off the side of the plate. She reaches out to pick it up when her heart skips a beat.

Through the glass panel, she sees her. The person she never wanted to see in her life again.

Jessica James.

And she's wearing a baseball cap.

Is it definitely her? Christina strains her neck, squinting as she watches the tall young woman with long dark hair fade into the distance. But this woman's hair is straight. Jessica wears her hair curly. At least she always used to.

Christina pushes the chair away from the table and goes after her. The woman, dressed in tight leggings, heeled boots and a black puffa jacket, is slotting money into a vending machine. Christina stands by a wall watching her. She bites her knuckle.

The woman bends down, sticks her hand into the mouth of the vending machine and pulls out a chocolate bar. She turns around, confirming Christina's suspicions. The exposed midriff, heart-shaped full lips, winged eyeliner, yes, it's undoubtedly Jessica.

What the hell is she doing here?

Has she come to visit Michael?

Is she the person who visited him on Thursday?

Christina's heart is beating so fast she can feel it in her chest. She wants to go after her and confront her, ask her what she's doing here.

But she can't.

Not after last time.

Christina had lost her temper. She didn't mean to. Jessica was in one of the music rooms at school. A keen pianist, she was practising for an upcoming grading. There was no one else about.

So no one heard Christina tell her to stay away from her husband. Her parting words ring in her head.

'You're pure evil, Jessica. The world would be a far better place without girls like you.'

TWENTY-SEVEN

Not this. Not again. Not now.

Christina sits in the doctor's waiting area with a pale-faced Abi, who has now been complaining of chest pain.

'I should be next,' Abi says. If she's worried, she's hiding it well. She does look off-colour, doesn't she? Or is the warm-toned light synonymous with doctors' waiting rooms making her daughter appear so pale?

Christina is hiding it well, too, yet inside she's a wreck. Call her oversensitive, but ever since Abi's cancer diagnosis when she was four years old, however minor an ailment her daughter complains about, it drives Christina into a frenzy of anxiety. It's completely understandable with what Abi went through. Any mother would be the same.

There's also Michael to worry about. The doctors have reported there are no signs of any permanent brain damage. His broken body is healing, but she remains guarded. He still has no recollection of where he went that night of the accident. But there are questions she still needs answered. Questions she has not yet felt it appropriate to tackle with him.

The pressure of recent events has become unbearable. Two

weeks have passed since her life spiralled out of control. Christina can feel the weight of her worries in the constant tenseness of her face and the nausea in the pit of her stomach. And she has barely slept in a fortnight. The thud of her car hitting her husband swims before her every time she shuts her eyes.

She is staring into space when her phone rings. It's DS Macintosh. Another person lurking about at the top of her stress list. What does he want now?

She silences the call, letting it ring until it clicks into her voicemail then waits a minute and listens to the message. Her jaw clenches. He wants to speak to her again.

'Who was that?' Abi asks.

'Anne-Marie,' Christina lies, internally berating herself. She changes the subject. 'Tell Dr Hadley exactly how you feel. Don't hold back.'

Abi rolls her eyes. 'I won't, Mum. Stop fussing over me. I'm sure this is a waste of time.'

Christina sees herself in her daughter, the strength she has had to summon over the years to get through the bad times: her parents dying young within three months of each other, Abi's cancer, Adam's infidelity, and the bitterly painful divorce that stripped her emotions bare.

She shuffles in the seat, trying to get comfortable. 'Never a waste of time. You know that.'

'When do you think you'll be going back to work, Mum?'

'I'm not sure. There's Michael to consider. It probably won't be until after Christmas now.'

'You're going to miss all the festivities.'

Christina snorts. 'That's the last thing on my mind. There's too much else to consider.'

'So Christmas is cancelled.'

'Certainly not. We'll stay at home this year, though.'

Since Sebastian's father died, the family have always spent

Christmas Day at Sophia and Sebastian's house. Nancy refuses to go anywhere else. But she'll have to this year. 'Everyone will have to come to us.'

A ping accompanied by the screen lighting up instructs Abi Carter to head to Dr Hadley in room five.

'Come in, come in,' Dr Hadley says in his well-spoken baritone voice, beckoning Abi and Christina into his cramped consulting room. He gestures to the two chairs next to his desk. 'Season's greetings. Is it too early to say that?' He laughs. 'No, never too early.'

There's something comforting about Dr Hadley. He has been the family doctor since Christina moved to the area with Adam over twenty years ago, and throughout Abi's cancer diagnosis and treatment, he was a towering pillar of support. 'What can I do for you?'

Abi rubs the area to the left of her chest bone, explaining the pain that has been troubling her. 'It's here.' She describes the tightness that comes and goes. 'I'm sure it's nothing really.'

'You let me be the judge of that.' Dr Hadley pushes his chair away from his desk.

'She has had some headaches, too,' Christina says, her heart thumping in her chest. She wrings her hands, silently praying all is OK with her daughter.

'They were nothing, Mum.'

After checking Abi's chest, Dr Hadley takes her blood pressure and measures her oxygen levels. 'I don't think there's anything to worry about here.' His authoritative tone is reassuring. 'I think this is muscular pain, but let's do a full set of bloods just to be on the safe side.'

Abi jumps off the bed and readjusts her shirt. 'Told you,' she mouths to Christina.

'She's got her annual scan after Christmas at Great Ormond Street,' Christina says anxiously. 'It's the last one before they move to five-yearly.'

'That should put your mind at rest.' The doctor picks up the phone. 'If I send a young lady to you for some bloods, can you fit her in, please?' There's a pause before he adds, 'Perfect, I'll send her down right away.'

'I'll see you in the waiting room,' Christina says, as Abi leaves the room.

Christina remains seated after her daughter has left. 'Can I have a quick word, please, Doctor?'

TWENTY-EIGHT

'Sure, how are things?' Dr Hadley finishes typing his notes. 'I heard about your husband. How is he?'

'Getting there.'

'That's good news.'

'There's talk about him coming home at some point soon. They think he'll make a faster recovery in familiar surroundings.'

'Quite so. Patients recover much faster in the home environment. Is your house set up for him? Once a patient is discharged, they're no longer the hospital's responsibility. Do you have help?'

'My brother and sister are around.'

'If we can be of assistance, let me know. You'll need to be on your A game when he gets home.'

'That's what I've been thinking, too. There is something you can help me with, actually.'

The doctor smiles kindly. He clasps his large hands and peers over the top of his spectacles, eyeing her face wisely. Empathy has always been one of Dr Hadley's strong points.

He's too nice. Emotion comes over her. Since the accident,

she finds it hard when people are nice to her. She clears her throat. 'Do you remember when my ex-husband and I split up?'

With her current frame of mind, the memory tightens the knots in her stomach. It's a day she'll never forget. The pain was like nothing she'd felt before. It was as if someone had suddenly opened a trap door beneath her and displaced her into another world.

She continues. 'You gave me some sleeping pills. I've barely slept this past two weeks, and I was thinking I could do with going back on them. Just for a while to get me strong again. In preparation for Michael coming home, really.'

The doctor bashes the keyboard with his forefingers, bringing up her file. 'You do have a lot going on, don't you?'

What an understatement!

Add the threat of a potential prison sentence to those worries, and it's no wonder she's sitting opposite him asking for pills to help her sleep.

'Is there any other reason you aren't sleeping, apart from all the stress with Abi and your husband?'

Can he sense her guilt?

'No,' she lies.

She actually hasn't had a full night's sleep since the incident with Jessica James. She feels as if it's written in the lines that have burrowed their way into her face recently. But she doesn't want to discuss that with the doctor.

After giving a talk on the use of sleeping tablets as a short-term measure only, the doctor returns to his keyboard and prepares a prescription. 'Let's start you on a month's worth. I'd like to see you again in four weeks' time. In the meantime, you know where I am if you need anything. Don't shoulder the world on your own. If you need a chat about anything, we go back a long way.' He whips the prescription off the printer and hands it to her. 'Understood?'

Christina nods, choked up. She doesn't deserve his compassion. She takes the piece of paper from him, relishing the thought of a good night's sleep. 'Understood.'

'Oh, and if Michael should come home in the meantime, you'll need to rethink about taking them. Remember, you need to be on your A game. Anything else?'

Her phone rings. Her stomach turns. It's the DS again. 'Sorry,' she says, silencing the call. 'No, nothing else.'

'I'm pretty sure it's nothing of concern with Abi. I'll arrange for the bloods to be sent off straight away. I should have them back in a few days. Get a good night's sleep and try not to worry.'

That's easy for him to say.

Christina sits in the car, waiting for Abi, who has popped into the supermarket to buy a bottle of water. She gets her phone out of her bag and texts Anne-Marie, telling her she's on her way to the school.

Anne-Marie has blocked out time in her diary after this appointment for them to have a coffee, but now the time has come, Christina can't face going into the school building. She has shut herself off since the accident, only able to face her family and people where circumstances have forced her to do so.

In her usual fashion, Anne-Marie immediately replies. Christina has never known anyone as efficient. However, that's what it takes to reach the heights of headteacher of a school like St. Christopher's.

Sure, but I have something for you. I'll bring it out to the car. A-M

While typing out a reply, her phone rings, startling her. It's

DS Macintosh. She can't ignore it again. Her fingers shake as she answers the call.

'Christina! We finally get to speak. I was beginning to think you were ignoring me.' He clears his throat. 'It's just a courtesy call. I went to the hospital this morning to speak to Michael.'

She clenches her jaw. Shouldn't she have been there?

'I did try to call to let you know.'

She tries to control the panic in her voice. 'What did he say?'

'Nothing. He has no recollection of what happened that night. I wondered if he has said anything different to you?'

'No. That's the message I got as well.'

'Leave it with me. I'll try again in the coming days. It's good he's on his way to recovery, though. I'd hate to think I have a murder on my hands.' He ends the call.

She bites her knuckle.

Murder?

TWENTY-NINE

After a kiss goodbye, Abi gets out of the car at the school, slamming the door as she waves. The noise goes right through Christina.

Anne-Marie, a tall and very attractive woman, appears from the front building holding a shopping bag. She has recently had her hair restyled into a Cleopatra look. The long black bob with a bluntly cut fringe suits her. Climbing into the front seat of the car, she opens the bag and hands Christina a bunch of flowers and a box of chocolates. The earthy-honey waft of the lilies from the bouquet fills the car.

'How're things?' Anne-Marie asks. 'Everyone is so cut up about what's happened.'

Christina takes the gifts. 'Thanks. He's getting there.'

It's odd being outside school with Anne-Marie sitting beside her. School life feels like another world away. There's a distance between her and her friend Christina has never felt before. She unclicks her seatbelt and turns to Anne-Marie, bending her knee towards her body.

'We're all so worried.' Anne-Marie hooks her glossy hair behind her ears. 'How is he?'

'Improving. There're no signs of permanent brain damage, which is good. But he has been through a massive trauma.' Christina's voice breaks. 'His body and mental state need time to heal, they tell me.'

Anne-Marie pats Christina's knee. 'Of course. However, take the positive. There's progress.'

'I'm sure he'll get there, but I don't know when he'll be back at work. But then again, you know Michael.'

'We're not expecting either of you back anytime soon, so don't even think about it.' She gives a tight-lipped smile of empathy. 'Getting our Mr Blake fully recovered is your priority now. We're all rooting for him. Are you sure you don't want to come in for a coffee? People would love to see you.'

Christina shakes her head. She can't face anyone. 'If you don't mind, I'll get going.'

Anne-Marie hesitates. 'It's upper sixth's parents' evening tonight. Are you coming? I'll understand, of course, if you don't.'

Damn. She had forgotten about that. 'Sure.'

Anne-Marie looks at her awkwardly. 'I don't want to put more pressure on you. We're all aware of the strain you must be under at the moment, but a few of Ben's teachers have raised concerns about him.'

Christina straightens her spine. 'Since when?'

Anne-Marie flicks her head. Her lustrous dark hair gleams in a rare moment of sunlight shining through the window. 'Since he returned after the summer. I really don't want to trouble you with this, Christina, but he has got worse these past few weeks.'

'What kind of concerns?'

'He's not putting in his usual level of effort.'

'OK. And? There's something else, I can tell.'

'I don't want to burden you.'

'I need to know, Anne-Marie. Just tell me straight.'

'You would've seen on his half-term report that his grades have dropped. And Mr Paton informed me that he's late handing in his history coursework.'

Christina runs her hands through her hair. 'I picked him up on his grades dropping. He said it was because of a couple of bad test results. He assured me all was OK, but if I'm honest, he has been very moody lately. I've put it down to teenage hormones.'

Anne-Marie hesitates, before adding, 'There've been a few behavioural issues as well.'

Christina frowns and bites her knuckle. 'Behavioural issues?' What the hell is Ben playing at? He's always been a conscientious kid. This is all she needs right now.

'Nothing too serious, but I think I need to let you know. When he drives his car into school, he hasn't been parking up at the sports fields. He parks in front of the houses on Vixen Drive, which all pupils know is a no-go. I've reminded him once, yet he has ignored me. And this morning, a resident complained that he was speeding along the road.'

'That's not OK.' Christina grimaces. 'Not OK at all. I'll have a word with him.'

'Also, he was rude to a teacher,' Anne-Marie adds.

'What did he say?'

'He swore. You know we make it quite clear we do not tolerate disrespect of our staff in this school. I've had a word with him about it.'

Christina blushes. 'I'm so sorry.'

'And I'm sorry for having to tell you about all of this when you have so much else going on. I'm hoping it's a short-term phase he's going through and have put it down to the stress at home after Michael's accident.'

'I'll be there tonight. What time does it start?'

'You would've received an email to book slots with each teacher, but it was sent the night of Michael's accident, so you would've had more pressing things to deal with. If you want to come, I can arrange times with each of his teachers. If you'd rather not go tonight, I completely understand. You can meet the teachers at a later date. Online, perhaps?'

'I'll be there.' Christina exhales a large breath. Ben's A levels start in less than six months. 'This is not a time for him to be messing around.'

'I'll message you slots when I've looked at each teacher's schedule. In the meantime, please send Michael our love.' Anne-Marie reaches out and squeezes Christina's hand. 'I wish I could do more for you.'

Christina bites back tears. 'Thanks.'

'Is there any update on who did this?'

Christina feels the usual heat rise up her neck again, spreading to her face. She opens the window. This is what she can't deal with. The shame of what she did is a constant torment. She shakes her head. 'The police have nothing to go on.'

'Strange, isn't it? With all the technology around today.' Anne-Marie opens the car door. 'Don't worry. It'll all come out in the end. These things always do.'

THIRTY

Will you and Sebastian go and see Michael this evening, please? I've got to go to Ben's parents' evening. X

Christina won't have time to get to the hospital after the parents' evening. Hopefully her sister can help out. Sophia has offered many times.

Her sister quickly replies.

Of course. Anytime. X

Thanks. He's in a bit of bother at school. I need to be there for him. X

What's happened? X

I'll tell you later. X

Ben's car pulls into the driveway a little too quickly for her liking, throwing up shingle when he skids to a stop.

Christina confronts him as he walks into the kitchen. 'What the hell's going on?'

He tosses his backpack onto the breakfast bar. 'What now?'

Christina rolls her eyes in frustration before she lets him have it. 'Don't you think I've got enough going on at the moment?'

'What do you mean?' Ben says, defensively.

'School.'

He slumps onto a stool. 'What about it?'

'I spoke to Anne-Marie this morning. You're not keeping up with your homework, and—'

'It was one history essay,' he protests. 'I've sent it in now.'

'And you were rude to a teacher. Swore at them. What were you thinking?'

'It was Mr Paton. He was being a prick about the homework. I was a day late handing it in. What's the big deal?'

'Don't refer to teachers in that manner. It's not right, Ben. I've brought you up better than that.' Christina perches on the edge of the stool next to him. 'The big deal is, this is your final year at school. You've always done so well.' She squeezes his arm. 'I love you too much to see you screw things up now.'

He folds his arms across his chest, defensively, staring at the window across the other side of the room.

She gives his arm another encouraging squeeze. 'It's your future at stake here.' She hesitates. This is new territory for her. Both Ben and Abi have always been the most studious of kids. 'I know things are pretty stressful around here, but is there something else troubling you at the moment?'

The scowl on his face deepens. 'What do you mean?'

'Something is clearly up.'

He jumps off the stool. It crashes backwards to the floor. 'There's nothing up,' he says, grabbing his rucksack and leaving the room. 'I just wish everyone would leave me alone.'

She picks up the stool, angered that he left it on the floor.

Striding to the door, she calls after him. 'And, by the way, a resident reported you speeding along Vixen Drive this morning. And if you disobey school rules again by not parking up by the sports fields, you're banned from driving in. And we're going to parents' evening tonight. Make sure you're ready.'

'Whatever,' he calls out.

Damn. She didn't handle that well.

What the hell has got into him?

THIRTY-ONE

Parents' evening doesn't go quite as Christina expected.

Ben is sullen, keeping to monosyllabic answers or grunts. His teachers are supportive, even offering extra help. She just hopes he will actually take them up on it.

The difficult thing is seeing all of her and Michael's colleagues, the well-wishers, and facing questions about the investigation – but she's here for Ben. It has always been easy to put him and Abi before everything else.

She stands up after thanking the history teacher Ben swore at, who is surprisingly pleasant, and turns to Ben, but he has wandered off towards the adjacent hall where they are due to meet his English teacher.

A blonde-haired woman dressed in a navy business suit and high heels grabs her arm. 'Mrs Blake?'

Christina squints. Does she know this woman? She thinks hard, not wanting to embarrass herself.

'We haven't met before. I'm Cathy Silver.' She turns to the girl standing next to her. 'This is my daughter, Nina.'

A wave of heat flushes through Christina.

Nina is Ben's age. She has long dark hair and heart-shaped lips.

'I heard about your husband,' Cathy says. 'How dreadful. How is he?'

'He's on the road to recovery, thank you.' What does this stranger want?

'I need to thank him,' Cathy says. 'We're indebted to him.'

Christina raises her eyebrows. 'What for?'

Cathy smiles, her teeth perfectly straight and toothpaste-white, and glances at her daughter. 'He has helped my Nina no end this year, and now she's been invited to interview for a place at Oxford.'

Christina smiles at Nina. 'Congratulations.'

'He made her change her mind about applying to drama school. Said it would be safer for her to get an English degree first. Lots of famous actors have done that, he told her. Eddie Redmayne studied History of Art at Cambridge before going into acting full-time. And Kate Beckinsale went to Oxford.' Cathy turns to her daughter again, her voice a thread of enthusiasm. 'Isn't that right, darling?'

Nina nods.

'And he helped her no end with her UCAS application, didn't he?'

Nina nods again, blushing.

'So we've a lot to thank him for. He's such an excellent teacher. I heard about his accident. Dreadful.' Cathy shakes her blonde locks, her eyes wide. 'Shocking, isn't it? There are such inhumane people on our roads.'

Christina glances at the screen at the front of the hall, counting down the seconds of each ten-minute time slot.

'Anyway, we won't keep you. Please pass on our thanks to your husband and good wishes for a speedy recovery.' She takes her daughter's arm and wanders off.

Christina watches them go, uneasy. Nina's sullen look, and now seeing the way she walks with such a confident swagger exuding self-assuredness and a hint of defiance, reminds her of Jessica James.

She needs to get out of here.

THIRTY-TWO

Michael is connected to fewer machines, and the visiting times are far more generous, on Jarrad ward, allowing Christina to spend more time with him. But he is never very communicative when she is there.

A doctor drops by. He scrutinises Michael's recent scan, pleased with the progress Michael is making. His ankle is healing nicely and other than the pain from a bruised spine and the spasmodic headaches, he is recuperating well. 'Patients in the ICU can lose about two per cent of muscle mass a day, so it's good to see you up and about,' he says to Michael, who is sitting in a chair beside the bed, a pair of crutches propped up against the side. 'And I see the physio has been. It's all heading in the right direction.'

'The swelling on his face has drastically reduced, too,' says Christina. 'It's practically gone.'

The doctor nods his agreement. 'We need to think about getting you home in the near future.'

'The sooner I get out of here the better,' Michael says, grumpily.

Christina shifts uncomfortably in her chair.

The doctor nods. 'Let's aim to get you back with your family by Christmas.'

'That's great news, isn't it?' Christina says, when the doctor leaves, despite having concerns about his homecoming if she's honest. Michael is an athletic man. He is going to take a lot of looking after. She's anxious about having to face it alone. Yes, her brother and sister will help her. Nevertheless, she knows Michael's impatience along the road to recovery will prove challenging.

But at least he is alive.

'And I've got some more good news. Abi's bloods came back OK.'

'Good,' Michael says, staring at his plastered foot.

'I've bought you a book.' Christina digs into her bag and hands Michael the Amazon order she placed last night. 'I thought it might help pass the time.'

Michael opens the brown envelope and removes a copy of *The Kite Runner* by Khaled Hosseini. A book he was talking about before the accident. One he has always meant to read but has never got around to.

Michael shuffles in the chair. 'Thank you, darling.'

Christina is taken aback. When did he last call her darling? She can't remember. It feels good. Really good. Tears well up in her eyes. Darling. How can one simple word fill her with so much hope? He used to call her that all the time. Is she hoping for too much in thinking she may finally get the old Michael back? 'We're going to get you better. You see.'

He turns his head away.

It confuses her. Did that word of affection slip out by mistake?

Christina gets up, pulls the curtain around the bed and perches on the side of the mattress. 'Listen, Michael, there're some things I need to ask you that've been bugging me.'

Now is not the time. Christina believes she has just had a

connection with the man she has been sorely missing for so long. He called her darling. But she can't leave it any longer. Now she has properly got his attention, she wants to ask him about why he hasn't been at the cycling club. It's tormenting her. She has to have her questions answered.

He lifts his head to stare at her. It's unnerving, a contrast to the warmth of his words only moments ago.

She starts with some good news. 'I met Nina Silver and her mum at Ben's parents' evening.'

'Did you?'

'She's got an interview at Oxford.'

A smile appears on his face. A smile of achievement. 'That's brilliant news. Bright girl. Very bright. When she puts her mind to it. She has been on the Oxbridge programme. I taught her in my first year at St Christopher's and again last year in her first year of sixth form.'

Christina clenches her jaw, stopping herself from commenting that Nina looks like Jessica James.

Michael puts the palms of his hands on his forehead. 'I've got a terrible headache. Do you mind going? I need to sleep.'

She clenches her jaw. There are still so many things she wants to ask him – about the cycling club, and the leather gloves she found in his car – but she backs down. She doesn't want to upset him. She's not being fair to him. He has been through a significant trauma. A trauma that she is responsible for.

And deep down, she knows he is only going to lie.

THIRTY-THREE

A few days later, Christina gets the news from the hospital. Michael's coming home.

When she returns from walking Wilf, she finds her brother in the lounge, shifting the furniture around to make room for the single bed they plan to fetch down from the attic room.

'Why didn't you wait for me?' she says, helping him nudge the sofa under the window.

'Didn't you get my message?' Ted wipes a layer of sweat from his forehead. 'I was between jobs, so I thought I'd drop in and make a start. I was thinking. And I don't want to pry, but are you sure it's a good idea for him to be down here? You know, given everything that was going on before the accident. Wouldn't it be better if he was upstairs?'

'It did cross my mind. But he thinks it'll be too difficult getting up and down the stairs with his ankle.'

The front door slams shut, startling them both. Wilf barks.

'Who the hell is that?' Christina dashes to the lounge door to see Ben stomping down the hallway.

'What're you doing home?' she asks.

Placing a hand on the banister, Ben swings himself around

the staircase like he used to when he was a kid and races up the stairs. 'I've got a free.'

'Shouldn't you be at school studying, then?' she calls after him.

'I forgot a file.'

Didn't parents' evening mean anything to him?

Christina is preparing two cups of tea, when the front door slams shut again. She looks out of the kitchen window. Ben is climbing into his car. He didn't even say goodbye. She tuts. What happened to the sweet boy who used to brighten her world? Now all he does is fill it with a daily bucketful of angst.

She takes a cup of tea to Ted.

'Was that Ben I heard?' he asks.

'Yep. He came home for a file. He didn't even say goodbye on his way out. He's so moody at the moment.'

'It's his hormones. He'll grow out of it. Remember us when we were that age?'

'I don't recall treating Mum and Dad like he treats me.'

'I do! Don't you remember? When I was about Ben's age and Dad found some pot in my bedroom. He went ballistic. I wasn't allowed out for a whole month.'

'I'm worried about him. There's something up with him.'

'Like what?'

'I don't know.' She sighs.

'Let him be. He's just a normal youngster finding his way in the world. He'll grow out of it.'

She shakes her head before going upstairs to strip the bed in the spare room.

The light is on in Michael's study. She frowns. Did she leave it on? She hasn't been up here since she charged his iPhone. She steps inside the room to switch it off, pausing to breathe in the smell of Michael's leather jacket before going to the spare room and stripping the bed.

'This should do for now,' Ted says when the spare bed is in place downstairs. 'You OK? You've gone very quiet.'

'It's all getting on top of me. I'm apprehensive about Abi's scan. Ben is playing up. And I'm worried about Michael coming home, if I'm honest. And DS Macintosh is trying to get hold of me again, too.'

'What does he want now?'

She shrugs. 'He didn't say. He has just left a voicemail asking me to call him. Every time he contacts me, it freaks me out. It's not getting any easier dealing with what I've done. I'm scared, Ted. Like, terrified.'

'You've got to stop it. The police haven't found anything. They'll lose momentum. Michael will mend, and we can all get our lives back together.'

'There's something else I haven't told you. Only because I forgot. I saw Jessica James at the hospital. That freaked me out, too.'

He knits his brow. 'What was she doing there?'

'She could've been visiting someone else, family or something. But get this. When Michael was first in the ICU, one of the nurses said he had a visitor. Someone wearing a baseball cap, but no one can remember any more details.'

'And you think it was Jessica?' Ted sits on his haunches, stroking Wilf's neck.

Christina shrugs. 'What should I do?'

Ted stops stroking Wilf. 'Kill her. And him.'

Christina stares at him in horror.

Ted laughs. 'I'm only joking, of course.'

'I bloody well hope so.'

'It would solve all your problems, though.'

'Ted!'

Standing up, he laughs and punches her arm, a habit of old that she's about to return when her phone rings. She takes it out of her pocket. 'It's the police.'

'Just answer it. Get it over with.'

Christina swipes the screen to accept the call.

DS Macintosh's voice booms down the phone.

She listens intently. When she ends the call, she relays his message to her brother.

'He's on his way to the hospital to speak to Michael again. I'd better get up there.'

THIRTY-FOUR

Christina arrives ten minutes before visiting time officially begins.

The ward is a relatively calm sea of blue curtains pulled around each bed. The lull before the storm of afternoon visitors.

Standing at the side of Michael's bay, Christina peeks through a gap she has forged in the curtain. Michael is sitting in the chair. DS Macintosh is perched on the end of the bed.

A Place In The Sun is playing quietly on the TV. A couple are relocating to a sunnier climate. They've had enough of life here in the UK. How Christina wishes it were her and Michael moving somewhere miles away from the crap that has landed on their doorstep.

'What I would do for a bit of sun right now,' the DS says. 'It's freezing outside. I think we might be in for snow. My kids would love that.'

Michael laces his hands in his lap. 'How can I help you, Detective?'

Is that an air of disdain Christina detects in her husband's voice?

The detective removes a notebook from his jacket pocket. 'I'll try not to keep you. I imagine you tire easily. How are you?'

'Getting there,' Michael replies. 'The sooner I get out of this place the better.'

Christina's heart is beating in her ears. What she's doing is wrong. Yet she needs to hear what her husband has to say. Wouldn't any wife do the same in the circumstances?

'How can I help?' Michael says again. He definitely sounds a little curt.

The officer coughs. 'As you're aware, we're looking into what happened the night of your accident. When we spoke before, you had no recollection of that evening. And I wanted to know if anything more has come back to you. Maybe something has nudged your memory?'

'I'm sorry, I can't help you. As I said, the last thing I recall is coming home from work that day.'

'We have a period of time unaccounted for. Can I just go through with you again what we know to date? It may spark something, you know, jog your memory.'

'You can. But I really don't know what good it'll do.'

The detective removes an iPad from his leather satchel and turns it on. He searches through it. With his thumb and forefinger, he zooms in and shows the screen to Michael.

Christina looks around, her pulse racing, wondering if anyone can see her. There's no one around.

'This is a map of the surrounding area,' DS Macintosh says. 'We carried out door-to-door inquiries in the days following the accident and gathered as much CCTV and video doorbell footage as possible. From what your stepdaughter told us, and from the doorbell footage, we know you were walking up Bridge End around ten past eight that night. You were seen getting in a car by a woman in one of the bungalows along that road.'

Christina frowns. She didn't know that. Who saw him?

'Did I?' Michael says.

'It wasn't raining at that point, and it's clearly you. You have no recollection of this?'

Michael shakes his head.

Christina bites her lip. Her husband is lying. She's sure of it.

The DS continues. 'Unfortunately, as it's rather out in the sticks where you live, and what with the weather being so atrocious that night, that's all we know from this avenue of inquiry.' The DS points to a different part of the screen. 'The next we see of you is someone dropping you off at The Black Horse pub at ten-thirty-six. Therefore, someone must've picked you up from Bridge End and taken you somewhere for roughly two and a half hours before dropping you off at the pub. It would be great to learn who picked you up, and where you went.'

Michael shrugs. 'I've already told you. I don't remember.'

Undeterred, the detective continues trying to jog Michael's memory. 'You went inside The Black Horse and ordered a pint of beer. The owner reported you appeared agitated. You didn't talk to anyone. He said it was most unlike you. You just sat at a table in the corner, drank that one beer and left. Another thing that doesn't stack up is why you left your phone at home.'

'I'm always mislaying my phone. Christina is always threatening to buy me a lanyard to attach it round my neck.'

Lanyard? Christina stifles a gasp.

Her husband is definitely lying. She has never mentioned anything of the sort.

'So there are certain things you do recall?' the detective says.

'I beg your pardon?'

'The lanyard, forgetting your phone. You remember how forgetful you are.'

'I do, but I don't remember anything after coming home from work that day.' Michael raises his voice. 'Don't you think I'd tell you if I did? I want to know who ran me down and left me for dead as much as you.'

Christina winces.

There's an awkward pause before the DS continues. 'A couple more questions, then I'll leave you alone.' He laughs, trying to lighten the mood. 'I'm under strict instructions from the wife to pick up a parcel from the post office before they close. I've missed it three days on the trot now. There'll be hell to pay if I don't do it today.'

Michael lowers his head, moving it from left to right as if he is stretching his neck.

'Michael, I must ask this. Is there anything you care to share with me? Strictly confidential, to go no further.'

Christina can't believe what she is hearing. What exactly is the detective referring to? She strains to hear Michael's reply.

'I'm not sure I follow, Detective,' Michael says.

'Did you go and see someone you may not wish your wife or stepchildren to know about?'

'No.'

'Or is there someone out there who may have a grudge against you?'

Michael laughs, resulting in what appears to be a genuine uncontrollable cough. He holds his ribs. 'What do you mean? Like a professional hit?'

DS Macintosh persists. 'Anyone who wishes you harm?'

'I'd like to think not.'

The detective strokes his beard. 'I gather there was an incident at school last year, involving' – he refers to his notebook, flicking through the pages – 'a pupil named Jessica James.'

Hearing that name makes Christina want to be sick.

Michael's voice, though weak, is sharp. 'It was nothing. A teenage crush that got out of hand. The school carried out a thorough investigation. I was vindicated.'

'But it resulted in Jessica having to leave the school. She couldn't have been happy about that.'

'No. Of course not. But she's moved on.'

'How do you know that?'

Michael pauses, appearing deep in thought. 'Teachers at school have told me. Look, I can't remember anything, simple as. Not where I went, not who with, and not why I didn't take my phone. When I do – if I ever do – you'll be the first person I tell.'

'OK. Let's leave it there for now, shall we?' The DS returns the iPad to his satchel. 'Thank you for your time. Rest assured, Michael, the answer is out there. And I'll do everything in my power to bring the perpetrator to task, because, believe me, when I get my teeth into something, my jaw stays locked until I get what I'm looking for.'

THIRTY-FIVE

'What makes you think he's lying?' Ted asks.

Christina is sitting with her brother in the kitchen, eating a Chinese takeaway. The kids are out with their dad. She shrugs as she plays with her food, pushing it around the plate with her fork. 'I know from that conversation he had with the detective he's hiding more than he's letting on.'

'You've hardly eaten.' Ted pushes the silver container of prawn toast towards her. 'Take the last one. I've had my share of these.'

'He does know where he went that night. I'm ninety-nine point nine per cent sure he does.' Christina picks up the bottle of Pinot from the table and refills her glass. She may have lost her appetite for food, but she hasn't lost her desire for wine. It's the only thing keeping her sane. 'I don't want to distrust him. But I can't help it.'

'Where do you think he went?' Ted asks. 'I've racked my brains, and I can't work it out.'

'I haven't got a clue. And what about him not being at the cycling club?'

'Why don't you ask him?'

'I'll have to pick my time to tackle him on that one. I've pushed him enough already. I need to wait until he gets a bit better. I don't want him to think I've been checking up on him.' She sips her wine. 'And I don't want to cause a scene. His headaches are dragging him down. And then there's his Facebook account.'

Ted picks up another pork ball with his chopsticks and chucks it in his mouth. 'What about it?'

'I told you. He's deleted it.'

'You never told me that.'

She plonks her elbow on the table and massages her brow. 'I'm sure I did.'

'Well, you didn't.'

She chews her knuckle, despite the pain. How could she have forgotten to tell him that?

'Why did he delete it?' Ted asks.

'I don't know. I found out at the same time as I discovered he hadn't been to the cycling club for months. I'm sure I told you. Isn't that something you'd tell your wife?' She frowns. 'And then there's the bloody gloves.'

Ted balances his chopsticks on the edge of his bowl and dishes out the last of the egg-fried rice. 'You need to talk to him. Get it all out in the open as soon as possible.'

'You're right.'

Ted's phone buzzes. He glances at the screen and smiles.

'Your new girlfriend, Mel?' Christina asks. She has been so wrapped up in her own world, she had forgotten all about his new love interest. She pokes his arm. 'It is, isn't it? When am I going to meet her?'

'Not yet. She's currently sat at Heathrow waiting for a plane to L.A.'

'L.A.?'

'She's half American. Her dad's from San Francisco, so she's off to spend Christmas with her family.'

'Show me a picture of her,' Christina says, intrigued at this new beau her brother obviously likes. She's pleased. It's been a long time since he was in a relationship. A serious one, anyway.

He flicks the screen of his phone and turns it to her.

'Wow! You're punching above your weight there, bruv. She's stunning,' Christina says of the captivating blonde with ice blue eyes he has his arm around. She pokes his arm again. 'You're blushing.'

'It's official. I've fallen head over heels.'

'You dark horse, you.' She squints at him. 'You know, I thought there was something different about you.'

He sticks his nose up. 'She's gone for a month, though. I'm not going to see her for thirty whole days.'

'Why don't you go out there as well?'

'I can't afford it.'

'Why? You must have some cash stashed away after all the hours you work.'

'I'm saving up.'

'What for?'

'Well... when she gets back... we're talking about getting a place together.'

Christina's eyes widen. 'This has moved fast.'

'I've been seeing her a few months. After all my previous disastrous attempts at love, I wanted to make sure.' Ted empties the remaining pork balls onto a plate. 'I'll save these for Abi. She loves them. Anyway, getting back to you. I wish I could do more to help you.'

'I haven't a clue what he was doing that night, why, or with whom. I'm going to find out, though.'

'How're you going to do that if he really is feigning amnesia?'

Christina pushes her plate away. 'I'm working on it.'

She was the one who hit Michael, yes. But she needs to ditch the guilt, and the fear of getting caught out, and move on. Twice before in her life she has survived adversity. When she thought Abi was going to die. And when Adam cheated on her. She can do it again.

THIRTY-SIX

Who picked Michael up that night? Where did he go? Who dropped him back at the pub?

Christina hopes the landlord of The Black Horse public house, Paddy O'Brian, and maybe his wife, Birdie, can help her answer the questions that have been buzzing around her head constantly. Whether there's much to be gained from quizzing Paddy, she doesn't know.

She has to at least try, though. It's a start.

How to approach the conversation kept her awake for most of the night, despite the sleeping pill she took. On the odd occasion she and Michael will pop into the pub for a drink. She certainly wouldn't consider either of them regulars, though. And they haven't even been in for a while. But when she telephoned this morning, Paddy was open to showing her the CCTV footage of the night.

She walks Wilf down to the pub, a whitewashed lath and plaster building with a slate roof that looks as if it's about to collapse. It looks more like a farmhouse than a pub. As she strides across the parking area, she hopes she'll be able to glean something, anything, more about Michael's movements that night than the police have.

She doesn't have long.

That bloody detective called again before she left, filling her with the same anxiety every time she sees his name flash up on the screen: is it all over for her?

And this time it wasn't just a courtesy call like last week. Instead of the usual 'No news, but we'll keep looking' update, he said he would be passing by and wanted to pop in for a chat. That was enough to set off the tremble in her hands alone. But, despite her probing, he had been cagey on why he wanted to speak to her so urgently.

The door to the pub is heavier than she remembers. She's out of strength as well as energy. Heads turn to admire Wilf as she walks across the flagstone tiles, which is not unusual. Because of his size, he commands attention wherever he goes. A spaniel appears from under a table, growling. Its owner grins at Wilf and pulls his dog back.

She approaches the bar where Paddy is serving a customer. She's not sure if he recognises her or not. 'Hello, Paddy. I'm Christina.'

Paddy acknowledges her presence with a nod and a smile.

'I'll be with you in a minute.' He passes a customer their change. A short, stocky man with a full beard that could do with a trim, he is every bit the stereotypical pub landlord. 'Birdie is downstairs changing a barrel. Can I get you a drink?'

Christina stares at the colourful bottles of gin decorating the shelves behind the bar. Are they tempting, or what? 'I'll have an orange juice, please.'

Paddy turns one-eighty and leans from the waist to grab a small bottle from the under-counter fridge. Pouring its contents into a glass, he passes it to Christina. 'On the house.'

Birdie, as graceful and chirpy as her name implies, appears

and turns on a beer pump. Paddy whispers something to her before beckoning Christina. 'Come with me.'

'Leave your dog. I'll find a treat for your boy,' Birdie says, delicately clicking her agile fingers towards Wilf.

'That's kind of you.'

'How are you?' Paddy asks as she follows him through the greasy-smelling kitchen and up a narrow, steep staircase that leads to a small room. Boxes of crisps, nuts and paper napkins clutter three-quarters of the room; the remainder is used as an office.

'As well as can be expected.'

'Sure. You've got a lot going on. Excuse the mess.' Paddy kicks a box to the side. 'I'm decorating the storage room downstairs.'

'Don't worry about it. You should see my son's bedroom.'

'Been there, done that.' Paddy laughs fondly. 'Had four of the blighters. Never gave us a moment's peace. Still don't.' He leads her to a small desk with three monitors. One shows a live, black-and-white feed of the bar area downstairs. Christina watches Birdie pulling a pint while Paddy boots up his computer from sleep mode and navigates to what looks like the pub's surveillance software. 'Won't take a mo.' He taps his fingers on the desk.

On screen, Christina watches Birdie hand the pint of beer over to a waiting customer and grab a card machine to take payment.

Paddy turns one of the monitors for Christina to gain a better view. 'As I said when we spoke this morning, there's not much to see, I'm afraid.'

The CCTV footage is grainy. The torrential rain was on nobody's side that night. Or perhaps it was. Maybe Michael had planned it like this, the weather distorting his movements in the blurry images.

'Here we go.' Paddy points at the screen. 'This is what I showed to the police.'

The footage shows the beam from a set of headlights to the left of the pub. Unfortunately, the car is out of shot, hidden by a line of vast conifer trees. Paddy traces his finger along the screen. 'Here he comes, walking up to the entrance.'

Christina squints, leaning her head towards the monitor. Not that it allows for more clarity. It's definitely Michael.

'Look.' Paddy points to the right-hand side of the screen. 'The car must've reversed to turn around. Shame we don't get a better view of it. We might've been able to see the make and model.'

'The police must've caught the car on some other CCTV somewhere,' she says.

'That's what the officer said they'd be looking at. But he told me it won't be easy.'

'Why?'

'The weather, for one. It'd be difficult to identify with the rain having been so bad that night. And whoever was driving that car could've gone in a number of directions.'

Disappointment rides through Christina as Paddy replays the clip.

'What was he like that night? Was he acting strange at all?' Once the questions leave her lips, she realises how ridiculous they sound. How could Paddy tell whether someone who seldom ventured into the pub was acting strange?

'He seemed agitated. Not the Michael we know. I tried to talk to him, but he wasn't his usual chatty self.'

'Usual chatty self?'

'We usually put the world to rights when he drops in on his way home from work.'

Christina is stunned. Confusion overcomes her. As far as she knew, Michael always came straight home from school. 'How often does he do that?'

Paddy leans backwards in the chair, lacing his fingers behind his head. 'Michael often pops in for a couple of pints after work.' He bites his lower lip. 'Sorry, I feel like I've said too much.'

Gritting her teeth, she fakes a smile. 'Not at all. He loves it here.' She takes a deep breath. When will she be free from the lies?

Lying is like a snowball. The more you roll it, the larger it becomes.

And it's not just her who is lying.

THIRTY-SEVEN

She storms off home with Wilf.

When Michael comes home from school, he often goes straight to the fridge, grabs a beer, opens it and takes a sip before even removing his coat. Some days, she is still working in her study and he doesn't even say hello before grabbing that beer. Is it to disguise the smell of what he has already consumed at the pub?

With the mounting unanswered questions and secrets, a fleeting thought occurs to her. What if, as DS Macintosh said, Michael being run over was a targeted attack, and it wasn't actually him who she struck that night but an animal? Is that a possibility? That she struck a deer, as she had thought, and someone else hit Michael?

The brief moment of hope disappears as quickly as it had come. Is this the state of her desperation and guilt? Of course it was her. She is clutching at straws of hope that are far too thin to get a proper hold of.

The question still remains. *Where* did he go during the two and a half hours unaccounted for?

She shivers with the cold. Perhaps he *is* having an affair. The thought makes her feel sick to the core. Michael's not that type of guy. She's pretty sure. His work is his world. Besides, he knows how much Adam's infidelity had nearly destroyed her.

But what if he was – *is* – having an affair, and the police find out? Would they think that gives the wife a motive and so delve further into her, and discover what really happened that night? She can imagine the front page headlines of the local papers: *Wife mows down her cheating husband*. It doesn't bear thinking about.

When she gets home, the house is silent. Going into the kitchen to make a cup of tea, she notices a bag of shopping from yesterday that still needs emptying. She's not in the mood, but no one else is going to do it. She takes a tin of shortbread out of the bag. Michael's favourite. Every year, she buys him some. Reflecting on the times when they used to be happy, she sighs heavily. What went wrong?

Jessica James is what went wrong.

She started his decline.

Christina sighs, reluctantly emptying the rest of the shopping, trying to take her mind off everything, but the conversation with Paddy has bothered her too much.

A car pulls onto the driveway. She darts to the window.

It's the DS. His visit had slipped her mind. Paddy has filled it with too much else.

She reluctantly goes to the front door.

The DS looks worn out, as if he's also had too many sleepless nights.

She takes him into the kitchen and offers him a drink.

After the usual pleasantries, he provides her with what he calls an update, not that there's much new to report. He and the team continue with their investigations. 'I paid Michael another visit at the hospital earlier.'

She folds her arms over her chest.

'He's still adamant he can't remember what happened that night.'

Why has he come here to tell her that? Does he think Michael is lying as well?

The detective pauses, his thumb and forefinger stroking his chin. 'Could I ask you about Jessica James?'

Christina's jaw tightens. 'What about her?'

'About what happened with her.'

'Nothing happened with her.' Christina emphasises the word *nothing*. 'She claimed he made an advance on her. He got suspended while the school carried out a formal investigation. She later admitted she had lied. She's a nasty piece of work, DS Macintosh. It's as simple as that.' Christina is being unprofessional. She shouldn't speak about a pupil like that, even one who is no longer at the school. 'The whole debacle traumatised him. And it cost him his promotion. He was all set to take over the role of deputy head, but he was passed over for another candidate. He blames Jessica.'

'I've spoken to Jessica.'

'What did she have to say?'

'I'm sorry, I can't discuss confidential conversations with you.' The DS looks her directly in the eye.

It's wholly uncomfortable. She holds his gaze.

'Do you think Michael's keeping anything back?' he asks.

Christina was right; the DS doesn't believe Michael either. About him not remembering, but there was also something in his tone when mentioning the Jessica incident. What has she told him? 'I'm certain he'd help if he could.'

He twists his lips to the side. 'Let's hope his memory returns.' He drums his fingers on the worktop in agitation. 'Keep me posted if anything changes.'

Christina sees him out and leans her forehead against the door.

Was that it? That was what she'd wound herself up about?

She has had enough of the lie she's living. She's utterly exhausted. Half the time she can't even think straight.

She wants it all to end.

THIRTY-EIGHT

Michael has been moved to Sarton ward, a more general ward, where the nurses are stretched to the max like an elastic band ready to snap. The gentleman in the adjacent bed continually cries out for his wife, not that he ever appears to have any visitors.

'I think we can start preparing for your return home.' The doctor looks up from the file he is holding. 'What do you say?'

'At bloody last.' Michael glances up from the screen of his phone. Beads of sweat glisten on his forehead.

'Are you still feeling weak?' the doctor asks.

'If I say yes, will that delay my release?'

The doctor laughs. 'No. Be aware, though. The most common physical problems reported by ICU patients are severe weakness and fatigue. The nurses will talk to you about taking care of yourself when you get home, but don't even try to resume your normal life straight away. It'll set you back. Activity is the key to recovery, but softly, softly. Avoid haste, and you'll get there quicker.'

Christina supresses a smile. Michael won't pay a single bit of attention to the doctor's advice.

'When can I go?' Michael asks.

'It won't be today. I want one more scan first. Just to be on the super safe side. I'll get my assistant to arrange it and schedule an appointment in a few weeks to have that off.' The doctor points to the plaster cast on Michael's foot. 'Leave it with me.'

Michael looks pleased.

'Can we talk?' Christina asks when the doctor slips out of the gap in the curtain pulled around the bed.

'You seem agitated?' Michael says.

'There are a few things on my mind, and I want to get them cleared up before you come home.'

He holds a pillow against his chest.

'I see you got into your phone.'

He smiles. 'You were wrong about the passcode. I hadn't changed it.'

She squints at the screen he is holding up to her as he types six digits into the locked screen. The six digits of his date of birth.

'See. You must've been mistaken.'

She stares from the iPhone to him and back at the phone. That can't be. Was she so consumed with fear that evening that she typed the passcode in wrong? But she tried three times. She couldn't have got it wrong three times, could she?

'What is it you wanted to ask me?'

Confused, she collects her thoughts. She must've been so stressed that night, she did type the wrong code in by mistake.

'I bumped into Paddy from The Black Horse. We got talking and he mentioned that you stop at the pub every night after work.'

Michael scoffs. 'That's a bit of an exaggeration. I sometimes stop there for a pint. What of it? You're not going to hold that against me, are you?' he replies light-heartedly, laughing almost.

She can't let it go. 'It's not that you stop for a drink, but rather you've never told me.'

'It's just never come up. I don't have to tell you everything.'

Is he being cagey? Or is her mind wielding the ugly stick of paranoia?

Christina tries to make light of it, to keep the conversation alive. 'It would've been nice to invite me along on the odd occasion, that's all.'

He shrugs.

'Michael, look,' she says gently. 'I'm just trying to help you piece together your movements to see if it can help spark a memory of who dropped you off at the pub the night of the accident.'

'Just leave it, Christina. If my memory returns, then I'll tell you. I want to move on with my life now. Get better and get back to normal.' He reaches for the remote control and switches on the TV, channel-surfing until he gets to the news reporting that the war in Ukraine continues despite the call for peace talks.

It irritates her. Isn't life depressing enough without seeing disasters around the world unfold?

'There's something else,' she says.

'What?' He absently stares at the TV.

She swallows. Perhaps she should leave it, but she can't stop herself blurting out, 'Why have you deleted your Facebook account?'

He flicks her a quick look. 'I did that a while back.'

'Why?'

'Why do you think?'

'I don't know.'

'I would've thought it'd be obvious.'

She frowns. 'Well, it's not.'

'I'm done with social media. I don't want anyone to find me.'

'Why?'

'Do I have to spell it out for you?' His voice breaks. 'I don't ever want a pupil to be able to find me again.'

Her shoulders drop. That makes sense. Jessica James. 'I don't understand why you didn't tell me.'

He shrugs. 'I'm sorry. It never crossed my mind. I was never big on Facebook, anyway. You know that.'

This, at least, she knows is true. Michael has always been a watcher, never a networker, when it comes to social media. Anne-Marie asked him to set up Instagram pages for St Christopher's football and rugby teams. A task he delegated to another teacher. But Christina is still put out that he didn't mention about deleting his account to her. Is she being unreasonable?

'Another thing. Why didn't you tell me you don't go to the cycling club any more on Sundays?'

'Who told you that?'

'Dermot.'

'Why did you speak to him?'

'I thought he might want to know about the accident. It'd be good for you to have some friends visit when you come home, you know. And I thought you'd want him to know that you wouldn't be at the club for a while.'

He stares at the TV.

Her hands ball into fists. He isn't listening to her, or he's pretending to ignore her on purpose.

'So where do you go if you're not at the club?'

The depressing news on the TV fills the void in their conversation.

'Michael,' she snaps. She doesn't mean to, but he's not being fair.

'I have been to the club.' He slowly turns to look at her. 'Just not every week. Not often at all, actually.' He is contradicting himself.

'Why?'

He scratches his neck. 'They are all too slow. It's annoying. I'm always having to stop to wait for them. I can get twice as far if I go on my own.' He lifts his foot and points to the plaster cast. 'I guess that won't be the case any more.' He stares hard at her. Are his eyes full of blame, or is that her paranoia playing nasty tricks on her again?

She bites her knuckle. 'Why didn't you tell me?'

'Tell you what?'

'That you stopped going to the club.'

'It didn't occur to me.'

'I feel you're keeping stuff from me.'

He screws up his face. 'Why would I do that?' He clutches his head.

'Are you OK?'

'I keep getting this pain.' He touches the side of his head. 'Right here.'

'Have you told them about it?'

'I mentioned it to the doctor earlier. He said it's most likely the after-effects of the trauma. He's going to prescribe some different painkillers. I don't want to make too big a deal of it. Otherwise, I'll never get out of this bloody place.'

'You need to make sure you're fit to leave, darling. It could be a warning sign that something else is wrong.' She opens her mouth to ask about the gloves she found in his car but quickly shuts it again. It's not the right time.

But she knows something for sure.

As clear as day, he's lying to her.

But why?

THIRTY-NINE

Michael is home. Christina can barely believe it.

He shakes his head. 'I need to rest. The journey has taken it out of me.' He sits down on the sofa.

'I'll get going, then.' Sophia picks up Lily asleep in her car seat. 'It's good to see you're getting better, Michael.'

He smiles at her. 'Thanks for coming to pick me up.'

'Yep, that was kind of you,' Christina adds. She was so nervous at the thought of driving home with Michael she had asked her sister to drive them.

'Anything I can do any time, just call.'

'Can I get you anything?' Christina asks Michael, conscious of the strain in her voice. She's a ticking timebomb of nerves ready to explode. She didn't realise how much his presence would be a constant reminder of her guilt.

He shakes his head.

'I've got a few jobs I need to do,' she says to her husband, before following her sister to the door. 'I'll keep my phone in my pocket. Just call if you need me.'

He nods and closes his eyes.

Sophia puts her coat on in the hallway. 'He's looking a lot

better. Better than you do, actually. Something's going on with you, I know it. What's happened?'

Christina looks at Lily snoring. She sighs. Oh, the blissful years of being a small child.

'Chrissy, what's up? You can tell me.'

Where does she even start? The fewer people who know about what she did that night, the better. 'I'm good. All good. Just trying to get my head around everything that has happened.'

Sophia opens the front door. 'You know where I am if you need me.'

After seeing her sister out, Christina unpacks Michael's bag he brought back from the hospital and sorts the washing before checking on him. He's asleep.

She heads upstairs. Stopping at the large sash window at the top of the stairs, she looks out at the trees stripped bare by winter. The garden is a mess. In excess of two acres, it's far too big for them to keep on top of. It was OK when she was married to Adam. He paid for a gardener. And a cleaner. Unnecessary luxuries, in Michael's opinion. He's a tidy person, unlike Adam, so she gave up the cleaner when he moved in, and then the gardener as Michael took over the garden. But he lost interest. As he did in everything early last year.

Passing the kids' empty rooms, she turns the corner of the hallway to the bathroom. She's cold and drained. A hot bath will do her good while Michael is asleep. A noise startles her. What was that? It sounds like someone running across the floor above in Michael's study. She unlatches the door to the two attic rooms and flicks the light switch. She swears. The bulb must have blown. The only light is coming from the small casement window between the two rooms that doesn't open. Pictures hanging on the wall have been knocked askew from where she and Ted brought the mattress and bed down for

Michael's homecoming. She straightens each one as she slowly climbs the narrow staircase.

When she reaches the top, she pauses. The noise has stopped. She looks across to the spare room. Did it come from there? She opens the door to Michael's study but can't see anything. Did she imagine it? She tries the spare room. Nothing.

She bites her knuckle. It's red raw. A visible sign of the weight of her guilt. And the madness it's causing, if she's now hearing things?

Stepping into the study, she pulls out Michael's squishy leather chair that used to belong to his dad before he passed away. It is one of the few pieces of furniture Michael brought into their marriage. For a man of thirty-four years old, he had few personal possessions, yet, that's his character. She snorts, thinking of how different Michael is from her ex-husband. Adam is a possessions man. A greedy sod. The more, the better for him.

She switches on the desk lamp. It feels wrong being up here without him. But with each passing day, her curiosity grows like a vine, its ugly thorns tormenting her. She needs to know where he went that night.

Opening the top drawer of his desk, she pauses, dejected. For the first few years of their marriage, she used to bring him cups of tea up here while he was working, marking tests or preparing lessons. Now she's about to probe into his belongings.

'For your efforts, I shall read you a poem,' he would say, selecting a poetry book from the many publications lining the shelves.

She would sit on the floor, her back against the wall, sipping a cup of tea while he read one of Elizabeth Barrett Browning's love poems to her. It was one of the happiest times of her life.

When did he stop doing that? She can't remember.

She searches through the drawer before closing it.

The answer is in this room. Where exactly, she doesn't know, but it's somewhere. She can feel it in her bones. Opening the drawer beneath, she hunts around. Again, she finds nothing out of the ordinary.

But she will find out where he went that night. And with whom.

FORTY

Three days have passed since Michael came home, and Christina is feeling the pressure.

She hasn't been able to take the tablets Dr Hadley prescribed in case Michael needs her. But at least they graced her with a few good nights' sleep in preparation for his return.

She has spent the past three nights on the sofa. His heavy breathing has kept her awake more than she has slept. Still, at least he is here. And he's alive. And she's not a killer.

It's been her biggest fear these past few weeks. That he could die. And that would make her responsible for his death. How would she ever be able to live with herself?

Now they are out of the woods, she can't help but berate herself for how callous her thoughts all seem. Is she only thinking of herself, or is this indicative of what their relationship has become? Even before these tumultuous events, she sensed her marriage was on a tightrope, ready to take a tumble at any moment.

Standing up, she wanders over to the kitchen window. Silver and dark snow clouds veil the morning sky. A hint of a white Christmas is on its way. Abi would love that. She has always wanted a white Christmas.

Usually, Christina loves Christmas. She decorates the outside of the house and garden with icicle lights and LED illuminated figures – snowmen, reindeer and cheery Santas – but she hasn't had the time or the inclination this year. She should do it for the kids' sake. What was the lesson she learnt from Abi's illness?

Live for today because you never know what tomorrow holds.

Too bloody right you don't.

A knock at the door startles her.

Sophia bundles into the hallway holding Lily on her hip, who looks like a giant marshmallow squeezed into the snowsuit Christina bought for her before she was even born. In the other hand she is holding an oven dish covered in foil. 'I've brought you a shepherd's pie.'

'Michael's favourite.' Christina hugs her sister. 'Thank you.' Her sister has been a lifesaver since the accident, and especially since Michael came home, stopping by with their favourite meals to save Christina having to think about what to cook for dinner.

'No problem. It's good to get out, to be honest.'

Christina takes her niece for a quick cuddle, jiggling her on her hip. 'Look at you, you gorgeous being.'

Lily chatters away in the language only she understands.

'You should start working again,' Christina says to her sister.

Sophia used to work with Sebastian. A weird choice of career, Christina has always thought. Not what she ever thought her sister would end up doing, but Sophia is good at her job. Very good. Then Lily came along and she gave up working altogether.

'I can't bear to leave this little one.' Sophia reaches out and playfully pinches Lily's chubby cheek. 'Who would look after you?' She holds up the shepherd's pie. 'I'll put this in the fridge.'

Footsteps pound down the stairs and Abi appears. She grabs her cousin, laughing. 'What a great outfit. I need a snowsuit like that.'

'Where's Ben?' Sophia asks.

Christina rolls her eyes. 'Out.'

'Why the eye roll?'

'He should be studying.'

'Why don't you go out, Mum?' Abi says. 'Have a break.'

Her daughter's compassion never ceases to amaze Christina. She's going to make a great doctor one day.

The thought is appealing. So much still needs to be done for Christmas. 'I could do with heading to the shops.'

'Do it,' says Sophia. 'We can hold fort here, can't we, Abbs?'

Abi is removing Lily's snowsuit, large grins all around. 'We sure can.'

'We'll be fine,' Sophia says. 'Just go.'

There's a forecast of blizzard-like conditions, Christina hears on the car radio. The roads are beginning to ice over, and she encounters a salt spreader on the way into town.

The shops are rammed with it being so close to Christmas. She flits from one to another, picking up small presents for the kids. Usually, Christmas is carefully planned out in advance. She enjoys the shopping, carefully choosing unusual gifts for everyone, but this year it's a chore.

She spends a fortune, filling her basket with a pretty dress for Lily and gifts for the family she's not even sure they'll like. She wishes it were the first of January and it was all over. The mad Christmas rush isn't helping.

As Christina makes a hasty exit, lost in thoughts of Michael, a man appears, standing right in front of her, blocking her way.

It's a familiar face, but she is confused. It doesn't belong here.

'Christina, I thought it was you.'

'DS Macintosh. Sorry, I didn't recognise you. How are you?' Christina forces a smile. He is like an unwanted friend who keeps showing up uninvited.

'Cyril, please. I'm totally flustered. I've gone and done it again and left my shopping to the last minute and am now clueless about what to get for my wife. Apart from that, fine. You?'

Christina leans against a shop window. A group of carol singers start singing 'We Wish You a Merry Christmas', rattling their collection tins and waving a portable payment machine at the crowd gathered around them. She finds it depressing. There's nothing merry about her Christmas. It's the worst she has ever had. 'It's all a bit last minute. I've had a lot going on, as you can imagine.' She lifts her full reusable bags. 'My sister and daughter are looking after Michael,' she says, as if she needs to defend herself as to why she has left her husband. 'I've just about managed to get everyone something.'

'It can't be easy for you after everything that has happened.'

Here we go, always the police officer. 'My family have been great. We'll manage.'

'The importance of a tight family,' the detective responds. 'Look, Christina, I haven't tried to hijack you here. I mean that.'

She stiffens, weary with trying to hide in the corners of a police investigation. What's coming now?

'It's just that...' He pauses as if he is determining how to phrase what he wants to say. 'I have to be honest with you. I think Michael knows more about what happened that night than he is saying. And I can't understand why he's not opening up.'

'What do you mean?'

'Well, I can buy the fact that he didn't see who ran him down. I get that. But I sense he can recall what he was doing that night. What's more, I think you think the same as me. He is holding out on both of us.'

Christina remains silent, wary of saying too much or too little. Scared she is going to spill the sickening truth about her role in the accident.

The DS continues. 'I question why he wouldn't want to help us find the person responsible for his injuries. Unless he knew who they could be.'

She could be mistaken, but she doesn't like the look in his eyes. 'You honestly think he has an idea who they are? I don't think so. He would've said. I grant you, he has been acting strange. But he has for a while.' She pauses to clear her throat. 'Even before the accident, I felt he was down. For the reasons I already told you. That's all. Then this happened, and it has compounded how he is feeling. I personally think he just needs some counselling. And time to recover.'

'You may well be right. If anything crops up that you think will help with the investigation, be sure to let me know, won't you?'

Her pulse races. Why is he even saying that? 'Of course. Why wouldn't I?'

There's an awkwardness as if the detective wants to add something else. He nods. 'I must get on. These Christmas presents won't buy themselves. Although I wish they would. Happy Christmas to you and all.'

He backs away and heads into a women's clothes shop.

Christina fishes in her bag for her purse to pay the parking fee when she realises how much she is shaking. She needs to get a grip when faced with the police. But she can't help herself. The detective caught her unawares. And she didn't like the message he delivered or the way he looked at her. Is he on to her?

FORTY-ONE

There is what feels like crowds of visitors over the following days, bearing gifts and Christmas cheer.

Seeing people again unsettles Christina. It's as if she has been holed up for weeks watching the drama being played out from afar, but since Michael came home, what she did seems more real. Some days she feels as if his eyes are full of blame. Ted keeps telling her to get a grip. It's all in her head.

Michael isn't enthused to see any of his visitors, which is most unlike him. They are the closest friends he has down south.

Dermot from the cycling club turns up holding a bottle of bourbon wrapped in festive tissue paper. 'For when you're better, mate! Good to see you after so long.'

'Being around people gives me a headache,' Michael says, when Dermot leaves. 'I just want to be on my own.'

'I understand, but we need to start getting you back into the real world.' She sweeps her arm around the room. 'It's not good for you to be cooped up in here. How about you start coming upstairs for bed? I saw this YouTube clip of a woman getting up the stairs on crutches.'

His face turns red; his eyes bulge. 'Get off my case, will you?'

His hostility bites like the frosty weather. Christina swallows the tears that are constantly on the brink of falling. Thoughts of the recent conversation with DS Macintosh come flitting back.

'Sorry. I don't feel strong enough yet.' Michael smiles at her. It's better than him yelling at her. But there's something odd about his twisted smile that leaves her with a chill of unease. Or is it her imagination?

The day before Christmas Eve, Anne-Marie drops by on her way home from town. Today she is dressed in green leggings and a pink and green paisley smock embellished across the chest with silver beads, and her hair is tied in a swinging ponytail instead of its usual loose bobbed style. It's unusual seeing her friend in a different outfit from the smart trouser suits she wears to work.

Christina struggles to sum up how Michael is doing. 'The headaches remain a problem,' she says.

'And how are you coping?'

'I'm OK.'

'And the kids?'

'They're good.' It's a lie. Abi is good. Ben is still incredibly moody, though. He seems to have got worse since Michael arrived home. She has tried to talk to him, but he remains as uncommunicative as her husband.

Anne-Marie follows her to the lounge to see Michael.

Before she opens the door, Christina says, 'He sleeps a lot and doesn't want to do anything other than sit and watch TV. With a lot of persuasion, I can get him into the garden for some fresh air, but that's about it. He hates the crutches. I'm wondering if he's a little depressed.'

'That's not unusual for people recovering from such trauma,' Anne-Marie says. 'He has been through a lot, you know. Be patient. Why don't you leave me alone with him for a while? Sometimes people find it easier to talk when no one else is around, especially loved ones.'

'Do you want a drink?'

'I'm fine. I met a friend for coffee in town.' Anne-Marie opens the lounge door. 'I'll see you in a bit.'

Christina busies herself in her study, wrapping the last of the Christmas presents for the kids. She's still trying to find the festive mood but is not having any luck. She searches for the final gift to wrap. A book she bought for Abi. She can't find it. Perhaps she left it in her car.

She wraps her coat over her shoulders and goes outside. It's bitterly cold, a westerly wind whipping through her as she opens the boot of her car. There's the book, under a bag she keeps in the car for unexpected stops at the supermarket. As she slams the boot shut, she remembers she hasn't picked up the post today. Slipping her arms into her coat and zipping it up, she hurries along the driveway. She finds the key on her keyring to the mailbox and opens it. Gathering up the post, she runs back to the house.

Anne-Marie is still with Michael. Christina goes to the lounge to offer drinks, but stops at the door, hearing them talking. At least they are having a conversation. It's probably best she doesn't disturb them.

Returning to her study, she opens the post at her desk. She can't take anything in, as if she is going through the daily functions of life but not really living it. It's the same as she felt after Adam left their family home. The ongoing police investigation, and the gaping holes in Michael's existence before the accident, constantly plague her. She's no closer to finding out the truth about where Michael went the night of the accident. It's dragging her down.

She opens a letter detailing Abi's upcoming hospital visit for her scan. There's been a slight change in the time of the appointment. Christina sighs and puts the letter aside. Abi hasn't felt any more chest pain since seeing Dr Hadley, but the scan next week is another constant thorn of worry in Christina's side. She tosses unwanted leaflets about local care homes and new windows for the new year into the bin before getting to the Christmas cards.

A stab of guilt hits her for not sending any this year. It's usually a tradition she keeps up with despite the cultural move to donate to charity instead of sending cards. She opens the biggest one first, purely because she's inquisitive. Who sends such big cards?

Ripping the seal, she pulls out the card. She frowns. Instead of Santa or robins, a large threatening eye stares at her. What the hell?

Opening the card, panic surges through her as she reads the typed message stuck on a heart-shaped, red piece of paper.

Happy Christmas, Christina.
I was THERE
I SAW what you did.
I'll be in TOUCH.

FORTY-TWO

At first, Christina thinks it's a joke.

She rereads the message three times, before the reality sets in.

Her pulse is racing. She runs to the kitchen to fetch her phone. Closing the door, she paces to the window. When Ted answers her call, she whispers, 'Something terrible has happened.' The fear in her voice is unmistakable.

'Calm down,' Ted says.

Christina relays the contents of the note in a hushed voice.

'I'll be right over.' He hangs up.

She places her mobile on the kitchen worktop, transfixed by her hands trembling uncontrollably.

Someone saw her run her husband over.

But it was so dark that night. The weather was atrocious. No one in their right mind would've been out. The only person who could've seen her was Michael. Yet that doesn't make sense either. He wouldn't have come back home, to the person who hit him, if he'd seen anything.

Besides, he has hardly left the lounge. And he certainly

hasn't been upstairs. How could he have typed that note, let alone delivered it to the mailbox on those crutches?

But someone had seen her.

This can't be happening. She needs a drink. She grabs a bottle of gin and pours a generous measure into a large glass, topping it with tonic water from the fridge.

Taking a large glug, she stares out of the window, trying to control her breathing. A flurry of snow appears in the air. She would find joy in that sight at any other time.

The door opens. 'Bit early, isn't it, Mum?' Ben pulls a face.

Christina glances at the clock. Her son is right. It's only four o'clock. 'It's Christmas,' she says, faking a smile.

He frowns at her. 'You're acting very strange at the moment. Are you all right? You're all jittery.'

Me, all right? She wants to tell him that people in glass houses shouldn't throw stones. Instead, she says, 'I'm fine.' It's a lie, of course. Her world has been a mess for weeks, months even, and it's just exploded.

'Abi and I are waiting for you in the snug.'

The snug is Christina's favourite place in the whole house. It's a tiny room next to the main lounge and with an open fireplace, a corner sofa covered with cushions, and a large flatscreen TV, it's the perfect place to chill out.

'What for?'

'She's put on *It's a Wonderful Life*. Apparently, you've promised her for three days in a row to watch it with us.'

Has she? Christina laughs openly, the irony not lost on her. Her life is far from wonderful.

'We always watch films together at Christmas, and we haven't seen a single one. It's now the twenty-third.' Ben steps closer to her. It's unnerving. He hasn't been particularly nice to her for a long time, and now he's being gushingly sentimental about Christmas films. 'Have you been crying?' he asks.

'Don't be silly.'

'Your cheeks are all red.'

She glosses over his observation. 'Ted's coming over. I need to have a quick chat with him.'

'Are we going to watch it or not?'

Christina snaps. She can't help it. 'Not at the moment, Ben.'

'Honestly, we'd be better off at Dad's. At least he knows how to celebrate Christmas.'

Her son's words are like a kick in the guts. What's most upsetting is that he knows how much his choice of words hurts.

He storms out and slams the kitchen door, just as the front door bangs shut.

Why is everything so complicated?

She runs to the hallway and shouts, 'I'm sorry. I'll be there soon, kids. Don't start the film without me.'

Ted walks in looking harassed. That makes two of them.

'Drink?' she asks.

'I'll have a beer.'

Leaving him with the card in the dining room, she grabs a Peroni from the fridge. She can't stop her hands shaking as she rummages through the utensils drawer for a bottle opener.

'What do you make of it?' Christina asks, opening the bottle of beer and handing it to him.

'Where's the envelope?' Ted asks.

'There was no postmark, if that's what you're asking. Just my name and address typed on a sticky label.' She sighs. 'Who would do such a thing?'

'Someone who likes playing games by the looks of it.' Ted takes the beer. 'Jessica James?'

'She has crossed my mind. But what would she have been doing out at that precise spot on that night?'

They both stare at each other. Ever since they were young, they have had a look. One that says they're thinking the same thought. 'She dropped him off,' they say in unison.

'Oh, hell.' Christina takes a gulp of gin.

'She's not old enough to drive, is she?' Ted says.

'She was seventeen when it all kicked off with Michael, so she's eighteen now. She drives her mum's car – a silver Ford Focus. I've seen her out and about in it.'

'I thought she was younger than that.' Ted guzzles his beer.

Christina frowns. 'But the car that dropped him off at The Black Horse drove off in the opposite direction. Jessica lives up at the top of Bridge End.'

Ted takes another swig of beer. 'She could've gone back home the long way.'

'Perhaps they've been together all along?' The thought cuts her like the sharpest of knives. Christina hugs her arms around her body as if she is trying to protect herself from the extra torment this latest development in her life is causing. 'I can't believe that, though.'

Ted raises his eyebrows. 'Can't or don't want to?'

Christina empties her glass. A warm feeling runs through her as the alcohol reaches her bloodstream. It's temporarily comforting. 'Both. What's the end game for her, though?' She waves the card in front of her brother's face. 'Someone saw me knock him over.' She thumps the palms of her hands against her temple. 'This is my worst nightmare. Imagine Michael finding out. We'd be over for sure. He'd report it. I'd go to prison. What about the kids?' She looks at her brother pleadingly. 'What do I do?'

'I don't know.' He shares her pain. She can see it in his furrowed brow. 'I guess you need to sit tight until they make their next move.'

'You think more of this is coming?'

He points to the note and quotes, 'I'll be in touch.' He looks at her. 'I think so.'

The lounge door slams shut.

Christina grabs the card and slips it under the tablecloth.

'Is that Michael?' Ted asks.

'No, Anne-Marie – my friend, mine and Michael's boss.'

So engrossed in the unfolding drama, Christina had forgotten her friend was there. 'Stay there. I won't be a minute.'

She runs out of the room, greeting Anne-Marie in the hallway.

Something's wrong, Christina can tell. Or is she self-reflecting? 'You were in there for quite a while. How was he?' she asks.

Anne-Marie looks at her questioningly.

There's something off about her. Christina is sure of it. There's an awkwardness between them. One that's never been there before.

Anne-Marie's hair is no longer tied in a ponytail, which strikes Christina as odd. Anne-Marie takes a deep breath, her face softening. 'I think he's a bit down, to be honest. That's normal for someone who's been through what he has, though. It's going to take time.' She squeezes Christina's shoulder. 'I'm sorry. I need to rush off. I didn't mean to stay so long. There's still a lot I need to do. I'm not sure how I'm going to fit it all in. Have a lovely Christmas, and I'll see you on Thursday.'

'Thursday?' Christina frowns.

'My birthday.'

'Of course. I forgot.'

'Don't feel pressured to come. I know you have a lot on.'

She can say that again.

FORTY-THREE

The house falls into quietness.

Ted is staying the night. He joined Christina for a glass of gin that turned into three – or was it four? – as they flopped on the sofa in the snug with Abi and Ben watching a Christmas film. A rare evening with her kids, Christina should've been content. But Ted had to keep nudging her to laugh at the funny bits knowing she wasn't concentrating. How could she?

'You don't need to sleep in here any more,' Michael says when she joins him in the lounge in her pyjamas. He is already in his bed. 'It can't be comfortable. I'll be fine. Get yourself a proper night's sleep.'

Christina stands at the end of the sofa, fiddling with the tassels of his navy blanket thrown over the edge. The thought of going back to their bed is inviting. 'What if you need me?'

'I can always call you. Keep your phone on.'

'I'm not sure it's a good idea,' she says, concerned.

'If you could get me some more painkillers before you go up that's all I should need. In case I get another one of these damn headaches.'

She leaves him to fetch some more tablets from the kitchen,

hurt that he appears not to need her as much any more. She should look on the positive side. It's a step in the right direction that he doesn't want her to stay with him all night. 'Here you go,' she says, helping him to sit up.

'You need to stop fussing over me.'

She hands him the tablets with a glass of water and perches on the edge of the bed beside him. 'Michael, can I ask you something?'

'If it's quick. I'm tired.'

She pauses, overcome with awkwardness. Why is she having these feelings about her husband of six years? Is this a time to be probing him for answers? She can't stop herself. 'Something has been bothering me.'

His raises his eyebrows, silently waiting for her to continue.

'One day, when you were in the ICU, my car wouldn't start, so I took yours. I was looking for some change in the glove compartment to give to the tea lady collecting for the children's ward when I found a black pair of women's gloves.'

He looks at her intently, his eyes blinking rapidly.

There's silence. Why won't he answer her?

He laughs.

'What's so funny?' she asks cautiously.

'I guess you're wondering whose they are?'

She nods, his laughter making her feel silly and small.

'I found them.'

'Where?'

'At school one day, as I was walking to the car. I meant to hand them in and forgot. We should've given them to Anne-Marie today.'

She eyes him warily. It's a perfectly plausible excuse. But...

'You do believe me, don't you?'

'Of course I do.' She fakes a laugh. 'Why wouldn't I?'

'Good. What's up with you? You're jittery.'

That's exactly what Ben said. It's as if they've been discussing her.

'Nothing. Just the stress of everything.'

'Go and get a good night's sleep.' He lies down and turns his back to her.

When are things going to improve between them?

Christina checks on the kids before retiring. Abi is already in the land of nod, so she gently and quietly kisses her daughter's forehead. 'Goodnight, beautiful,' she whispers.

Abi returns a sleepy sigh and turns over.

Ben is on his phone, EarPods in. She waves goodnight from the bedroom door.

He nods at her before returning his gaze to the screen.

She leaves him be, nostalgic for the days when they would have a quick cuddle every night before bed.

Placing a sleeping tablet on her tongue, she swallows it with a swig of water. There's no way she'll be able to sleep otherwise. The message in the card dominates her thoughts.

Someone saw her run Michael over.

She still can't believe it.

Pulling back the duvet, she climbs under the covers, relieved to be in her own bed despite how cold it is. She remembers the days before Michael took to sleeping on the sofa – when she used to lovingly refer to him as her personal hot water bottle. He would get under the covers before her and warm the bed for her, and when they turned the lights out, he would spoon against her and hold her.

While waiting for the tablet to take effect, she picks up a book and attempts to read, but her thoughts are too distracted.

She left her husband for dead.

And someone saw her do it.

A creaking sound steals her attention. What was that? It's probably the house settling down for the night. She should be used to it. The old timber-framed dwelling makes all sorts of inexplicable sounds that still occasionally freak her out. There it is again. Is it Michael? Does he need her?

Feeling the need to check on him again, she throws off the duvet and slips into her dressing gown. Leaving the room, she stands leaning over the banister. The house is completely silent. She must've been mistaken. She runs downstairs to check on Michael. He is asleep. She returns upstairs and peers in Abi's room. The merest movement of the duvet gently rises and falls in time to her daughter's breathing. She checks on Ben. Even he is asleep. The darkness consumes her as she navigates her way back to bed.

At about one a.m., a beam of moonlight stretches into the room. She lies staring at it for what feels like hours, sweating. She checks the time. It's now gone two o'clock. It's no good. Against her better judgement, she takes another tablet and waits, desperate for sleep to follow.

The drugs and alcohol she consumed throughout the evening do not marry well. She falls in and out of a fitful sleep, plagued by vivid nightmares about the night of the accident. The thud when she hit Michael's body. The police informing her that her husband had been involved in a serious accident. Michael's bashed-up face when she first saw him in hospital.

A noise wakes her. Someone is moving around downstairs. It must be Michael, but then she hears talking. Ted must have gone down to see him. Or maybe it was Ben? She hauls herself out of bed and walks to the landing. It's dead quiet. She must have been mistaken.

When she finally descends into a slumber, the hand-delivered card weaves its way into her dreams. She sees a figure walking through the snow to the mailbox at the end of the drive. They are delivering a letter. But however hard she tries, she can't see their face.

She awakes again, feeling queasy. She shouldn't have taken the second pill. Is that movement on the stairs – the familiar creak as someone climbs? Or is she dreaming? She drifts in and out of consciousness, waiting. The second stair from the top – there'll be another creak as weight bears down on that one, too. There it is! Someone is definitely coming up the stairs.

Silence falls. Sleep claims her again, but only momentarily. Within what feels like barely a minute, she is wide-eyed, staring at a silhouette of a person illuminated by the snowy winter moon casting a shadow below the ill-fitting oak-panelled door. Christina tries to scream, but fear paralyses her.

There's a noise from above. Someone is in the attic rooms now, pacing around. She must go and see who it is. But she can't move. Someone is holding her down.

She awakes with a start, her head spinning and her throat as dry as sand.

'Happy Christmas Eve. I've made you a cuppa.' Ted is standing over her, holding a mug of tea. He is wearing the short-sleeved pyjamas he keeps here for the nights he stays, revealing the identical black panther tattoos on his muscled forearms.

Christina groans. She's groggy, punch drunk. 'I've hardly slept.'

'Me neither. I've bloody well been called to a job.'

'On Christmas Eve?'

'A client's got a leak in their kitchen.' He rolls his eyes. 'I'll be back as soon as I can. Sophia should be over soon.'

'Were you wandering around the house in the night?'

'No. Why?' Ted peeps through the gap in the curtains. 'It's snowed.'

'I thought I heard someone. I must've been dreaming.'

He nestles on the side of the bed, lowering his voice. 'Look, I've been thinking. About the note. It has kept me awake most of the night.'

'It has given me nightmares.'

'Say the worst happens, and this person, whoever they are, goes to the police. And they have proof it was you.'

She places the mug on the bedside table. 'Don't say that. You're scaring me.'

'If it happens, we need to have an answer ready about the car. My guess is, if it goes that far, forensics will be able to tell you've had work done on it.'

'What do I tell them?'

'You say you hit an animal, and I arranged to have it fixed, but it happened last month. At the beginning of November. I can get my mate to corroborate that story if need be.'

'Michael will know that's not true.'

'We'll say he must've forgotten about it.' He snorts. 'Let's face it. His memory is shot to bits at the moment.'

'What if this blackmailer has photographs?'

'Chrissy, the weather was atrocious that night. You said no one was about. It was a dark, empty road.'

'This is hell.' She throws her hands to her head, trying to control her breath. 'I'm scared, Ted. Bloody petrified.'

'Just do as I say.'

FORTY-FOUR

Christina's halfway to the door of the pharmacy, having picked up enough of Michael's medication to see him through to the new year, when a hand lands on her shoulder.

She spins around to see a woman, around mid-forties, she vaguely recognises but can't place.

'Hello, Christina. I'm not sure if you remember me? I'm Mary, Elizabeth Haggerty's daughter, from Bridge End.'

Christina sifts through her troubled mind until she finds the memory she is searching for. Mrs Haggerty lives in one of the bungalows along Bridge End, a few hundred metres from Ivy Brook. Michael calls her the local curtain twitcher because he says she is always at her lounge window. Christina often bumps into Mary and her mother when she walks Wilf along the route across the fields that back onto Mrs Haggerty's garden. 'Mary. How are you?'

The woman appears agitated. 'Like everyone else! Trying to get Mum's medication before Christmas starts. How's your husband? Mum told me what happened.'

'He's on the mend, thank you.'

'Mum was so upset when the police came around. I hope she helped.'

'Helped?' Christina asks.

'Mum was the one who showed them the footage from her video doorbell of your husband walking past her house on the night of his accident.'

'I didn't know it was her.' There are a handful of houses along that stretch of road, and DS Macintosh never said which one he had obtained the evidence from.

'I hope he gets well soon. Please give him my regards,' Mary says.

Christina is about to walk away but stops. 'Do you think your mum would mind if I popped over to look at that footage?'

'I'm sure she'd be delighted with the company. Pop in some time.'

'I will,' Christina says, waving goodbye.

Christina has spent the morning since running errands staring blankly out of the kitchen window, fearing what's next. Wilf sits at her feet.

All she wants to do is go back to bed and spend the day under the covers. Taking two sleeping pills on top of drinking all that gin last night was a stupid idea. Why did she do that?

'Mum!'

'Sorry, what did you say?'

'Why do you keep looking out of the window? Are you waiting for something?' Abi sticks a bagel in the toaster.

Christina leaves the window and pushes an orange in her daughter's direction. 'Have a piece of fruit with that. Any more chest pains or headaches?'

Abi shakes her head. 'Stop asking. I'll tell you if I do. How's Michael today?' Abi seems to be warming more towards him since the accident.

'I'll take you out for a walk in a bit,' Christina says, smiling down at Wilf nudging her leg. 'Michael's resting. He says he needs to build his strength up for the big day.'

'Where's Uncle Ted?'

'He had to go to work.'

Abi blinks. 'On Christmas Eve?'

Christina explains about a leak in the kitchen Ted fitted last week. 'He can't get hold of the plumber who worked on the job for him.'

'That's not fair,' Abi says. 'Not on Christmas Eve.'

'That's what happens when you have your own business. The buck stops with you.'

'I'm never going to have my own business. Are we watching another Christmas film? I enjoyed that last night. Ben did as well. I think it might have to be two. He wants *Home Alone*. I want *Elf*. We can't decide.'

'How many times have we seen *Home Alone*?'

'Don't complain. At least he's up for spending time with us.'

'True. True,' Christina says. 'What's he like when you go to Dad's?'

'What do you mean?'

'Does he spend all his time in his room?'

'Dad takes us out a lot, so he can't.'

'Is he as moody when you're there?'

Abi shrugs. 'We do more there, so it's hard to say.' Her daughter maturely changes the subject. 'What time are Sophia and Sebastian coming over with Lily?'

'They're not.' Christina reaches for a netting of brussels sprouts. She needs to get all the vegetables prepped for tomorrow, and she hates preparing brussels. The smell will turn her stomach even more than it's already turning.

'Why?'

'Uncle Sebastian has got to work.'

'Who's died?' The toaster pops up the bagel. Abi takes it out and smears it with butter.

'How should I know?' Christina yawns. She's going to need an afternoon nap at this rate.

Abi sits at the breakfast bar, munching the bagel and licking the butter that oozes onto her fingers. Wilf leaves Christina's side and sits by Abi's feet, hoping for some morsels.

'You didn't answer me. Why do you keep looking out of the window?' Abi asks.

'I'm checking to see whether there's going to be more snow,' Christina replies, hating herself for the lies she keeps having to tell. Her eyes are drawn to the window again as Abi describes an operation to separate conjoined twins attached at the abdomen that she has been reading about this morning. She wishes they'd installed that video doorbell now. Not that it would've done any good. The mailbox would be out of range, anyway. They need some CCTV installed.

'It took eighteen hours, Mum,' Abi says. 'Can you imagine working for eighteen hours?'

'Or waiting?' Christina says. 'That's worse.' She knows. Waiting for Abi to come out of the brain surgery she had when she was four was the worst thing Christina has ever had to endure. She had spent the whole ten hours in complete anguish.

Abi describes the details of the operation, how the surgeons separated the twins and reconstructed their shared intestines to ensure they each had functioning organs. It's making Christina queasy. 'One of them haemorrhaged, Mum. I wonder how much blood loss there was.'

The postman's van pulls up outside the entrance to the house. He gets out and shoves a delivery into the mailbox.

Christina drops the vegetable knife on the chopping board and rushes out of the kitchen. Not bothering with a coat, she grabs her keys, opens the door and runs to the mailbox through the flurry of fine snow as the van disappears.

With trembling hands, she finds the key and opens the mailbox, preparing herself for the inevitable. A gush of wind whips through her sweatshirt, chilling her to the core.

A single white envelope lies inside the black metal box.

She grabs it and flips it over.

It's a bank statement.

Taking several deep breaths, she returns inside. She's not thinking rationally. Her thoughts and actions make no sense. The card she received was hand delivered. It didn't come via the postman.

A mix of emotions tears through her. Part of her is relieved there's nothing else. Another part is strangely disappointed. At least she'd know where she stood if there was another note, and she could stop fretting about what was to come. Then she could work out a way to deal with it.

For now, it's as if there is a noose around her neck, and someone is about to pull it tight.

FORTY-FIVE

It's another restless night. Different people sending her threatening messages plague the nightmares of Christina's short bursts of sleep. Messages that take all forms: texts, emails and letters. She awakes early, saturated in sweat, yet shivering. She wants this all to be over. We all want closure. That's what the DS said.

The house is quiet. Too quiet. How she misses the days when Abi and Ben burst into the bedroom at a ghastly hour on Christmas morning, barely able to contain their excitement as they announced Santa Claus had already come. They would bounce up and down on the bed, pleading with her to get up. She moaned and groaned about it at the time, but, now she looks back, it gave the start of the day that Christmas feel. She sighs, mournful. She'll never get those days back.

When she gets up, Ted is already on culinary duties, having offered to take on most of the cooking today, thankfully. The radio is playing Bruce Springsteen's 'Santa Claus is Comin' to Town' as he lines up pots and pans on one side of the kitchen, preparing breakfast on the other.

She wills herself to find the Christmas spirit. It's a struggle. 'I didn't hear you get up,' she says, reaching for the kettle.

'I want to get ahead of myself. Military precision is what is required today.' Ted mocks a salute. 'I'm glad you've already prepped all the veg.'

'Want some tea?'

'Tea? I've been waiting for you to get up and get me a glass of Buck's Fizz.'

'You're kidding me?'

He laughs. 'What happened to the girl who didn't even go to bed on Christmas Eve?'

'Kids! That's what happened to her.'

He laughs. 'Happy Christmas, Chrissy.' He leans over and kisses her cheek. 'Love ya.'

'Merry Christmas,' she says. Not that there's anything merry about it. This is the worst Christmas she has ever had. 'Thanks for your help. I don't know what I'd do without you.' Embracing him, she can't help looking over his shoulder and down the snow-covered drive towards the mailbox.

No. Not today.

Surely, whoever has threatened her won't leave another card on Christmas Day?

FORTY-SIX

Christina has already checked the mailbox three times by the time the sound of snow crunching under car tyres announces Sophia and her family's arrival at midday.

Michael is taking a nap, and the kids are sitting at the breakfast table, setting up their new Apple Watches among the cutlery and plates on the table set for nine. Discarded wrapping paper, gift tags and ribbon litter the floor. Ted is stressed over the turkey. 'It's looking rather pink. Don't you think?'

Christina checks the meat. 'It could probably do with another half an hour.' She rushes to the door to greet her family. Sophia steps in first, holding Lily, rosy-cheeked from the cold wind.

Christina takes Lily, genuinely smiling for what feels like the first time in days to see her niece.

Sebastian follows, laden with presents and Lily's foldaway highchair, with his mother in tow. They thump their feet as they enter. Her brother-in-law is as white as the snow he's left on the doormat.

Christina hopes he's not coming down with something. The

last thing Michael needs is a virus or infection. 'Are you OK, Sebastian?' she asks, jiggling Lily on her hip.

'I had the flu jab yesterday,' he says. 'It's made me feel a little off-colour.'

'On Christmas Eve?'

'I've been so busy lately. I missed three flu clinics, so as I was seeing the nurse for something else she agreed to give me the jab. It never usually affects me, but it hasn't agreed with me this year.'

'Man flu,' Sophia says, rolling her eyes. She takes Lily back from Christina. 'I need to give her a quick feed.'

'I'll do it,' Christina says.

'Best leave it to me. She's being tricky at the moment. Are you OK? You look more off-colour than Sebastian.'

'I'm fine.' Christina shepherds them to the lounge as per her brother's wishes. Ted's stress levels rocket off the scale when too many people invade his space in the kitchen.

Nancy flumps on the sofa next to Michael. 'Who's going to get me a drink, then?' she asks in her usual forthright manner. 'It is Christmas after all.'

'What would you like?' Christina asks.

'A sherry would be nice. If you've got any.'

Christina turns to Ben. 'Could you help with the drinks, please?'

He nods and takes everyone's orders.

Lily struggles from Sophia's grasp and throws herself into Michael's arms.

'Steady on, tiger,' Michael laughs.

It's the first time Christina has seen him laugh properly since before the accident. A wave of relief washes through her. Is it because it's Christmas, and he feels duty-bound to put on a brave face? Or is the road to recovery in sight? Please let it be the latter.

When Ted is ready to carve the turkey, he announces for everyone to take their place at the table.

Michael bursts Christina's bubble by declining to come to dinner.

'He says he's got a headache,' Ben says.

'Shall I take him some more painkillers?' Sophia asks.

Christina counts hours on her fingers. 'He's not due any.'

'Here, take him some dinner.' Ted passes Sophia a plate of food. 'I'll get a tray. You never know, he might eat it. He told me he doesn't like eating in front of people since the accident because he dribbles sometimes.'

Christina stares at him. 'When did he tell you that?'

'When I was here the other night.' Ted stirs the gravy.

Christina is put out. Michael hasn't shared anything like that with her. She stops at the kitchen window and stares at the mailbox. Her heart misses a beat.

Ben whispers in her ear. 'I think Sebastian's mum's a bit tipsy.'

Christina cocks her head around the arch into the breakfast room to see Nancy sitting at the head of the table drinking a glass of sherry. Her flamed cheeks are as red as the scarlet blouse she is wearing, and she is singing her rendition of 'Fairy-tale of New York', belting out from the smart speaker Ben has hooked up to a Christmas playlist, completely out of tune.

Lily bangs a wooden spoon on the tray of her highchair, babbling.

Sebastian tells Nancy to quieten down.

Abi fiddles with her watchstrap, stifling a smile.

Ben sniggers. 'Look at her. She's being so funny.'

'You shouldn't have kept filling her glass,' Christina says. She should berate her son for encouraging Nancy to drink more, but she doesn't want to ruin the family mood. Besides, it's the liveliest she has seen him for months.

He shrugs and joins his sister at the table.

Christina welcomes the normality of family life, even if Michael isn't with them. It's been a while since laughter has filled this house.

Sophia returns from the lounge with the tray of food. 'He's fallen asleep.'

'Put the plate in the oven,' Christina says. 'I'll take it to him after we've eaten.'

Abi helps Ted and Christina serve a meal to be proud of, while Nancy entertains everyone with catty remarks. It's as if the sherry has drowned her inhibitions and left her completely without a filter.

Everyone dives in, but Christina still hasn't found her appetite she left at the kerbside of her husband's accident. She pushes food around her plate, sipping wine and feeding Lily in the highchair beside her for enjoyment.

Her niece grabs a Yorkshire pudding out of her hand and stuffs it in her mouth, giggling.

A mobile chimes.

'Bloody hell. Who's that?' Nancy can't seem to contain herself. 'No phones at the dinner table,' she barks, unfairly directing her comment at Abi and Ben.

Sebastian frowns, patting his jacket pockets. 'Sorry, I think that's me.' He takes the ringing phone out of his pocket, silencing it as he leaves the room.

Nancy scowls. 'I hope that's not work related.'

Ben signs a gun pointing at his temple to Abi, feigning someone's demise as everyone continues eating.

Minutes pass before Sebastian returns. He looks toward Sophia and then Christina and Ted. 'I'm so sorry,' he says. 'I have to go. There's been a death out in Bradstock.'

Sophia throws him a dirty look. They start bickering, her sister implying that she doesn't want to be left alone with his pissed mother to deal with.

Ted relays a story of one of his clients' outlandish Christmas decorations that must have cost a fortune, stealing the attention from Sophia and Sebastian's disagreement that has turned into a row.

Nancy joins in as Sebastian stuffs down his dinner before expressing his apologies, kissing the top of Lily's head and leaving the room.

A minute later, the front door slams.

'I suppose if you're gonna go, you're gonna go,' Ted says, trying to placate Nancy and Sophia, both equally irritated by Sebastian's disappearance. Nancy even bursts into tears.

Christina shakes her head but remains surprisingly calm. The commotion is rather amusing compared to the turmoil in her life.

After everyone has left or retired for the night, and she has checked on Michael, who is fast asleep, Christina finds herself gazing toward the kitchen window again in a trance-like state as she finishes the last of the washing up. She's staring at the only thing that seems to hold her attention at the moment.

She vowed she wouldn't be lured into checking the mailbox a thousand times a day. They would be winning, whoever her tormentor is. Once everyone was here, it had taken all her being to resist the urge to slip outside to look.

After another check on Michael, who is fast asleep, she fills a glass with water and turns out the light. At the bottom of the stairs, she pauses. She can't. She just can't go to bed without checking the mailbox.

Leaving the glass on the side of the stairs, she reluctantly walks along the hallway and opens the front door.

FORTY-SEVEN

Cold winter air rushes at her.

The driveway is in darkness, the night eerily quiet. Removing her phone from her pocket, she flicks on the torch. Only when she's halfway down the driveway does she realise she's still wearing her slippers. Snow seeps through to her socks, soaking her feet. With trembling hands, she forces herself to unlock the mailbox.

Bile rushes up to her throat.

Sitting inside the black metal box is another large card.

Christina glances around, imagining a person in the shadows, gloating at her expense.

What a stupid thought. Whoever left her this unwanted Christmas present has long gone.

Snatching the card, she bangs the mailbox shut and runs to the house, looking over her shoulder every few steps. She locks and bolts the front door; the taste of what little Christmas dinner she managed to eat sours in her mouth.

Rushing into her study, she throws the envelope addressed to her the same as before on the desk. Her breathing is erratic, coming in short, sharp bursts. It's unbearable. Her legs give way, prompting her to sit down. She clutches her throat, trying to calm her racing heartbeat. Hesitantly, she opens the envelope.

Inside she finds a card with the same picture as before of an eye stuck to the front. Opening the card, she holds a hand to her mouth, stifling a cry as she reads the message stuck on a heart-shaped, red piece of paper.

Happy Christmas, Christina.
It's going to be £10,000 to buy my silence.
To keep you out of PRISON
Drop the cash in the bin at the bottom of the steps opposite DIDIFORD railway station.
8 p.m. Thursday.
Come ALONE.
Or I go to the POLICE.
I KNOW what you did to your husband, Christina.
I KNOW.

Christina drops her head in her hands. The smell of leftover turkey has drifted into the room. Along with the note, it makes her gag.

She rereads the instructions. The words on the card appear fuzzy, fading in and out of focus. Wiping the beads of sweat coating her brow with the sleeve of her dress, she struggles to breathe. The final indicator of a panic attack.

She forces herself to inhale deeply, slowly through her nostrils and out through her mouth.

Repeat.

She's been here before. During Abi's treatment, when she was scared she might lose her daughter. She'd held everything together then, only just, because she couldn't let Abi see her fear. She can at least try now.

She flips the card over and continues the breathing regime,

muttering, 'You're not having a heart attack. You're going to be OK.'

At least five minutes pass before the alarming feelings subside. The emotional strain has taken its toll, but she is in control again. Ted. She needs to speak to Ted. She places her hands on the desk and pushes herself up, tucking the card down the front of her dress.

She hurries upstairs. Not wanting to disturb the kids, she quietly opens the door to the spare room. The waft of Jack Daniel's hits her. The room is in darkness, save for a faint beam of light shining through the gap in the curtains. Ted is asleep, snoring heavily, oblivious to the wretched news she is about to share with him.

'Ted. Ted.' Her tone is soft but urgent. 'Wake up.' She clicks on the bedside lamp and kneels by her brother's side.

He grumbles.

'This is serious.' She shakes his shoulder. 'There's another card.' She pulls out the evidence from the front of her dress.

'Shit.' He shields his barely open eyes from the bright light.

She swivels the head of the lamp in the opposite direction.

'Let me see.' He takes the card, wrestling himself into a sitting position. 'Shit,' he repeats as he scans the words.

'What am I going to do?' Christina whispers.

'Nothing,' Ted replies, his voice croaky from slumber.

'Nothing? I can't do nothing, Ted.'

'You seriously don't intend paying it, do you?'

'What else can I do?'

'If you pay that money, they'll come back for more. I guarantee you. What's the saying? Never give in to blackmailers.'

'Ted, I could go to prison.'

'Do you have that sort of money?'

'It would pretty much clear out my savings, but I could. I've got back-up.'

'Back-up?'

'The money for the kids.'

'What money?'

'The funds from the divorce settlement that I put aside for them for when they go to uni, or whatever they decide to do.'

He leans against the velvet headboard. Running his hand through his hair, he rereads the message. 'Let's sleep on it.'

Christina scoffs. 'Sleep? You're joking. I won't be getting a wink's sleep tonight. I'm going to have to pay this, aren't I? You must be able to see that.'

'And then what? What happens when they come back for more, and you don't have anything to give them?' Ted's voice is urgent, pleading Christina to see sense. 'Because they will be back.'

A moment's silence passes. Christina clutches her chest. 'I'll have to deal with that when it happens.'

FORTY-EIGHT

Christina stands in the queue at the bank, willing the cashier to hurry up so she can make the withdrawal.

Because it's a large sum of money, she called yesterday and ordered the cash. It should be ready to pick up straight away. All she needs is to get to the front of this bloody queue. Her head is pounding from anxiety and lack of sleep, not to mention the argument she had with Ted this morning when he dropped in for a coffee to talk to her.

He thinks she's a fool for giving in to her blackmailer. 'Think seriously about what you're planning to do,' he whispered. Not that he needed to. The kids were upstairs and Michael was in the lounge. 'These are ruthless people.'

She looked at him horrified. 'You think it's more than one person?'

He shook his head. 'No. I was referring collectively to the bastards who blackmail people.'

'I can't let them go to the police,' she told him. 'How will Michael react when he finds out I nearly killed him? And the thought of what'll happen to the kids if I get put in prison doesn't bear thinking about.'

Ted didn't have an answer.

The overhead lighting in the bank is bright. It isn't helping the thumping pain in her head. She closes her eyes for a moment, listening to the hum of customers going about their business.

The grumpy couple in front of her are arguing about how much the wife spent on Christmas. It has left them broke. When it's their turn at the counter, they dump bags of counted coins from a supermarket bag to exchange for notes to see them through until payday.

Christina opens her eyes, watching the couple.

They collected the coins in an old glass jar, the wife tells the cashier. 'There's five years' worth in there.'

It's depressing to watch and to listen to.

But not as depressing as her situation.

When it's her turn, the cashier asks, 'Doing something nice with the money?'

'Having my house renovated,' Christina lies.

She can hardly tell the truth.

FORTY-NINE

Given the situation and her 'meeting' this evening, Christina considered cancelling her visit to Anne-Marie's. But it's her friend's birthday, and she feels obliged to go to the gathering Anne-Marie throws every year. Especially this year since her daughter is away with her dad on a skiing holiday.

Usually, Michael comes along. So do Abi and Ben when it's their year with her, as they grew up going to playdates with Anne-Marie's daughter. But with Michael out of action, she told the kids to stay at home with him. She doesn't intend on staying long.

She sits in her car a few spaces from Anne-Marie's house, watching the wipers squeal and squeak, swiping flakes from the windscreen, while she tries to pluck up the courage to get out. People from school she hasn't seen since the accident will be there, and her tolerance for socialising at the moment is pretty non-existent.

She considers leaving the large manilla envelope stashed with cash in the glove compartment but decides it's too risky. The last thing she needs is for someone to break in and steal the last of her savings.

She switches off the engine. One cup of tea, and she can make her excuse. Anne-Marie will understand, and people know she has a lot on at home.

If only they knew the half of it.

Anne-Marie opens the door, and Christina is engulfed by the powerful floral scent of Opium perfume from the birthday girl.

Anne-Marie is dressed in a black polo jumper and a pair of green sequin trousers, her choice of clothes as unusual as the décor of her house. 'I was hoping you'd come.' Anne-Marie takes the bouquet of lilies and pip berry stems that Christina bought from the flower stall outside the bank. 'I've missed you.'

Christina removes her coat. Water from melted snow drips onto the parquet tiled flooring from her boots. The sound of chitter chatter humming over Fleetwood Mac fills her ears.

Anne-Marie frowns. 'You've lost weight.'

'It's been a stressful time.'

'Here, let me take that for you.' Anne-Marie grabs her coat. 'I'll hang it up.' She points at Christina's bag. 'Want me to take that as well?'

Christina tightens her hold of her handbag, securing it against her chest. 'It's fine. I'll hang onto it, thanks.'

Anne-Marie steps backwards, apologising. She frowns. 'How are you?' She hangs Christina's coat on a hook and leads her into the kitchen, passing a woman drinking prosecco Christina doesn't know.

'As well as can be expected.'

'How's Michael?' Anne-Marie reaches up to a shelf and pulls off a pink vase with turquoise polka dots. It appears an unlikely match for a bunch of lilies and red berry stems, but Anne-Marie will undoubtably turn it into a centrepiece.

'He's talking about going back to work.'

'That's positive. Is he ready, do you think?' Anne-Marie

runs the tap and fills the vase with water, arranging the flowers like a pro.

'His ankle is healing really well, but he's still suffering from these terrible headaches. The doctor prescribed some new tablets. They seem to be helping a little. I can't see him back at work though until the headaches are fully under control.'

'Absolutely not. He needs to be fully recovered. But I know Michael. I bet he's chomping at the bit to get back to work. I can't see him as a good patient.'

'You can say that again. I should return as well.'

'Only when you're ready.'

'I'm going a little stir-crazy at home.' Christina is worried about her job, even though she knows Anne-Marie would say she shouldn't be.

'Any news from the police?'

Christina swallows back tears. She shouldn't have come here. She's not ready to socialise. It's emotional talking about her husband, knowing what she did. 'Nothing. And he still has no recollection of what happened that night. Where he went, with who or why.'

Anne-Marie stops arranging the flowers, a lily in her hand. 'Where do you think he went?'

Christina's voice breaks. 'I'm scared.' Her eyes well up. 'I'm scared it was another woman.' She pauses. What on earth was she thinking saying that? Anne-Marie might be her closest friend but she is also her husband's boss. Still, saying it out loud does lift a little of the weight that has been clinging to her shoulders.

'Don't be so silly. Michael would never do that to you.' Anne-Marie laughs, brushing it off, but she doesn't appear entirely convincing.

Christina has an insatiable urge to confide in her friend about what she has discovered about Michael since the accident. How he often used to stop off at the pub before he came home. How he stopped riding with the cycling club. And all the business with his iPhone. And the leather gloves he claims he randomly found. But it feels wrong to discuss her husband with his boss. It's inappropriate.

'Michael isn't the type to cheat. Besides, I keep him far too busy.'

Is Anne-Marie trying to convince Christina or herself? 'Can I ask you something, Anne-Marie?'

'Ask away.'

Christina swallows. 'We never really spoke about it. The Jessica situation.'

'You know I can't talk about that.' Christina's not surprised. Anne-Marie kept her professional integrity throughout the whole incident, even though it must have been difficult.

'You would've told me if you'd had any suspicions about Michael, wouldn't you?'

'Goodness, Christina. Where has this come from?'

Christina shrugs. 'I don't know. Between you and me, Michael hasn't been particularly nice to me since the accident.' She needs to be careful here. She wants to confess how she feels about the Jessica situation, but what if she's wrong, and it's nothing? She could feed a seed of doubt in Anne-Marie's mind that could get Michael in serious trouble.

'He's been through a traumatic time. Unfortunately, you're the closest to him, so of course he's going to take it out on you. Michael's a good man. We just need to help him through the difficult times ahead.'

'I know. I'm sorry. I don't know what made me say that. My head is all over the place.'

Anne-Marie laughs. But it's not her usual laugh. It's too hollow, rehearsed even. 'Come on. Let's go and get you some food.' Grabbing a glass from the worktop, she fills it with prosecco and hands it to Christina. 'Come on, people are dying to say hello to you.'

FIFTY

Christina reluctantly lets her friend steer her through to the lounge, where around twenty others are gathered in small groups chatting and drinking beer and prosecco.

People turn to greet her, waving enthusiastically.

She wishes she could return their eagerness. A limp lift of her hand and a fake smile is all she can manage.

The dining table is crammed with dishes of cooked food centred around an elaborate cheese board embellished with small bunches of black grapes and cranberries. Anne-Marie must have been cooking since Boxing Day. 'You need to have a piece of my turkey, mushroom and cranberry pie.' Anne-Marie picks up a knife and cuts a slice.

Christina's stomach turns. What she needs is to leave.

The room is closing in on her. She is feeling claustrophobic. And the noisy chatter above the music that is too loud is unbearable as if she is listening to a choir singing out of tune. It's pounding through her like a pneumatic drill. 'Not for me.'

She admires the Christmas tree, a real one adorned with old-fashioned, multi-coloured flashing lights and baubles. The angel is hunched over and her head squashed against the ceiling. She looks wholly uncomfortable – exactly how Christina feels right now.

Anne-Marie smiles. 'Had too much turkey? I can't say I blame you. It does get a bit repetitive, doesn't it? Have a sandwich instead.' She grabs a red and white striped plate. 'I've got sausage with warm red cabbage and beetroot slaw.' She pauses to smile. 'I know. It sounds a strange combination, but I guarantee you'll love it. Or there's Brie, ham and fig mini rolls.'

Christina can't face eating, but politely agrees to sample the feast. 'I'll try the sausage.' She almost knocks it out of Anne-Marie's hand trying to catch her handbag as it slips from her shoulder.

She's saved from her friend's questioning look when the doorbell rings. Anne-Marie hands Christina a sandwich and disappears.

Several people swarm towards her like bees to a hive needing their fix of sweet gossip. Their voices come at her in unison.

'We've missed him.'

'It's not the same without him... or you.'

'When's he coming back?'

It's as if she's a stranger in a room full of friends who have known each other since birth. She holds her handbag tightly against her chest, sipping her drink while answering questions the best she can and forcing a smile at unhelpful remarks. Since when did she become so fragile? This isn't her. She's stronger than this.

'Why haven't they caught who did this yet?' asks a geography teacher.

Enough. Christina can't stand it any longer. She excuses herself and wanders into the kitchen. She'll find Anne-Marie and say goodbye. Her friend will understand. But Anne-Marie isn't in the kitchen. She must have popped upstairs or to the toilet.

Conversation flows from the conservatory, where a teaching assistant is talking to her husband. Christina's burning ears steer her closer to their conversation. She stands by the PVC side door that leads to the garden, listening.

'That's the one I told you about. The one whose husband supposedly had an affair with that pupil. The girl had to leave the school. Jessica James her name was. She finished her A levels online. There was talk of her younger sister, Holly, leaving too. She's still there, though. She didn't want to lose her friends. Jessica's currently working at her parents' pub, The Farmer's Arms. The one at the top of Bridge End. Remember when we went there, and I got that awful food poisoning?'

Christina's stomach convulses in repulsion.

'You shouldn't say things like that,' the woman's husband says, berating his wife.

'It's true, apparently. And it's not the first time.'

What's that meant to mean? Christina grits her teeth.

'The chap's still working at the school,' the husband says. 'He'd have been ousted if there were any truth in it. You know how protective that place is about its reputation.'

'It was never proved. When they investigated, Jessica admitted she lied, and Mr Blake came back to school.'

'There you go, then. Case closed.'

'It cost him his reputation, though. And his promotion. He was going for the deputy head position. Poor Anne-Marie. We all felt sorry for her. But how can you make a teacher your deputy with that kind of sordid behaviour rumoured about them?'

The woman's husband responds irritated, as if he is defending the brotherhood. 'If he were innocent, it shouldn't have mattered. You can't pass someone over for promotion on that basis. Surely, there must've been a better candidate. Who got the job?'

'An external woman with more experience.'

'There you go, then. You need to be careful,' the husband barks. 'What have I always said? Your big mouth is going to get you in trouble one day. Let's go and get some food.'

A tide of anger rips through Christina. She grabs the edge of the sticky worktop marked with fingerprints from spilt drinks and finger foods.

She wants to shout at the woman. That is her husband she's gossiping about. But she hasn't got the bandwidth for a show-down. The strap of her bag digs into her shoulder. She's got more pressing issues to worry about.

Christina hurries to the hallway, tears threatening to burst. She grabs her coat and quietly slips out of the front door.

Climbing into her car, she drives home faster than she should.

Along Bridge End she passes the house where Elizabeth Haggerty lives. She grimaces. She had completely forgotten she told Mary when she bumped into her in the pharmacy just before Christmas that she would drop in to see her. She'll have to go some other time.

Blinking, she focuses on her driving, realising she has veered into the middle of the road. Not something you want to do on a road like Bridge End.

There's too much on her mind. She glimpses at the passenger seat, wondering if the money she has stashed in her handbag is heading into the hands of the young woman who she can't seem to escape.

Jessica James.

FIFTY-ONE

'It'll be murder out there. There's another cold snap coming, along with all the snow,' Michael says as he hobbles into the kitchen. He has taken to getting around without his crutches. They annoy the hell out of him. 'Leave the phone. You don't need it.'

Christina is surprised at his concern. Guilt overcomes her for lying to him. 'I won't get another chance. Anne-Marie's going away.'

She hopes he doesn't detect the deceit in her voice. Yet she has no option. However bad the roads may be she needs to deliver the money, but she can't tell him that. Saying she left her phone at Anne-Marie's was the only excuse she could come up with. She swallows hard, unsettled by her husband's long, hard gaze.

He shuffles over to sit on a stool at the breakfast bar. 'The roads will be like sheets of ice. Death traps.' Irritated, he scratches the skin around the top of the plaster cast. 'I can't wait to have this bloody thing off. It's been nearly five weeks of hell.'

'Only one more day. You're lucky. Anne-Marie told me her sister broke her ankle in a skiing accident and was in plaster for seven weeks,' she says. 'Are you sure you're OK with Sophia taking you to the appointment? I feel terribly guilty I won't be there with you.'

'I'll be fine.'

'It's sod's law the appointment came through on the same day as Abi's scan.'

Michael picks up the local paper. 'I said it'll be fine,' he says bluntly.

On her way out, she leans over to kiss him. 'Anne-Marie won't be back for a couple of days. I can't live without my phone. I'll be back as quick as I can.'

She sits in her car facing the house, waiting for the ice to clear from the windscreen.

The wipers clunk and scrape. She is freezing, despite her thick woolly hat and full-length quilted coat. The cold has seeped into her bones. No amount of clothing can protect her. In the footwell lies her handbag containing the phone she supposedly left at Anne-Marie's house.

And the fat manilla envelope with ten thousand pounds.

She continues questioning herself. Is she doing the right thing? Will the note she wrote accompanying the package make any difference? The one that tells her extortionist that they can't ask her for any more money.

Ted had laughed when he stopped by and saw her writing on the envelope: *You've got my life savings. I have no more cash, so don't bother coming back for more.* 'You're kidding yourself,' he said.

'You're not helping me with comments like that.'

'Only speaking my mind, sis. As always.'

But Ted has agreed to go with her, staying out of sight, to provide the moral support she desperately needs.

Christina stares at the house. Pangs of anxiety overcome her. Maybe she should've called her sister to come over and sit with Michael. With Ben out, despite her saying she didn't want him driving tonight, that leaves Abi in the house alone with him. What if something happens? But Sophia would have insisted on picking up the phone from Anne-Marie's house herself, which would have ruined Christina's plans. 'Keep calm,' she says out loud, her breath fogging the air and further misting the inside of the windscreen.

She reaches in her bag and clicks her phone off silent. It immediately rings, making her jump. She takes it out of her bag.

It's Ted. 'I've got a real problem here.'

'Please tell me you're still coming.'

'My bloody van won't start.'

'You're kidding me.' This is all she needs. She can't even pick him up as he lives in the opposite direction to where she has to drop the money.

'I'm going to keep trying. If not I'll call a cab,' he says. 'I'll meet you there. Don't do anything until I arrive.'

Her voice fades with dread. 'I'll have to deliver it if it gets to eight o'clock. I can't risk anything going wrong.' Her voice is frantic.

'I'm so sorry, Chrissy. You know I'd never let you down. Just wait for my call.'

She swiftly hangs up and throws the phone back in her bag. What is she thinking? Anyone looking out from inside the house would see her on the phone.

Reversing the car, she turns around and starts her journey to the train station. A journey that proves fraught with danger. Michael wasn't joking when he said it would be murder on the roads tonight.

On two occasions, the car slides uncontrollably, the steering wheel light and unresponsive on the ice. If there had been oncoming vehicles, she would have ploughed straight into them. The thought of Ben out in his car tonight fills her with utter dread.

Eventually, Christina reaches the station. Parking in a side turning, opposite the bridge that crosses the railway line, she sits and stares at the steps leading down to where she is to leave the money. She has allowed for plenty of time, too much time. She's fifteen minutes early.

Turning off the engine, she is spooked by how quiet the world outside is. Snowflakes fall on the windscreen. The faint moonlight casts flickers of shadows from the surrounding trees against the bright white of the snow-covered ground, amplifying her growing unease.

The wait is painful. She counts the minutes in the silence of the car, each anxious breath producing puffs of cloud against the frosty air.

Does the blackmailer know she is here? Is she waiting in the shadows, watching her? She? Why does she think they are female? Her enemy could easily be male. Yet somehow, she doesn't think so.

If only Ted were here.

She glances at the clock on the dashboard. Seven minutes to go. She calls Ted, only to get his voicemail. Should she go now and get this over and done with? The instructions were clear: eight p.m.

A train rushes by, rattling the tracks, scaring the life out of her. She grips the steering wheel, her knuckles as white as the falling snow. It's a surprise trains are even running, given how ghastly the weather is.

Lowering her head, she focuses on her breathing until the illuminated clock on the dashboard tells her it's five minutes to eight. Removing the envelope from her handbag, she shuffles it down the front of her coat when it suddenly dawns on her. What if this isn't about the money? What if her blackmailer is waiting for her with a knife? Or a gun? She tries to dismiss such thoughts. She's being neurotic. They're not out to harm her. There are easier ways for them to do that if they had wanted to. They are simply out to hurt her bank balance.

But just in case, she will chuck the money in the bin and run.

She tries Ted one last time before zipping her coat to her neck and climbing out of the car. She can't wait for him any longer. Michael and Abi will start worrying where she is.

The wind whistles around her, drowning out the distant hum of traffic.

She clasps the envelope against her chest. The chill in the air is tangible, cutting through her layers to her bones. She can't wait to get this over and done with.

A rustling noise behind her makes her freeze. She spins around. No one is there.

She crosses the road. Her boots provide some protection, but her feet are numb from the cold. An eerie feeling overcomes her, as if she is being watched.

The snow dampens the sounds around her, acting as acoustic insulation, muffling vibrations and noises, so the only sound she can hear is her own racing heartbeat.

She peers down the steps, into the abyss.

Beginning her descent into the blackness, her heart beats in her ears. The narrow, steep steps are camouflaged in snow and are flanked to one side by a tall wall and dense high bushes to the other.

Damn Ted for not being here.

She digs her phone out of her pocket and finds the torch-light to pick out the path. Holding the black metal handrail, she slowly creeps down the steps, swearing under her breath for the mess she has found herself in.

Finally, she reaches the bottom. She scans the shadows, seeing if anyone else is present. Though what she would do if there were, she has no idea.

The hushed whispers of wind play tricks on her mind, merging with the rhythmic beat of her pulse in her ear. She needs to get the hell out of here as quickly as possible.

She searches for the bin where she was instructed to leave the cash, shining her phone's torchlight this way and that. There it is. Opening her coat, she stuffs the envelope inside the empty metal drum. She takes a moment to stop and listen, ensuring no one is nearby.

A chill goes through her where the bulk of money had provided extra warmth.

Dropping her phone, she moans as the torch light disappears, throwing her into total blackness.

And, terrifyingly, a powerful hand clasps her shoulder.

FIFTY-TWO

Another hand unceremoniously covers her mouth as Christina attempts to scream. It silences her. Her life flashes before her. Is this how it's all going to end?

She turns her head and swears to see her brother.

Keeping his hand in place, Ted whispers, 'Shush.'

She stares at him, horrified, wriggling to break free. 'What the hell are you playing at?' she whispers urgently. 'You scared the hell out of me.'

Ted holds up two fingers, mimicking walking, signing for her to return to the car. He mouths, 'I'm going to stay and wait.' He nods to the steps. 'I'm going to find the bastard doing this.'

She hesitates. It feels wrong leaving him here to deal with her problems.

'I mean it. I said go.' He pulls the generous hood of his parka over his head and withdraws into the trees. 'Just do as I say.'

Christina follows his orders, disorientated and shocked to see him. She climbs the steps back towards the sanctuary of her car, where she sits to catch her breath. She can't take much more of this. She starts the engine, exhausted and emotional.

A coating of white blankets the roads as she negotiates the

journey home. Snow falls furiously, blurring the windscreen quicker than the wipers can clear it. It needs to stop. Otherwise the trains won't run in the morning, and she'll have to drive into London for Abi's appointment. Another worry.

She shakes her head, clutching the steering wheel, still unable to comprehend how she got into this mess. Her arms ache at the tension building through her hands and up to her shoulders. A gust of wind hits the car. Her heart hammers as she fights to control it skidding, her breaths coming fast and heavy.

As she reaches Bridge End, she calms a little. Home is in sight. Her breathing settles until she hears the dull grumble of an approaching engine.

She gasps.

The oncoming vehicle has veered onto her side of the road and is heading straight for her. Instinct kicks in.

She swerves hard to the left, her tyres sliding out of control on the snow. The vehicle's dazzling lights sweep past her in a blinding flash, the proximity of the near miss shocking her to the core.

Eventually, her car comes to a halt, ramming into a snow-piled verge. She glances in the rear-view mirror. The red tail lights of the offending driver are rapidly receding into the darkness behind her. Her hand rushes to her mouth. She bites her knuckle so hard, pain shoots through her. Was that an innocent mistake from the other driver? Or is someone trying to kill her now? They've got money out of her and now they want to get rid of her? She can't decide if that's logical or not.

Abi is standing at the kitchen window when she arrives home, ice cold and shaken. Her daughter rushes to the front door, opening it wide as Christina heads up the path. 'Where've you been, Mum?'

The wind blusters flakes of snow into Christina's face. She

hurries inside and shuts the door. Never before has she been so relieved to be home.

'You said you'd only be half an hour,' her daughter cries.

Christina throws off her coat, trying to disguise the panic in her voice and her shaking hands.

'The roads are bad. Some idiot nearly ran me off the road. I'm so sorry, darling.' She hugs her daughter tightly, choking on the lies she has to keep telling.

'Mum, you're hurting me.' Abi wriggles her body from Christina's grip. 'Dad called. He said he'll pick us up tomorrow and drive us if the trains aren't running.'

'Have you heard from your brother?'

Abi shakes her head. 'I've only just come down here to get some water. I haven't seen him. I'm going to bed. I'm tired.'

'I'll be up soon,' Christina says.

She needs a large glass of wine.

On second thoughts, something stronger. With trembling hands, she finds the leftover brandy she was saving for the Christmas cake that she never got around to making and takes a swig neat from the bottle.

She checks her phone, desperate to hear from Ted and her son. It's now a quarter to nine. She was out for well over an hour. Has Ted been waiting there all that time? There's nothing from him, but a text from Anne-Marie sits among her messages. Her friend is sorry she didn't get to speak to her again before she left the party. Perhaps they can meet in the new year before the new term begins? Christina types a hasty reply. She apologises for leaving without saying goodbye, adding she would love to meet up, and will be in touch. She tries Ben. He doesn't answer. Damn him. Where is he? She drops him a text asking him to let her know what time he'll be home.

She heads to the lounge. Michael is sitting on the sofa in the dark, save for the glow from the Christmas tree lights and the

TV. He has the news on again, not that he appears to be watching it. 'You've been ages,' he says.

'You were right. The roads are truly awful. An idiot up Bridge End tried to run me off the road.'

'Get your phone?' he asks.

She nods.

'Are you all right?'

It's as if he is looking straight through her. It's eerie in this low light.

'I'm fine,' she says. 'That driver scared me.' A good cover for the truth about why she is so truly shaken.

'Could you get me a bourbon?'

She hesitates. 'Do you think that's sensible?'

'Just a small one. I haven't had any alcohol since the accident.'

'I'm not sure you should mix it with all the painkillers you're taking.'

'I can get it myself.'

'Michael.' She pauses. She wants to tell him it's not a good idea. But she knows him well. If he is set on having a drink, he'll have one. 'I'll get you a glass.'

Christina reluctantly fetches two glasses from the kitchen. While she is there, she checks the window. There's still no sign of Ben. It's not helping her stress levels. She checks her phone. Nothing. And there's still no news from Ted.

'Make it a large one,' Michael says when she returns to the lounge. 'It might kill this damn headache once and for all.'

'I'll join you.'

'Good,' he says.

She pours a small measure from the bottle of bourbon Dermot bought for Michael into each of the glasses and hands one to him.

He takes a sip. 'I have something to tell you,' he says.

Her heart jolts.

'My memory is coming back. I'm beginning to remember what happened that night.'

FIFTY-THREE

The dark look in his eyes is scary, sinister almost.

Christina stares at him, reeling.

Is this it?

After all that has happened this evening. After all she's done to stop him from finding out, is he going to tell her that he saw her that night?

She's lightheaded. She has to sit down. 'Tell me.'

'Cheers,' he says, raising his glass.

'Cheers.' Clinking her glass against his, she tries to collect herself. She wants to shout at him: *Come on, spit it out.*

'So, what do you remember?' she asks, as casually as she can manage.

He shakes his head, staring into his glass. It's as if he is tormenting her, stalling before he delivers words of accusation that he saw her that night. 'It's really weird. I feel like I'm at the cinema, watching myself walking home in a monochrome movie scene. It was raining hard.'

'Walking home from where?' Christina asks.

'The pub. But I only know that because that's what you and

the police have told me. I wasn't dressed properly. I only had on my blue jacket.' He sighs. 'Why wasn't I wearing my winter coat?'

She shrugs, holding her breath.

'I don't know, either. I must've had other things on my mind when I left here that night.'

'So you don't remember leaving the house?'

He shakes his head. 'The hood of the jacket wouldn't stay up. I had to hold it in place over my head.' He snorts. 'That's a strange thing to remember, isn't it? When I can't remember why I went out in the first place.'

Christina's jaw tenses. That's the part of his memory she wants to return.

He takes another sip of bourbon. 'The lights of the car were approaching me too fast. The driver was speeding, that's for sure.'

That's not true. She wasn't speeding that night. She picked up speed after that hairpin bend, but she never went over the limit.

Her hands are trembling around the glass. Has he noticed? She rests the glass on her lap.

'What maniac does that in such bad conditions?'

'Someone too desperate to get home, I guess.' She shifts her body, unable to get comfortable. Something about him is unnerving her.

He takes another sip of bourbon. 'I looked around. I remember now.'

He looked around? She tightens the grip around her glass. She wants to cut to the chase and ask him if he saw who was in the car, but he appears to be in a trance, and something is telling her she shouldn't push too hard.

'The rain was too fast, too powerful. The driver couldn't possibly have seen me. I tried to jump aside, but I must have caught my foot. There was no deceleration as they hit me and catapulted me into that ditch. They must've felt their car crash into me, though.'

He sounds almost as if he has rehearsed this – carefully chosen the words to haunt her.

'Perhaps they thought it was an animal.' She is conscious how feeble her voice sounds, but she wants him to know the truth.

'Animal?' He laughs, almost maniacally. 'No, there's no way they could've mistaken me for an animal.'

She wants to scream at him. *But it's true.*

'It didn't hurt,' he continues. 'The car stopped. The driver got out. Only briefly.' He tells her that he must've passed out at that point because all he remembers is a floating sensation as if he was flying in the clouds.

'This is terrible, Michael.' Two tears drop down her face. She swipes them away with the back of her hand. 'I'm so sorry you had to go through this.'

'I regained consciousness at some point.' He goes into every excruciating detail about the wet grass and muck he was lying in and how he could taste the mouthful of sodden mulch.

It's as if he is teasing her, trying to punish her by dragging out his words. Does he know it was her who ran him down? Or is she going crazy, her mind playing games she doesn't want to join in with?

He tells her how, lying there, sleeping felt like the easiest option. 'That's when I thought I was going to die.'

'Oh, Michael. I—'

He raises a hand to quieten her, slowly, as if it's an effort. He stares into space. 'It was like sleep was calling me. There was a calmness, a serenity about it, that was so appealing. But I knew it wasn't my time. I made the conscious decision to live, but I knew to do that, I needed to get help.'

How can he remember such detail yet doesn't recall why he ended up walking along that road alone at that time of night?

He describes the momentous struggle over the shallow bank to the road, clawing his way through the wet grass, groaning with inarticulate pleas for help. The pain in his back was excruciating, and his head was pounding like someone was beating him with a baseball bat. 'I was lying in the middle of the road. A light appeared.' He squints. 'A single light this time, slower than before. I must've blacked out again because the next thing I remember is a hand shaking me and someone shouting: "Stay with me, pal. Help's on the way. Listen to me. You're gonna be OK."'

That must have been the motorcyclist that the police told her had found him.

'They kept telling me not to move. To stay still. At first I thought it was Ben, but the guy was wearing a motorcycle helmet.' His eyes meet hers. 'A decent human being.'

Christina wrings her hands. He knows it was her. She is sure of it. But how is that possible?

He taps his fingers against his glass.

'What happened next?' The suspense is killing her.

He tells her how everything happened so fast after that. Flashing blue lights, the urgent, piercing wail of a siren, doors opening and closing. 'The motorcyclist kept repeating himself, "He was lying in the bloody road. I could've hit him." Then I turned cold, so very cold, and I thought that was it. My life was over.'

His words are wrenching. She wants to reach out and touch him, feel his arms around her, lovingly like they used to hold her.

But something feels off.

'So what about where you went that night? Who picked you up along Bridge End and dropped you back at the pub?' Her voice wavers. 'Where did you go for all that time, Michael?'

He empties his glass and hands it to her. 'Sorry, my head is throbbing. Would you mind getting me some more painkillers?' He nods to the foil strip on the table. 'That packet is empty.' He turns his attention back to the TV.

She is sure he knows the answer to her question.

But why won't he tell her?

FIFTY-FOUR

With trembling hands, Christina grabs a glass from the kitchen cupboard and a bottle of Merlot from the wine rack. She pours herself an outrageous measure and takes a large mouthful.

She needs to speak to Ted. But there's still nothing from him. And where the hell is Ben? He should be back by now. She considers dropping him another text but is too worried it'll disturb him if he's driving. After another sip of wine, she finds a new box of Michael's painkillers from the larder and fills a glass with water. When she returns to the lounge, he has turned off the TV and moved to the bed, the only light now coming from the Christmas tree.

Christina turns on a lamp.

He squints, lifting his hand to shy his eyes away from the light. His shoulders are slumped, his eyes downcast as he glances at her. It's a strange look, creepy almost. One she's never seen before. He clutches his head. 'I've got a headache from hell. The worst I've ever known. I feel like my head's going to burst.'

She shouldn't have given him that bourbon. What if his

body can't cope and he dies? What will the blackmailers have to say about that? That she actually killed her husband?

She is being silly. Of course he's not going to die. He's getting better.

She hands him the glass of water and presses the tablets from the foil packaging into his cupped hand. 'Do you think I should call the doctor? Or an ambulance?'

'Absolutely not. I couldn't bear to go back to that place.' He takes the tablets from her hand. 'Hopefully, these'll do the trick.'

He looks dreadfully pale. Or is that the light? 'Can I get you anything else?'

'Will you stay with me? Just for a few minutes,' he says.

She frowns, confused at the tone of his voice. That's the neediest request he has made of her in weeks, months... years. 'Are you OK?'

He nods, lies down under the covers and closes his eyes.

Sitting on the sofa, she waits for him to fall asleep.

And then she hears it. The comforting sound of the front door opening. She gets up and rushes from the room, bumping into a pale Ben in the hallway. Something has happened. 'What's up with you? You're as white as a sheet. Where've you been?'

He brushes past her. 'Out with Cal.'

'I've been so worried about you.'

He stops at the bottom of the stairs, rolling his eyes. 'You need to take a chill pill, Mum. You're gonna have a heart attack one day.' He frowns at her, as if he is genuinely concerned, before taking off like a rocket and shooting up the stairs.

She opens her mouth to retaliate but stops. Pick your battles. That's what all the advice says. He is home and safe. She'll reiterate her concerns to him in the morning. He's more likely to listen.

Before checking the doors are locked and turning off the lights, she looks in on Michael.

He is sleeping soundly.

She stands over him. Something isn't right. She can't put her finger on it other than to say he is scaring her. Or is she confused?

Heading upstairs, she stops at her daughter's room. Abi is sitting in bed reading a book. 'Are you OK?'

Abi pouts. The facial expression which Christina has learnt over the years means: No, I'm not OK. Christina parks herself on the edge of the bed. 'Are you worried about tomorrow?'

'I'm scared, Mum. I hate these scans. What if they find the cancer has come back? I can't bear to go through all that again.'

Her daughter's pain physically hurts Christina. She's as worried as Abi about the appointment tomorrow, but she has to be strong. For her daughter's sake.

'You said you were OK earlier.' She strokes her daughter's fringe across her forehead. 'What have I always told you? Think positive and only worry about what you can control.' She almost chokes on her words. 'Let's wait for the scan results. And if we need to worry, then we can worry. As it stands, you're well, so that's a good sign.' She kisses Abi's cheek. 'Now get some sleep. I'll see you in the morning.'

'Thanks, Mum. I love you.'

'Not as much as I love you.'

Christina falls into bed. She's physically exhausted, but her mind is whirling in overdrive. She's never going to get to sleep. She can't take a sleeping pill, though. They've got an early start in the morning.

Her phone rings. It's Ted. At last. 'What the hell?' she says. 'I've been worried sick. Where are you?'

'At home.'

'Thank heavens for that. What happened?'

'Nothing. I stayed until ten o'clock, but no one came. I'm sorry, Chrissy. I had to leave. It was so cold I thought I was getting hypothermia. I wondered if the person saw me and was waiting for me to go.'

'But you left the cash where it was.'

'Of course I did.'

'What now?'

'Your guess is as good as mine. Let's hope they heed your note and you never hear from them again.'

Christina sets her alarm for seven the next morning and goes downstairs to check on Michael one last time. Halfway down, she hears a noise coming from the lounge.

She stops.

He is talking to someone. Or is that her imagination?

She keeps feeling as if she is losing a grip on reality. What is real and what is not? She creeps down the rest of the stairs and opens the lounge door. She startles to see Michael sitting on the edge of the bed.

He is rocking backwards and forwards, exhaling a low moan.

She rushes to him. 'Whatever's wrong?'

'My head is burning.' He places the back of his hand on his forehead. He tells her how much his head is pounding, the pain intense, as if someone has attacked him with an axe and sliced into his brain. 'Get me some ice in a tea towel. Please.'

The uneasy feeling she had earlier taunts her. Is she going to lose him? She places her hand on his forehead. 'You're not hot.'

She fetches the thermometer from the plastic tray of medical accessories on top of the cabinet and sticks it in his ear. Another moan escapes his lips. After the beep, she reads the dial. 'Thirty-six point nine. Your temperature's fine. That's a good thing. I'll go and get the ice.'

She rushes to the kitchen and makes an ice pack. When she returns, he is lying down, the same guttural moans escaping his mouth. Seeing him curled up in the foetal position is more terrifying than seeing him lying in the hospital bed, and panic sets in again.

He can't die. It would make her a killer.

She places the ice pack on his forehead. 'I'm going to call an ambulance. Something's not right here.'

'No way. I don't want you to. It'll pass. Get me some more painkillers, can you?'

'You're dosed out. You can't have any more.'

He snaps. 'Just get me another two.'

She gently holds his arm. 'Michael, you can't. Please, you're worrying me. Let me call an ambulance. Or at least drive you to the hospital. Even if they just check you over. It'll give us some peace of mind.'

'If you call an ambulance, I won't get in it.' He grabs her wrist. 'If you don't get the painkillers, I'll have to get them myself.' He's hurting her, twisting before he releases her wrist to clasp his head again.

Reluctantly, she leaves his side to fetch them. He should be in hospital. What if she overdoses him by giving him more pills?

She returns to the lounge and sits beside him. 'Please let me phone for an ambulance.'

He snatches the packet of pills out of her hand. 'I said no. I'll take another two of these and get some sleep. The doctor said headaches are normal after what I've been through. Don't you remember?'

She can. But she can't remember him saying they would be this bad. 'Why don't I sleep on the sofa? Just in case you need me.'

'No. Go to bed. You look done in.'

What an understatement.

Upstairs, she perches on the edge of the bed. She taps 999 into her phone. This has got to be the right thing to do, hasn't it?

She is about to press the call button but stops. She'll just anger him more, and he won't get in the ambulance anyway. If he gets any worse, maybe she can persuade him to let her seek help.

She erases the numbers.

FIFTY-FIVE

Just after eight o'clock the following morning, Sophia arrives.

'I'm so glad you're here. Thank you for coming early.' Christina takes a jabbering Lily from her flustered sister. 'You look awful. Seriously, are you OK?'

'Ha, you're one to talk, sis.' Her sister stamps her boots on the doormat. 'Madame is teething. I feel like I was up with her all night.'

'Oh, you poor little angel.' Christina smothers Lily with kisses and then hugs her sister. 'You should've said. I wouldn't have asked you to come over so early. But I appreciate it.' She calls the kids from upstairs, telling them it's time to go. 'I'm too worried to leave him on his own. I've been checking him all night, and he does seem a bit better.'

'What happened?' Sophia asks, removing her padded, shin-length coat.

'He said it felt like his head was going to explode last night.' Christina holds up her thumb and forefinger pinched together. 'I was this close to calling an ambulance, but he wouldn't let me.'

Sophia's bag, overstuffed with Lily's paraphernalia, slips

from her shoulder. It drops to the floor. 'I knew it was bad, for you to text me at six-thirty in the morning. How is he now?'

'I've just given him another dose of painkillers. He can't have any more for four hours. So when you get back from having his plaster taken off. I wish he'd let me call the doctor.' Christina sighs heavily. 'I shouldn't be leaving him. I should be with him.'

'Abi needs you more than Michael today.' Sophia rests a hand on her shoulder. 'He'll be fine. I'll try to get him to call the doctor.'

'I'm wondering if you could persuade him to speak to someone at the hospital while he is having the plaster taken off.'

Sophia takes Lily back. 'I'll try. Don't worry. It'll all be fine here. Just go. You don't want to miss the train.'

'Thanks for all your help. I don't know what I'd do without you.' She kisses her sister's cheek. 'Oh, by the way, Ted is stopping by later.'

'Why?'

'He's fixing one of those video doorbell cameras for us and a security camera.'

Sophia frowns. 'Why?'

Christina would love to share more with her sister, but she can't. 'Oh, nothing. It's something Michael and I have been meaning to do for a while but have never got around to it. You know how it is. There's always something more important to sort out. I've always felt safe with Wilf around, but I feel more vulnerable now that Michael is laid up. Ted said he can put them up for us in no time.'

'What time's he going to get here?'

Christina shrugs. 'You know Ted. He'll turn up when he turns up. He's got a couple of jobs to sort out first, he said. Then he'll come over. I said you might or might not be here. Can you tell the kids I'll meet them in the car?'

Sophia looks distracted.

'Did you hear me?'

'Yes. Good luck. I hope it all goes OK.'

In the car, Christina whacks the heating up high and clears the windscreen of last night's snowfall as she waits for the kids. She rubs her gloved hands together. She should've parked in the carport last night, but she was too eager to get inside the house.

Her heart skips a beat as she glances in the rear-view mirror and sees the postman's van stop off at the end of the drive.

She can't stop herself.

Leaving the engine running, she grabs the key to the mailbox, and crunches through the frozen snow. The cold air brushes her cheeks as she stares at the mailbox getting closer with each step. Her pulse is racing. As it constantly is these days.

Ben was right. She's going to have a heart attack at this rate.

She opens the black metal box.

Grabbing the edge of the fence, she steadies herself as she picks up the pile of post from inside.

FIFTY-SIX

Fear rushes through her as she examines the letters, looking for another card. But there's only a credit card statement and a handful of leaflets.

She returns to the car and chucks the mail into the tray of her door, swearing at the kids. Why are they never ready on time? Never. She thumps the steering wheel.

Eventually, they arrive at the station to find the first train was cancelled. The next one arrives packed. Christina grimaces. The three of them have to stand.

The kids scroll through their phones. Christina can't work out if Abi looks white or if it's the hue of the inclement weather or the artificial lighting.

The train's vibrations jerk through her forehead as Christina leans against the window. Never has she felt so exhausted in her life. When she finally managed to drop off last night, Michael's explanation about what happened the night of the accident had governed her dreams.

Murmurs of conversation fill the packed carriage, an orchestra of jumbled discussions. She watches the white world flash by, wishing she could turn back the harrowing hands of time. She's going to regret going out that night with Ted for the rest of her life.

When the train pulls into the next station, a crowd shuffles on, squashing Christina further against the window. She turns. Her eyes widen.

A woman with long dark hair wearing a black puffa jacket and black leather gloves is sidestepping down the aisle. The same jacket Jessica James was wearing that night Christina saw her at the hospital. Is it her? The woman has her back to her, so Christina can't see her face.

The man next to her elbows her head, attempting to steady himself as the door snaps shut and the train leaves the station. 'Sorry,' he says. 'Are you all right?'

She looks at him vacantly. Her breathing has become shallow. She's sweating despite the sub-zero temperature. Christina bobs her head from side to side, trying to catch a look of the woman's face. A tide of dizziness overwhelms her as the mass of other passengers blurs around her. She slams her hands against the door. She's going to be sick.

Abi looks up from her phone. 'You don't look good, Mum.'

It's all got too much.

Her legs are like breadsticks about to snap. Christina panics. She's falling.

She still searches for the woman, even as she goes down. The train speeds on.

Abi screams, 'Mum!' as Christina's world turns black.

The overpowering luminous lights overhead momentarily disorientate Christina as she regains consciousness. They project a fierce glow across the troubled faces encompassing her personal space.

People have moved aside, cramming into the aisles of the

carriage. Ben is kneeling beside her, offering a bottle of water another passenger must have given him.

Abi is stroking her forehead.

Whispers of relief flutter around her.

A young girl peers at Christina curiously. A woman, holding the girl's hand, says, 'Don't stare.'

Christina shuts her eyes, trying to contain the nausea that is threatening to reach another level. She can't be sick – not on a train.

A man gets up and gives her his seat. Arms loop through hers, raising her off the floor to take up the man's kind offer.

The face of the woman in the puffa jacket comes into view.

It's not Jessica James. In fact, it looks nothing like her.

Christina drops her head to her chest. She is going crazy.

The Great Ormond Street Hospital for Children is busy today despite the time of year. Adam meets them at the multi-coloured seating area just inside the entrance. 'Dad!' Abi cries when she sees him. 'Guess what? Mum passed out on the train.'

Adam stands up, removing his designer scarf. 'Are you OK?' He appears genuinely concerned.

'I'm fine,' Christina says.

'You don't look fine. What's going on?'

'It was hot and crowded. All good now.'

Adam takes Abi's backpack and slips it over his shoulder. 'What the hell have you got in there,' he asks, feigning falling over. He clips Ben's shoulder, telling him to remove his EarPods, and hugs him.

Christina fakes a smile and nods. An odd sensation comes over her, remembering the times they've spent in this hospital for some of Abi's treatment. Adam was always so supportive. He took time off work for every appointment and insisted on sharing the overnight stays so Christina could go home and spend time with Ben. And he donated considerable sums to various appeals. He was a good husband. A perfect husband. Until she discovered he wasn't.

He glances at his Rolex watch. 'Shall we get a drink?' He looks from her to each of the kids and back at her. 'We've got time.'

'You bet,' Abi says. 'And a doughnut.'

Ben grunts, but Christina chances linking her arm through his as they walk past the reception. She asked if he wanted to stay at home today, but he had insisted on coming along. He has been as supportive as his dad when it comes to his sister's illness.

She finds a table in the café and sits down on one of the luminous green chairs, waiting for the others to get her a cup of hot chocolate. How many times have they sat here, taking a minute trying to gather strength to be brave in front of their daughter? Too many.

She remembers when Abi was sick, really sick. She had a mouthful of ulcers and was failing to thrive, so she had to have a gastro tube. Christina had to feed her through it. How she hated filling the syringes with the creamy liquid that was keeping her daughter alive. But she always managed to talk her daughter through it, keeping her calm.

Across the canteen, Adam is joking with the kids, waiting to pay. It's been a while since she has seen him with them, and although she hates to admit it, they are happy with him. Damn you, Adam Carter. Why did you have to cheat?

Her phone rings. It's DS Macintosh. What does he want now? She thought she'd get a break from him over the Christmas period and considers ignoring the call but knows she'll only stress wondering what he wants.

'DS Macintosh here. Can you spare a minute?'

She inwardly groans. This is all she needs right now. 'It's

not a good time. I'm at a hospital appointment with my daughter.'

'OK. I'd like to pop over again. Today preferably.'

Her chest tightens. 'Do you have news?'

'How about later this afternoon?'

Why did he ignore her question?

'Will you be home by then?' he asks.

She is irritated. Doesn't he realise today will be stressful enough for them?

'I'm around until eight o'clock,' he adds.

'Fine,' she says. 'How about five o'clock?' That will give her time to get home and get herself sorted.

'I'll see you then.'

'Can I ask what this is about?'

'I want to speak to Michael.'

'What about?'

'I'll discuss things with you later.' He ends the call.

The detective knows something. She can feel it.

FIFTY-SEVEN

'Remember what you always tell me, Mum? Don't worry about the things you can't control. You heard the doctor. He thinks the same as Dr Hadley. The chest pains weren't anything to worry about.' Abi appears more composed than Christina as they part ways outside the hospital.

'That's right. They're just being extra cautious.' Adam ruffles Abi's hair.

Abi brushes his hand away and puts on her woollen hat. 'Let's just wait for the scan results, Mum.'

She glances at Adam, feeling nothing but raw sadness. Why did he have to tear their family apart?

'We'll get going, then,' Adam says. 'Are you going to be OK?' he asks Christina.

'I'm feeling fine now.' Christina kisses the kids. 'I'll see you on Monday. Happy New Year. Have a great time,' she says with false conviction. How she hates them going to his place on any weekend, let alone during the holidays.

Christina watches them walk up the street in the opposite direction, where Adam has parked his car.

She wishes she'd driven. Snow covers the pavements, and

slush lines the gutters, but apart from a layer of brown mush and salt, the roads are pretty clear. She could've been home in an hour. There's no counting on how the roads are in the country, though. They still weren't that great when she left this morning.

The thought of going home is wholly depressing. She's got the detective to face later as well. She can't handle the Tube just yet. Being in the hospital has made all the old feelings come flooding back.

She wanders around in a trance. Finding a small café on Lamb's Conduit Street, she orders a cappuccino and a croissant. Not the healthiest of snacks, but it's all she can face. She calls Sophia, wanting to check up on how things are going at home. There's no answer.

She tries Michael. He doesn't pick up either. She's mildly irritated. Don't they want to know how Abi got on?

Then she closes her eyes, trying to breathe. What if something has happened to him? What if he has died? She berates herself. She has got to stop thinking about him dying.

She downs her cappuccino, forces herself to eat the croissant, and leaves the café.

In stark contrast to the outside temperature, the underground is stifling. Coupled with the relentless clatter of the carriages hurtling through the tunnels, the heat makes Christina feel queasy. The buttery croissant hasn't helped. When the Tube pulls into Liverpool Street station, she is relieved for the cold blast of air greeting her as she steps off the carriage.

She hurries up the escalators, hoping to catch the train due to leave in three minutes. Rushing across the concourse to the mainline station, she swears at the departure board. The train has been cancelled and the following one delayed by twenty-five minutes. Swearing again, she stands on the concourse with an expanding crowd of disgruntled passengers, their heads snapped backwards as they study the digital display informing them of further delays. She's going to get home later than five o'clock. So she's going to miss DS Macintosh talking to Michael.

She tries to call the DS, but she has lost her signal. The gremlins are sure out in force today. She dashes outside the station. When she manages to find a signal, she calls the DS again. The call goes to voicemail. She leaves a message, telling him she is delayed and asking him to come around at six o'clock. Michael doesn't answer when she tries him again. And Sophia. No luck. Then Ted. The same. Why isn't anyone picking up their phones?

For forty-five minutes, she wanders around the station, continuing trying to call everyone but has no luck. She returns to the platform where her train has now pulled into the station. Crowds of passengers swarm around the doors, waiting for them to shuffle open. She must get a seat. Despite what she told everyone, she hasn't fully recovered from her experience this morning, and standing again isn't an option. When the doors beep and open, she resists the people trying to wrestle her for a seat and plonks herself next to the window, utterly exhausted. She tries to ring Sophia and Michael again, but both calls go to their voicemail. She gives Ted a go.

'Finally! What the hell's going on?'

'What do you mean?' her brother asks, sounding harassed.

'I've been trying to call Michael, Sophia and you. All I keep getting is your voicemails.'

'The weather's been dire. There was a power cut at your house while I was there. Maybe that's affected phone signals. Anyway, I've fixed the doorbell for you and set it up on an app on Michael's phone.'

She grimaces. 'But I want it on my phone, not Michael's.'

'I had no choice. He asked me to. You can have it on yours as well. I'll sort it for you. Or Michael can.'

'What about the security camera?'

'The bloody thing was faulty. I'll need to pick up a replacement. I won't be able to fix it today. I'll have to come back.'

Damn. She wanted the security camera more than the video doorbell.

The journey home is slow. A broken down train in front keeps them waiting between stations for ten minutes, and a faulty door on a carriage towards the back of the train for another half an hour. She has worked herself into a frenzy by the time the train reaches her station. DS Macintosh hasn't returned her call. Did he even get her message? He might have turned up already.

Anxious to get home, she navigates her way along Bridge End, passing the spot where video doorbell footage picked up Michael on the night of the accident just past Mrs Haggerty's house. That reminds her. She must go and see her.

The closer she gets to her house, the more uneasy she feels.

It's dark as she approaches Ivy Brook. The car slides broadside under the icy conditions and she narrowly misses the brick pillar at the entrance to the driveway. She turns on full beam and screams in frustration to see DS Macintosh's car in the driveway.

'I'm beginning to think you don't sleep, Detective,' she says when she walks into the kitchen.

The DS is sitting at the breakfast bar with Michael. He laughs. 'Just committed to my job, Mrs Blake.'

'Did you not get my message?'

'What message?'

'I asked you to come at six o'clock.'

He shrugs. 'No, sorry. I didn't.'

'Where's Sophia?' she asks Michael, throwing down her keys.

'She left when Ted got here. I've been fine.' He places his hand over his forehead. 'Headache is better.' He lifts his foot. 'Plaster is off.'

The DS jumps off his stool. 'I'll be on my way, then.'

'I thought you wanted to talk to me,' Christina says, puzzled.

'No, no,' he says, shuffling into his duffel coat. 'Only Michael.'

She walks him to the front door. 'What did you want to talk to Michael about?'

'I just wanted to ask him if anything had come back to him about the night of the accident. We might have a lead soon, I understand. It appears his memory is slowly returning.'

FIFTY-EIGHT

Christina constantly checks her phone.

She doesn't want to miss a call from the hospital. They usually contact her the day after the scan to deliver the results.

When the second of January arrives, and she still hasn't heard, she calls Abi's consultant. His secretary is profusely sorry for the hold-up. 'The new year has delayed all sorts.' Her voice is gentle, encouraging and understanding. 'I'll get a message to the doctor to contact you straight away.'

Adam pulls up in the driveway as her phone rings later that afternoon. She nervously takes the call. Her heart is in her throat as the doctor delivers the news she has anxiously awaited for so many years. Abi doesn't need to be scanned for another five years. By which time, she'll be an adult and her care will move to a different hospital. How she has waited for this news for so long.

'Unless, of course, there're any problems, in the fondest of ways, I hope I'll never see you again.'

Her voice breaks. 'Thank you for everything.'

'I wish Abi all the best. And you, Christina. Your strength has helped your daughter and your family survive this.'

Christina stifles tears as she runs outside. The kids are getting out of the car. She races towards them, waving her phone, crying and laughing.

Adam gets out of the car. He knows her well enough to decipher her message.

She hugs Abi and Ben, holding them close. 'You've got the all-clear. No more scans for five years.'

Abi invites Adam into the embrace. The four of them stand like a family, hugging each other in joy.

Adam looks at her.

She knows what he's thinking. His eyes glassing over at the jubilation, and the regret.

The regret for tearing his family apart.

FIFTY-NINE

£100K, and then I'll leave you alone for good.
You've got ONE week to deliver.
Transfer details as attached.
Remember: YOU pay. I keep quiet.

Just when she thought things were on the turn, with the all-clear news about Abi's scan and Michael's mood improving somewhat now that his plaster cast is off.

It's late afternoon, but Christina is already on her second large glass of wine, when Ted arrives.

He reads the message, digesting its contents. 'I knew it. I knew they'd come knocking again.' He holds the envelope upside down and shakes it. A small card falls out. 'The bank account details.' He passes it to Christina. 'I guess whoever is doing this means business.'

'Keep your voice down. Michael will hear you.'

'But one hundred thousand pounds!' Ted's face is raging like a storm.

Christina tosses the card aside. 'I guess I have no choice.'

'You're not seriously thinking of handing over that kind of

money.' Ted plonks himself on the stool next to her. 'For a start, where are you going to get it from?' He stares at her questioningly.

'I have that money I put away for the kids.'

'The Premium Bonds?'

She nods. 'Fifty thousand in Premium Bonds I can cash in and fifty thousand in a high-interest savings account. At least then that'll be the end of it.'

The creases on her forehead deepen. The amount the blackmailer is asking for is the exact amount she has in savings. She bites her knuckle hard.

There are only three other people who know about those savings. Adam, Ted and Michael. Actually, there are four. Anne-Marie was her confidant throughout Christina's divorce. And of course, the kids. That makes six.

'Don't look at me like that,' Ted says.

'Like what?'

'Like I've done something wrong.'

'Sorry.' She rubs her thumb over her knuckle. The skin is broken and is as raw as her threadbare nerves. 'It's strange, isn't it?'

'It's all bloody strange.'

'I mean...' She points to the card. 'The amount they are asking for is the exact amount I have in savings for the kids.'

'It's a pretty round sum. You can't pay it, Chrissy.'

'What's the alternative? Either I pay it, or I go to the police and give myself in.'

'Just say no. Do nothing and see what happens.'

'What then? They go to the police. I'll have to confess and face the repercussions. It'll be a custodial sentence,' she says with conviction. 'You said so yourself. There will be no reprieve. I'll lose everything.'

Ted stares at the card, frowning. He slams his hand down on the worktop and picks up his phone. 'We must be able to trace who this bank account belongs to.' He angrily types on the screen.

Christina takes a gulp of wine. 'Surely it won't be that easy.'

It takes several minutes before Ted expresses his disappointment. 'It's an offshore account. Whoever it is has done their homework.'

Christina bites her knuckle again, despite the pain. 'Great, so that's a dead end.'

Ted continues scanning the internet. 'You still have to follow some rules and regulations. Hypothetically, given time, we could trace who the money goes to.'

'Yes, but we don't have time!' Christina says.

A thought occurs to her. Could Ben have told Jessica James about the money? Were they good enough friends back then for him to share that kind of information? She believes they were. She slams her fist on the card. 'It's Jessica bloody James. I'm telling you. I know it's her.'

'Really? She seems too young to do this kind of thing.'

'You don't know what that girl's capable of. She's clever. Sneaky. I'm going to confront her.'

'Steady on, Chrissy. Think about it. Say it's not her. Then what? She'll latch on to what's going on.' He laughs ironically. 'You could have a double whammy. Two blackmailers coming at you full throttle. If she doesn't report you straight away.'

'What should I do, then? Just pay it? It's only money at the end of the day.' She holds up her hands then drops them on the worktop.

'It was money for the kids!'

'I can sell this house at some point. And with Adam they'll always have enough money. They need their mum more.' Christina's face mirrors the concern on her brother's. She sighs heavily. 'I'm so sorry for everything. What a mess I've dragged you into.'

'Don't be silly. You're my sister, Chrissy. That's what families are for – to stand by you during the good and bad times. Look how much you've stood by me over the years.'

But bailing him out the time he lost his way ten years ago, when his business crumbled and his long-term girlfriend walked out on him, is nothing compared to what she has involved him in.

'So, the hundred-thousand-pound question is... is it worth paying up to get this person out of my life?' Christina asks.

Ted muses. 'Till they come knocking again.'

'It's her.'

'Who?'

Christina stands up. 'Jessica. She has something to do with this. I know she has.'

SIXTY

The one hundred thousand pounds is ready to make the transfer.

Two unsettling days have passed since the third card arrived. Christina has tried to keep herself busy.

Michael is eating a late breakfast in the kitchen, reading the news on his iPad, commenting on the unscrupulous imbeciles running the country.

'They're not all bad,' Christina says, faking a bright voice. She yawns. Sleep is still a zone she can't settle into. She has been saving her sleeping tablets for the weekends, as they make her feel groggy in the mornings. And they are running out.

'You seem distracted,' Michael says, not looking her in the eye.

She stops buttering her toast. How long has he avoided meeting her gaze? 'All good. I'm just getting ready to start work again. I need to run some errands today. Is there anything you want?'

He scrolls through the screen on his iPad. 'There's my prescription to pick up from the pharmacy. I'll need it for the weekend, but I could get it.' He started driving again the day after the plaster cast came off. She thought it was too soon, yet he was adamant he needs to get his life back on track.

'I'll be in town. I might as well get it.'

'Are you looking forward to going back to work?' he asks.

'Yes,' she lies. She's not. Will she ever be? The accident has changed her but she's worried about her job. 'When do you think you'll be going back?'

'I'm not sure,' he says.

She hesitates, knowing he won't like what she's going to say. 'Do you think it would be beneficial for you to have some therapy first?'

He finally glances at her, a foreboding look in his eyes. 'The only therapy I need is to see the person who did this to me suffer.' His voice is full of anger.

She gulps. 'Maybe they'll never find that person.'

'Perhaps you're right.' He now fixes his eyes on her. 'But I hate to think they'll get away with it, don't you?'

Her chest tightens. It's as if he knows. 'Absolutely.'

Christina dashes from the pharmacy to the post office and pops into a couple of shops. Her mind is in a whirl. She can't concentrate on a thing. Michael's strange behaviour has unnerved her yet again. And constant thoughts of the blackmailer plague her. The more she thinks about it, the more she is convinced Jessica James has something to do with it.

Stopping in a café, she finds a table and orders a cappuccino and a double espresso from a tired-looking waitress. She needs all the caffeine she can get. The café is buzzing, the cacophony of clinking plates, lively conversations and the hiss of the espresso machine intensifying her unease.

She downs the double espresso as soon as the waitress delivers the drinks. Her phone rings.

It's Anne-Marie. 'Are you ignoring me? Didn't you see my text?'

'No. What text?' Christina asks.

'Are you still in town? I was driving along the High Street earlier and saw you.'

'I'm in the café opposite the butcher's.'

'Stay put, and I'll pop in.' Anne-Marie ends the call.

Christina finds the text her friend sent half an hour ago, along with several messages she hasn't got around to replying to. She's fed up with people asking if the police have caught the culprit of her husband's misfortune yet. Part of her wants to scream *No, I'm still walking free.*

'You've survived bad times in the past, Christina Blake,' she whispers as she stirs sugar into her cappuccino. 'You just need to summon the strength to do it again.' It's hard when the whole world seems to be against you, yes. But not impossible. Move on. She needs to move on now.

The door opens and Anne-Marie wanders in. Her cheeks are flushed and she seems harassed.

'What's up?' Christina leans closer toward her. 'What's wrong with your mouth?'

Anne-Marie touches her cheek. 'I've just been to the dentist for a filling.' Taking the chair beside Christina, she removes her hat and tan leather gloves and flops them on the table.

'Nice gloves,' Christina says. 'Christmas present?'

'Yes. Mum bought them for me. I lost my previous pair. I thought I'd go for a different colour.'

After ordering a bottle of water, Anne-Marie digs in her handbag distractedly. 'Sorry, I'm rushing around trying to get a few chores out of the way before term starts. How're things?'

She's not seen her friend like this before. Is it because her mouth is numb from the filling? Christina stares at her. No, there's definitely something troubling her.

'How are things at home?' Anne-Marie asks.

Christina fiddles with grains of sugar spilt on the table, brushing them into a small pile before squashing them with her finger, as she updates her friend on Michael's progress since having the plaster cast removed. 'He seems to be improving. He has even started driving again.'

'You know, I was thinking. It's a shame Michael hasn't got family of his own to come and see him. People to help you out. Is there really no one?'

Christina shakes her head. She has always felt sorry for Michael in this regard. He is an only child, and so were his parents. 'You know his mum and dad died shortly before he moved down here. He has a couple of friends up north. He'll see them next weekend.'

'Are they coming to stay?'

'No, he's going up there.'

Anne-Marie shifts restlessly in her seat. 'How's he going to get up there?'

'By car. What's up, Anne-Marie? You seem troubled.'

'My tooth is hurting.' Anne-Marie touches her jaw. 'Has he ever talked about the previous school he worked at?'

'Hillywood, you mean?'

'That's the one.'

'Not really. Why do you ask?'

'I was just curious.'

'You must've asked for a reason.'

Anne-Marie shakes her head and sips her water.

But there must be a reason she asked that question. Why is her friend denying it?

SIXTY-ONE

When she gets home, Christina dumps her bags, changes into her walking boots and grabs Wilf's lead. She needs some fresh air. The catch-up with Anne-Marie has disturbed her. What was she trying to get at earlier?

The sun is lurking behind grey clouds, and it's freezing cold, the bitterness of winter stubbornly hanging around. Turning left out of the drive, Christina crosses the road to Bridge End, aiming for the fields at the rear of The Black Horse.

She strides with purpose, resolute. She's not a wicked person. She just made a mistake. A mistake she will continue paying for for the rest of her life.

Christina approaches the row of three bungalows along Bridge End, where Elizabeth Haggerty lives.

Damn! When she bumped into Elizabeth's daughter, Mary, that day in the pharmacy just after Christmas, she said she would drop in. Elizabeth has that video footage of the night of the accident. With everything going on, it completely slipped her mind.

Mary is in the garden putting out the rubbish. She waves to Christina. 'How's your husband?' she asks.

Christina clears her throat. 'Much better, thanks. I was passing and just remembered. I said I'd pop in to see your mum. I'm so sorry. I totally forgot.'

'No problem. You've had a lot to deal with. Would you like to come in now?'

Christina looks down at her boots and then at Wilf.

Mary waves her in. 'Don't worry. Mum loves dogs.'

Christina stalls. She hadn't geared herself up for small talk.

'Come on. Come in. My mum would love to have someone to talk to.' It's as if Mary is desperate for company for her mum, or perhaps she needs it herself.

Christina relents. She follows Mary to the front door where she kicks off her boots and steps into a small square hallway. The smell of baking fills the air. It reminds Christina of the comforting days of childhood when life was so simple. Her mum used to bake all the time.

Mary offers her a drink.

Christina declines. She has drunk enough coffee already today.

A voice sounds from a room to the right. 'Who is it, love?'

'Christina Blake. Remember I told you I bumped into her at the pharmacy?' Mary leads Christina into the lounge with Wilf following.

The room appears frozen in time, entombed in the 1980s. Elizabeth, a round lady with grey permed hair and jowls like a bloodhound, is sitting by the window in one of two floral-patterned armchairs that match the floral wallpaper.

'Didn't you see her walk up the path with me?' Mary asks her mother.

'I must've dropped off,' Elizabeth says, sharp-eyed. Her glasses catch a twinkle of light from a brown-coloured fringed lampshade.

Mary gestures for Christina to take a seat. 'Can I tempt you with a slice of apple cake? I've just taken it out of the oven.' She nods towards Elizabeth. 'It's one of Mum's favourites.'

Christina sits down, declining the offer of cake. Her appetite still hasn't properly returned.

'I'm sorry to hear about your young man,' Elizabeth says.

Christina nods. 'Thank you.'

'My Mary said you'd like to look at the pictures from my video thingy. Is that still so?'

Mary smiles. 'Where's your iPad, Mum? I'll show Mrs Blake the images.'

'Call me Christina, please.'

Elizabeth shrugs. 'I don't know what's happened to it.' She leans towards Christina as if she is relaying a secret. 'Screen's too small. I prefer the telly.'

While Mary goes in search of the device, Elizabeth continues. 'The police still haven't found who ran your husband over, so I hear. When the same happened to my Peter, they didn't catch the culprit either. So I know how you are feeling.' Elizabeth points to a large, framed photograph on the brick fireplace. 'My Peter was knocked down, and the devil drove off.'

Devil.

Christina's stomach turns. She should never have come here.

Elizabeth's eyes gaze into the distant past. 'He died instantly, though. That's what they told me, anyway. Who really knows.'

Christina crosses her legs. 'I'm so sorry. I never knew that.'

'Forty years ago, but it still feels like only yesterday. The police have more technology nowadays, though. Like my doorbell. I'm sure they've got a better chance of catching who did this to your husband than they did back in my Peter's day.'

Mary appears with the iPad and takes a seat on the sofa. 'Let me find the right screen, and we can show you what Mum showed to the police.'

It takes Mary several minutes to find the footage. Elizabeth relays more details of her husband's accident and the pain she and their children suffered as a consequence of what she describes as 'that monster's actions'.

Christina lowers her gaze. The older woman's words ring in her head.

That's what she is. A monster. Everyone keeps saying it.

Mary moves across the room. 'Here we go.' She perches on the arm of Christina's chair and passes the iPad to her, leaning across to press play. 'It's coming up now. Watch.'

A black-and-white clip of less than five seconds shows Michael passing along Bridge End at the foot of Mrs Haggerty's house. 'There you go.'

She watches intently but it's so short, it tells her nothing she doesn't already know. 'Is that all you have?'

'That's it.' Mary shrugs. 'There's nothing else. The police watched all the footage several times. So did we. Your husband doesn't appear coming back the other way.'

Christina thought she might see something that would tell her what Michael was up to that night. But she was kidding herself. What did she expect to find that the police didn't?

Elizabeth repositions her body in her chair. 'It's a shame it didn't show your man being picked up.'

Christina turns her head sharply. 'Sorry?'

'On occasions, I've seen him being picked up just up the road there.' Mrs Haggerty points a bony finger towards the window in the direction of where Jessica James lives.

Christina stares at her wide-eyed. 'How often?'

'I don't remember. My mind isn't what it used to be.'

'What type of car was it?'

'Oh, dear. I really couldn't say. I don't notice that kind of thing.'

'Was it a big car? A small car?'

'I think it was big. But all cars are big to me. Not like the Fiat I used to drive.'

'Colour,' Christina says with urgency. 'Do you recall the colour of the car?'

Elizabeth shakes her head. 'Like I said, dear. I struggle to remember things.'

'Did the car then pass your house? Would you have it on your footage?'

'No. They picked him up, turned around and went the other way. Isn't it strange – him walking up the road to meet someone? Surely they would come into your drive. It's big enough.'

It's precisely what Christina is thinking.

'Did you mention this to the police, Mum?' Mary asks.

'I can't remember.'

The police would've questioned Michael about it if she had.

But it gives Christina confirmation of her own creeping doubts.

SIXTY-TWO

Christina's heart pounds. History is repeating itself.

Michael is having an affair. He is cheating on her. Just like Adam did. But how can she confront him after what she has done?

Stomping around the fields towards The Farmer's Arms pub, she tries to vent her anger. The ground is sodden underfoot from all the rain that has refused to let up. A weird sensation overcomes her as if it's not really her walking across the fields but another person she is watching from the air above.

Is she brave enough to have it out with Jessica once and for all?

Does she have a choice?

When she arrives at The Farmer's Arms, muddy and cold, she looks through the window, her heartbeat thudding. It's very busy for a weekday lunchtime. But then it is a popular pub. Many of the rustic tables and chairs are filled with lunchtime eaters. It has a different vibe to The Black Horse. Even though it's just as old, the interior has been modernised as much as a nineteenth-century building can be. The furniture is modern, the floor tiled, and the walls are papered with botanical prints.

Jessica is serving pie and mash to a table of six. She is dressed in jeans and a white shirt; the buttons are unsuitably unfastened, exposing her cleavage. Her long dark hair is tied up in a bun making her appear older than Christina remembers.

She does a double take. A girl the spitting image of Jessica is waiting on another table. At first, Christina thinks she is seeing things, then she realises it's Holly, Jessica's younger sister.

Christina bites her knuckle through her gloved hands, doubting herself. Could Jessica and Michael really still be having an affair? The thought makes her heave. She moves away from the window. Now she's here, she's not feeling so brave. She can't just waltz in there and demand Jessica talk to her. She turns to the exit as a voice calls out her name.

'Mrs Blake.'

Christina stops. She recognises that voice. She should go home. But she can't. Spinning around, she sees Jessica standing outside the side entrance to the pub.

It's time to confront what deep down she has feared to be the truth for so long.

Christina walks towards the young woman, shaken. Wilf barks as if he senses Christina's tense stature. 'They can stop right now.'

'Sorry?' Jessica folds her arms across her voluptuous chest. 'What're you talking about?'

'The cards. They stop now,' Christina says firmly.

Jessica raises her eyebrows. 'What cards?'

Two customers walk out of the pub past Jessica. The woman, wearing a riding jacket and trousers, thanks Jessica for her hospitality.

Christina waits until the pair are out of earshot. 'You know very well what cards I'm referring to.'

As soon as she says it, Christina realises how stupid she

sounds. She shouldn't have come here. Jessica has hardly been the most reliable narrator in her stories over the past few years, so what's going to make her tell the truth now?

The young woman stands with her head dropped to the side. 'I don't know what you're talking about.'

Christina lowers her voice. 'What really happened with my husband, Jessica? I want to hear it from you. Did you and Michael have an affair? Are you still having an affair?'

'No,' Jessica says. 'You've got it wrong.' She suddenly seems so grown up, but tears shield a fire burning in her eyes. 'Go home. And leave me alone. I want nothing more to do with you or your family.' The young woman turns around and hurries back inside the pub.

The door slams closed.

Christina hurries after her but stops, berating herself. This is not her. Hot tears burn her eyes.

Jessica was right. She needs to go home.

She reverses her journey across the fields and strides purposefully along the track to Bridge End, where she crosses the road to the adjacent open farmland and onto the track she often takes when Wilf needs a longer walk. She wants to cry, but she's too angry for tears. Was Jessica lying to her?

She doesn't know.

She doesn't know anything any more.

SIXTY-THREE

'You OK, Mum?' Ben asks when he surfaces from his room shortly before noon on Saturday. 'Mum! Did you hear me? Are you OK?'

'Fine,' she lies, feigning a smile. The kids are going to their dad's today, and she doesn't want to give them a reason to worry about her. But Elizabeth Haggerty's revelation continues to torture Christina. It's all-consuming. She approached Michael about it, but he denied it. He said the old woman was batty and must've mistaken him for someone else. She's been stewing all morning, drinking one cup of coffee after another.

'Where's Michael?' Ben asks.

'He's gone away for the night.'

'Where?'

'To see his friends up north. He always goes up there this time of year, remember?'

Ben pulls a face. 'Is he up for that?'

She shrugs. 'Apparently.' He has come on leaps and bounds since Christmas and Christina thinks time away to spend with his friends will do him good. She tried to persuade him to take the train, but he insisted on driving, so she backed off.

'What time is Dad coming to pick you up?' she asks. 'He did say, but I can't remember.'

'Twelve-thirty,' Ben replies, strolling across the kitchen to stand beside her. 'We don't have to go, you know. We can stay here with you.'

She turns her head sharply to look at her son. 'Why would you want to do that?'

'You've been acting really weird lately.'

She stares him. There he is. The considerate young man who has been hiding in this moody teenager's body. She knew he was in there somewhere. 'You have to go. Dad got you those tickets ages ago. It'll be fun. Live for today.'

'You always used to say that, didn't you?'

'Say what? What do you mean?'

'You always said *live for today* when Abi was ill. Because you never know what tomorrow's going to bring.'

She ruffles his hair. 'What's happened to you? Where's my moody teenager gone?'

He smiles. 'I dunno. Michael's accident has made me think. I haven't been very nice to you lately, have I? I feel kinda bad about that. I'm sorry, Mum.'

'You were a kid dealing with a difficult situation.' She hugs her son, staring out of the window. With hindsight, she shouldn't have moved Michael in here so quickly. It wasn't good for any of them. She never had a chance to be on her own and deal with the hurt from her divorce. Michael came along at the wrong time.

Ben pecks her cheek. 'I love you, Mum.'

She turns and watches him walk away, her heart melting. When did she last hear those words from him? 'I love you too,' she calls after him.

After Adam has collected them, she wills herself to keep busy. She must stay occupied.

She takes her cleaning caddy and the vacuum cleaner upstairs to clean the kids' bedrooms. Wilf is behind her, faithfully following her like her shadow. Starting with Abi's room, she empties the bin into the large rubbish bag before running the duster around the furniture and vacuuming the floor.

The blackmailer's note is at the forefront of her mind. The money is due on Monday. And she's ready to make the transfer.

She lugs the cleaning gear into Ben's room. It's a different story compared to Abi's tidy room. The bed is unmade and the floor is littered with clothes. How many times has she reminded him there's a linen basket in the corner of the room?

Collecting all the items off the floor, she dumps them on his bed. She is running the hoover around when she stops to pick up a train ticket from the floor. It must've fallen out of one of his pockets.

Curiously, she studies it. That's strange. It's from 28 December. The day she delivered the first drop of cash to the blackmailer. She looks at the time: 20.08. She frowns. Ben went out that night. She didn't want him to because the roads were so bad. But he went to see his mates. So, what was he doing taking a train from Didiford station into London?

She slips the ticket into the pocket of her joggers.

After she has cleaned upstairs, she lies down on the sofa in the snug. She's wiped out. It's so quiet without Michael and the kids here, but she's happy to be alone, without the stress of worrying about others. She doesn't get peace for long.

Wilf positions his head next to hers, his constant whining a hint that she hasn't walked him yet today.

She sighs heavily but smiles at her faithful friend. 'Come on, then. Where's your lead?'

Twenty minutes later, she finds herself walking along the side of the gardens of The Black Horse. Smoke billows out of the chimney. They must have a fire going. She recalls the

Christmas before last when she and Michael went there for lunch one Sunday. There was a roaring fire blazing that day as well. It had been her suggestion. The school term had finished the Friday before, and she had just got over the flu. She didn't have the energy to cook but had fancied a roast dinner.

Michael was in a dark mood that day. Snow had arrived, and the roads were too dangerous for him to go for a bike ride. It took all of her persuasion to get him to agree to go to the pub with her. It was there she had first broached the subject of him getting some help after the Jessica situation. He obviously needed it. But no matter how hard she tried, he wouldn't listen. Would things have turned out differently between them if she'd managed to get him to see a therapist back then?

She continues along the footpath edging Ivy Road. Five or so minutes later, she stops. Her heart skips a beat as she realises she is walking parallel to the spot where she hit Michael. She recalls when the police secured the area with blue and white tape. A crime scene, of which she was the perpetrator.

It looks no different to any other area of the field, but it's as if she can feel Michael there. It's the earthy smell of the sodden ground. That's how he described it to her that night when he said his memory was returning.

Wilf barks.

She looks up.

His paws are digging at a spot on the ground. 'Come here, boy,' she calls out. They are near the road now, and she needs to get him back on his lead.

He ignores her.

'Wilf. Come.'

He's not having any of it.

She jogs over to him, her boots sticking in the mud making it difficult. 'What are you up to?'

He looks up at her, wagging his tail, his paw scraping at an object in the ground.

She bends down to pick it up. 'What have you found?' It looks like a phone. Brushing off the mud the best she can, she gasps loudly. She recognises it. But it can't be.

She furiously wipes off the mud. Dark smears smudge the screen. She was right.

It's Michael's old mobile phone.

SIXTY-FOUR

Christina places the old phone in front of Ted sitting at the breakfast bar. 'It's the one he had before he got an iPhone.'

'How do you know?' Ted asks.

She turns it over. 'The cycling club sticker on the back.'

The kettle clicks off. She pours two mugs of tea.

'Where exactly did you find it?'

'I didn't. Wilf did in the field adjacent to where I hit him. That's why Michael didn't take his iPhone out that night. He took this one. Whoever he was meeting, he was communicating with using this phone. I bet you.' She hands her brother a mug of tea.

Ted takes it from her, staring at the Samsung phone. He seems distracted somehow, not himself. 'I don't believe it.'

'Me neither.'

'Where is he?' Ted asks.

'He's gone away for the night,' she says.

'Where?' he asks, frowning.

'Up north. I told you. It's his mates' annual meet-up.'

'I remember now,' Ted says. 'Is he up for that?'

'My thought exactly, but he was adamant he wasn't going to

miss it. I thought it might do him good to get away for a bit.' Her stomach tightens as she prods the phone. She takes the stool beside her brother. 'It must've fallen out of his pocket when I hit him.'

'It's more likely he was holding it at the time.'

She flinches. 'How do I get into it?' It feels wrong to do this, but finding this old phone has clouded any good thoughts she has left for her husband.

Ted reaches across and takes a napkin out of the wire holder. He attempts to clean the phone before pressing the on button at the side. 'How come the police didn't find it?' He squints at the screen. 'It needs charging.'

Christina stands up. 'My charger will work.'

She rushes to the other side of the kitchen, unplugs the charger and takes it back to her brother. 'Here you go. This should work.'

Ted slots it into the wall socket. 'Fingers crossed and all that.'

They wait.

He fiddles with the end of the lead inserted into the charging port, shaking his head. 'It's kaput.' He shakes the phone. 'Water must've got into it. Or mud that I could've pushed in further when I put the lead in.'

'You're kidding me.'

'Or it's the charger. My bet is it's the phone, though. It's been out there a long time in all that snow and rain.'

Christina can't believe she's so close to figuring out Michael's movements that night. Yet so far away. 'What can we do?'

'Let's see if we can get it working.'

After a minute or so, Ted holds it up, shaking his head. 'No luck. It's knackered.'

'Can't you put the SIM card into a different phone?'

Ted gazes along the edges of the phone. 'Should be able to.

We'll need to get it out first.' Looking around, he reaches for a pile of paperwork at the side of the of the breakfast bar and removes a paperclip. He unbends it and pokes the tip into the holes beside the SIM tray. 'It's stuck.'

'You must be able to get it out.'

'It's not worth forcing it. It'll break.'

She kicks the side of the cupboard beneath the worktop.

'Steady on.' Ted tries to calm her.

'Why does everything have to be so bloody difficult?' She's at breaking point. She knows she's not going to like what she finds – which she is certain is going to be correspondence between Jessica and Michael – but she needs this. Needs something solid. Something to unravel everything that's happened.

She wouldn't mind betting DS Macintosh's forensic team would have the SIM card out and read within a heartbeat. Perhaps she should hand it over to him. But that could be signing her own death warrant. Wife caught husband having an affair and decided to get rid of him – what other motive would be needed?

'Here we go. Come on, you beauty.' The SIM card tray pops open. Removing the card, Ted studies it, grimacing. 'I'm not sure it would've survived either. Let's give it a go.' He picks up his own iPhone and takes out the SIM card before giving the card from Michael's old Samsung another clean with his shirt sleeve. 'If this wrecks my phone though, you owe me a new one,' he jests as he slots in the SIM card.

They both hover over the phone waiting for it to spring into action. 'It's not working, is it?' Frustration rises within her.

'Nope. Let me take it to a tech geek mate of mine.'

'Who?' she asks.

He ignores her question. 'Leave it with me. I'll see what he can do.'

'You sure know some shady characters, Ted.'

'All above board. Well sort of.' He laughs. 'He loves this kinds of stuff. He'll get it working.'

'Will you take it to him now?'

'Can I drink my tea first?'

She lays her head on his shoulder. 'Sorry.'

He squeezes her hand. 'This is killing me as much as it is you. I blame myself. I shouldn't have agreed to get your car fixed. I should've persuaded you to own up to the police about what really happened that night instead. Things would've turned out easier for you.' He slurps his tea before removing the SIM card and wrapping it in a napkin.

'It all sounds surreal, doesn't it? I keep thinking I'm in a bad dream.' Christina rests her elbows on the worktop. Clasping her hands together, she drops her chin on top of them. 'I went to see her.'

Ted looks at her, frowning. 'Who?'

'Jessica. I walked up to The Farmer's Arms and asked her outright if she and Michael were having an affair.'

Ted's jaw drops. 'What did she say?'

'She denied it. Told me I wasn't thinking straight and to go home.'

'You shouldn't have gone there. What good can come from it?' Ted stands up and places the napkin holding the SIM card in his pocket. 'I'll go and sort this out for you.' He grabs his van keys. They scrape along the worktop.

'Perhaps I'll come with you.'

'Why don't you try to get some rest? You're looking really pale.'

'Maybe.'

Rest? Who is he kidding?

SIXTY-FIVE

Christina is unsure what draws her up to the attic once Ted has gone.

Standing at the door to Michael's study, she stares at his possessions, breathing in the smell of his leather jacket hanging on the back of the door.

She walks towards the desk, her heart heavy. The high-pitched call of a bird sounds from outside the small casement window. She picks up the photo of her and Michael cutting their wedding cake. Reaching for a tissue from the drawer, she cleans the dust from it. The stand has come unattached from the back. Was that broken the last time she picked it up? She can't remember.

Propping the frame up against a pile of books, she studies it. They were happy then, weren't they?

Her phone pings with a message from Ted.

Lucky for us, my mate is in. He's on the case now. Will call soon.

She turns to the bookshelf. A book catches her attention. It's jutting out, not sitting proud of the others. She pulls it out and gulps. It's *The Collected Poems of Elizabeth Barrett Browning*, the book Michael often used to read to her from. She flicks through the pages. A piece of white card with a poem drops out. She reads it, speaking the last paragraph out loud.

All that I have I bestow on you
The very fibre of my being is yours
My body, my soul
For now and all eternity.

It's not of a professional standard, but it's well-written. Even she can tell that.

Her pulse races as she turns over the card to find a typed message.

To Michael.
Happy Christmas.
I wish we could spend it together alone, just us.
With love always. XXX

Her world turns one-eighty.

It is dated Christmas Day the year before last.

Christina knows who it's from. Michael used to tell her how Jessica made up poems all the time. Before that girl wrecked their lives, he often used to read his pupils' work out to Christina. She recalls him saying he was impressed with Jessica's poems. She had a natural talent, apparently.

And then one day, Christina realised he hadn't read one of Jessica's poems to her for a while. When she asked him why, he shrugged and said she had stopped writing them.

She rereads the poem on the card.

That's why.

Jessica had started making them too personal.

With trembling hands, she calls Ted. There's a rattling sound. He doesn't appear to be at home. 'Where are you?'

'I'm on my way to yours.'

'You'll never guess what's happened now.'

'Calm down, Chrissy.'

Trying to control her breathing, she clasps the poem in her hand. It's taking all of her resolve not to tear it into a thousand pieces. 'Did your mate get into the phone?'

The sound of Ted taking a deep breath sounds through the receiver. 'We did.'

'And?'

'Let's talk about it when I get there.'

She raises her voice until she is almost shouting. 'Tell me.'

'I'll be there in about ten minutes.'

'Tell me now,' she screams.

But the line has already gone dead.

Christina runs downstairs to wait for him. She paces the kitchen, not knowing what to do with herself.

Jessica lied to her.

Michael met with Jessica regularly, discussing literature and her Oxbridge application. Had that been a lie?

Christina's stomach turns. He'd been doing the same with Nina Silver, according to her mum at Ben's parents' evening before Christmas.

She walks to the window, willing her brother to hurry up. Placing a hand on either side of the window frame, she lowers her head and inhales deeply, slowly letting out long breaths. She must control her breathing. She will pass out at this rate.

Ted's van crunching over the shingle driveway makes her look up. She runs to the front door.

He gets out of the van, the hood of his top pulled over his head, and jogs towards her, a phone in his hand.

She hurries her brother inside and closes the door with a

bang. The sound echoes through the quiet house. 'And?' she asks.

He screws his face up. 'Let's go and sit down.'

'No, Ted. You tell me now.' She tries to grab the phone from him, but he pulls his hand away and strides up the hallway.

'You need to sit down and prepare yourself for this,' he says when they get to the kitchen. He drops onto a stool and orders her to sit beside him.

Her bottom lip is trembling, and her stomach churning.

He hands her a phone.

SIXTY-SIX

'Whose phone is this?' Christina asks.

'An old one of my mate's. It's got the SIM card in it.' Ted points to the screen showing an exchange of text messages. 'It looks as if he either started using this phone the night of the accident, or all previous messages have been wiped. My guess is the latter. I think he's been using this phone for a while. Brace yourself.'

She reads the exchange.

I need to see you.

What's happened?

I'll tell you when I see you.

Do you want to call?

Better not.

She's going out around seven-thirty. I can't drive. I've had a couple of drinks.

Shall I pick you up from the usual place?

OK. Give it until eight to be on the safe side. I'm worried about you.

I'll see you soon. Don't worry. I love you.

Not as much as I love you.

Christina doubles over. The pain is unbearable.

'I'm so sorry, Chrissy.' Ted reaches out to put an arm around her shoulder.

She shakes him off. She can't bear anyone's touch.

'Do you recognise the number?' he asks.

She stares at the screen and shakes her head.

'I tried calling it, but the phone's switched off. There's no voicemail message.'

Pulling the poem out of her pocket, Christina throws it on the counter. 'Read this. I found it in one of his books.'

Ted's eyes flit over the poem. 'What a bastard.'

Her voice shudders. 'It's from her.'

'Who?' he asks.

'Jessica,' she spits.

He studies it again. 'How do you know? There's no name on it.'

She bows her head, telling him about the poems Jessica used to write. 'It answers many questions.' She lifts her head. 'At least we know where he went that night, now.' Her voice breaks. 'After everything Adam did to me, too. Michael knew how much he destroyed me.'

'Could you be mistaken? Could there be an explanation?'

She gives him a look that tells him to stop clutching at straws. 'It's all here in front of me.' She picks up the phone and searches through it, looking for any other evidence to tell her she is wrong. 'Was there anything else?'

'I had a quick look, but it doesn't appear so,' Ted says. 'I think the sole purpose of this phone was to converse with her just over text.'

'I feel like I don't know him any more.'

Ted raises his hands, shrugging his shoulders up to his ears.

Christina pushes her stool away from the breakfast bar. The legs scrape along the floor. 'I'm going to go and see her again.'

Ted jumps up and grabs her shoulders. 'Stop, just stop.' He looks her in the eye and raises his voice. 'Don't you think he is the one you should be challenging?'

She sits back down.

'When's he coming back?'

'Tomorrow night.'

'Then you've got twenty-four hours to compose yourself before you confront him.'

SIXTY-SEVEN

Christina rummages through the drawers in Michael's study.

She has spent all night coming up with excuses to explain away everything she has discovered about him, but she knows it's pointless.

How she despises this man she has loved deeply for the past six years.

Anger overcomes her. Pulling the drawers off their rails, she turns them upside down, dropping their contents onto the floor. She kicks the mess, scattering objects across the carpet. Thoughts of Jessica and Michael together torment her. She drops to her knees and combs through the items with her fingers, trying to find a clue, more proof to confront him with.

She crawls over to the small cupboard built into the eaves. It's crammed full, mainly with plastic storage boxes of Michael's and a few items that there's no other home for: an old cycling helmet, books, clothes and some old pictures that belonged to his mother that he couldn't bear to part with. Yanking each item out, she tosses them aside until she gets to the boxes. What else could he have hidden from her? More poems?

She stops. Does she want to be doing this? What happened to the man she fell madly in love with?

He fell in love with someone else.

Some of the boxes are full to the brim with paperwork. Christina unclips the lids and rifles through the contents. One contains documents relating to the sale of his parents' house after they passed. Another box is full of personal documents. Her heart wrenches as she pulls out details of Michael's life: his birth certificate, academic awards and the photos of him growing up he had shown her when they first met.

She goes through every single item in every box. But she doesn't find anything that shows Michael in a bad light.

Until she finds another box behind a large bag full of old sports clothes.

She opens it. Inside, she finds a file marked *The Best of the Best*. She opens it to find essays from when Michael was at university. Work for which he achieved top marks. Underneath are what looks like copies of essays from other students that he has scored very highly. She recognises his handwriting. She flicks through them when a photo of a young woman falls out and flutters to the floor.

Christina picks it up. At first glance, she thinks it's Jessica. The young woman in the photo has long dark hair. But then Christina realises it's not her.

Perhaps she's an ex-girlfriend?

He'd had a few relationships before he met Christina but has never talked much about them, despite Christina's curiosity. The past stays in the past as far as Michael is concerned.

Christina turns the photo over. Her blood runs cold as she reads the inscription on the back. *Ellena Masterson, Hillywood, 2016*, and underneath, *Love E.*

That was the year Michael moved south. Hillywood was the school he worked at before St Christopher's.

Curious, she scrambles to her feet and takes the photograph

downstairs to her study, where she switches on her computer. She stares out of the window while waiting for the machine to fire up. It's getting dark. The kids will be home soon.

When the screen flashes, she searches for Ellena Masterson and Hillywood School. It's an independent school like St Christopher's. Michael left there to further his chances of promotion, he has always claimed. But now she thinks about it, he has never talked about it much.

It looks as if Ellena was a keen hockey player. Several photos of her fill the screen, playing in leagues and winning many medals. She was also the only student who won a place at Oxford that year. Christina's heart sinks. A place to study English.

This is making her feel sick. Very sick.

But that's where any mention of Ellena Masterson stops.

Christina tries to find her on social media. No one of that name remotely resembles her on any site. She returns to the Google photos of the school. It takes a while, but she eventually finds a picture of Ellena accepting a medal. Her mother, a local florist, Polly Masterson, was quoted as saying how proud she was of her daughter.

She searches for Hillywood Florists and finds an email address and phone number for a Polly Masterson.

She grabs her phone from her pocket. The train ticket she found in Ben's room yesterday drops out. Frowning, she places it on her desk. She calls Polly Masterson's number. There's no reply. Of course there's not. It's Sunday.

Opening her email, she types a message to Hillywood Florists asking for Polly Masterson to call her. She presses send.

The front door opens.

Christina jumps. She never heard a car.

'Mum, we're home,' Abi calls out.

Footsteps stomp past the study door.

Christina looks out of the window and sees Adam's car

leaving the driveway. She shoves the photograph of Ellena Masterson beneath the papers in her filing tray and gets up.

Abi appears and comes to hug her. 'I missed you, Mum.' The scan results have changed her daughter. It's as if she is lighter.

'I missed you, too,' Christina says, hearing footsteps running up the stairs.

Abi stands back. 'Mum, what's wrong?'

'I'm fine. How was the concert?'

'Good. You're acting odd. What's up?'

Her whole body is shaking. Christina shrugs, trying to throw her daughter off the scent of her concerns. 'I was just going through some admin. What's up with your brother?'

'He's had an argument with Dad.'

'What about?'

'He asked for an increase in his monthly allowance. Dad said no. He gives him enough.'

'I'll talk to him.'

Abi grabs Christina's hand, her eyes wide with alarm. 'What the hell, Mum! Look at the state of your finger.'

Christina withdraws her hand, staring at the inflamed, cracked skin around her knuckle.

'That's infected. You need to put some cream on.'

'I will do.'

'Why do you keep biting it? My scan was clear. Michael's on the mend.'

She'd love to open up to her daughter but could never burden her with her worries. 'It's healing. I'll be fine. I am fine.'

'What's for dinner?'

Dinner? Christina hasn't even thought about it. 'Didn't you eat with Dad?'

'No. You said you were going to cook a roast.'

Did she? She hasn't even been shopping. 'I'm sorry, I've been busy.'

'Are you OK, Mum, really?'

'Fine. How about fish and chips?'

Abi's eyes light up. 'Anytime!'

'I'll go and pick it up. I want to get an early night ready for work tomorrow.'

'Do you really need to go back so soon? No one expects you to.'

'I need to move on, Abi.' She fakes a mouthful of positivity. 'I need to get some normality back into my life.' The kids don't need to see their mum moping around any more.

She grabs the train ticket from her desk to talk to Ben about it. But she thinks better of that idea. If she confronts him now, after he's already had an argument with his dad, things could go downhill fast. Especially in her state, after all she's found out today.

Besides, it's not him she's after answers from at the moment.

SIXTY-EIGHT

She needs a glass of wine. But she has to drive to get dinner, so she settles for a Diet Coke, which she takes back to her study to check on her emails. There's no response from Polly Masterson.

Ted has left a message. He has been working all day. The man never stops. He is now going out to meet his new girlfriend, but he wanted to know if she was OK. He can drop in on the way, if she wants him to.

She considers asking him to come over. So much has happened; she needs to talk to someone. But she has to sort dinner for the kids first. She drops him a text to tell him she'll see him tomorrow.

Heading upstairs, she knocks on Ben's door. There's no answer. She puts her ear to the door. He is talking to someone. It sounds as if he is arguing with them, but she can't hear what he is saying.

She folds some laundry drying in the spare bedroom before returning and knocking on Ben's door again. There's still no answer. She listens. She can't hear anything. He must have his EarPods in. She opens the door and walks in. He is sitting on the bed, playing with his phone. 'Hello, Mum. How are you?' she says sarcastically.

'Sorry I didn't say hello,' Ben says. 'I was in a bit of a mood.'

'What's happened?'

'I asked Dad for some money. He said no. He's got so much.'

She perches on the side of the bed. 'That's not the point. He's good to you, Ben. You need to learn the value of money.'

'I know. I was out of order.' He lifts and drops his phone. 'I've already called him and apologised.'

'What do you need money for?'

'This and that.'

'Can I ask you something?' she says.

'What?'

She hands him the train ticket. 'What were you doing going to London that night between Christmas and New Year?'

He snatches the ticket from her hand. His jaw tenses. 'Where did you get this?' he snaps.

'I was hoovering earlier and found it on the floor.'

He thumps the bed. 'You shouldn't be in my room.'

She stares him out. 'You said you were meeting your mates that night.'

'I was.'

'So why did you go to London?'

'I didn't.'

'So what were you doing at Didiford station?' She needs to know he didn't see her there, dropping the money to the blackmailer. Otherwise, he'll be the one asking all the questions.

He rolls his eyes. 'Cal and Jake were going to a party in London. I was going to go too, so I bought a ticket but changed my mind.'

'Why?'

He pauses as if he is thinking of an excuse to give her.

She stares at him hard. 'The truth, Ben. I always brought you up to tell me the truth.'

'OK, you'll find out at some point, so I might as well tell you.'

Her heart sinks. What has he got himself involved in? 'What?' she whispers. She can't cope with more bad news.

His face reddens. He looks from her to his phone then back at her.

'What, Ben?'

'There's this girl, Maisy. I met her at a party last term. We've been seeing each other. She was going to go to that party that night, too, but she decided against it. So I cut out as well and went around to her house instead.'

Christina's shoulders drop. 'Why didn't you tell me about her?'

'I didn't know if she liked me for ages. But I've just found out she does.' He smiles coyly. 'I need to bring her around here to meet you.'

Christina is taken aback. 'I'd love that.'

She releases a large breath. At least she can trust her kids. Ben laces his hands and jiggles his little fingers when he's lying. A trait she picked up in him when he was young. He doesn't know she knows that. Sometimes mums need to keep these things to themselves.

She reaches out for a hug.

He opens his arms and hugs her tightly. 'I'm so sorry for being such a dick, Mum. I really am. You didn't deserve it. I know you've always put me and Abi first.'

She smiles. That's her boy. The lovely boy she knows. She draws away from him. 'I'm going to grab fish and chips for tea. What would you like?'

'Cod, please.'

Christina starts the car and rests her chin on the steering wheel while waiting for the heater to kick in and the windscreen to clear. Dusk is on the horizon, silhouetting trees against the darkening sky.

She's cold and so very tired. Perhaps a pizza delivery would've been a better idea than fish and chips. Her phone rings. It's Polly Masterson.

Polly apologises. She has only just picked up Christina's messages. 'Do I know you, Mrs Blake?' Her voice is as chirpy as a bird's.

'No. But I think my husband taught your daughter when she was at Hillywood School.'

Polly hesitates. 'I don't like the sound of this.'

'My husband, Michael.'

Polly spits out his name. 'Michael Blake.'

'That's right.'

'Why have you asked me to call you?' Polly's chirpy tone has dulled.

Christina needs to keep this woman on her side. She pours all the desperation she has been feeling into her voice. 'I found a picture of your daughter in one of his boxes while I was clearing out his study. And it's raised some questions because there was an incident with one of his pupils the year before last.'

'How truthful do you want me to be with you, Mrs Blake?'

'One hundred per cent.' Christina pauses before adding, 'Please.'

'He was grooming my daughter. When my husband and I found out, we gave Mr Blake an ultimatum. Our daughter was destined for better things. We didn't want her reputation ruined. So my husband had a man-to-man chat with him. Words along the lines of, if he didn't get the hell out of town, he'd find himself at the bottom of the river when my husband next went fishing.'

Polly clears her throat.

'Your husband isn't a good man, Mrs Blake. But I'm sure you already know that.'

SIXTY-NINE

Christina struggles to breathe.

She was right all along. Something was going on with Jessica and Michael. She goes over the last few years in her head. The signs were all there now she is looking for them.

She pulls Michael's number up on her phone and calls it but after three rings, hangs up.

Her mind is a scrambled mess. She needs to calm down first. And sort the kids' dinner.

She heads to the fish and chip shop in town. It's further away than the local one, but the kids prefer the chips from this one. And she must admit, it's worth the extra journey time. She turns onto Parson's Road, a short cut through country lanes that leads into town, when a car passes her going the other way. She looks in her rear-view mirror and slams on her brakes.

That was Michael, wasn't it?

What's he doing here? He isn't due back until later. Did he even go away? Did he stay here to see her: Jessica? Or did he come back early to see her?

Perhaps she is mistaken, her mind playing wicked games with her. She opens the door and peers at the vehicle in the distance. It's too far away for her to say for definite that it's Michael's car.

Performing a three-point turn in less than ten seconds, she races after the car which is now pulling onto the main road.

She is three cars behind the Volvo. There's no mistaking it's Michael.

She still can't work out why he is here. Where's he going?

A sudden thought occurs to her. What if Michael is the blackmailer? What if he saw her that night? But that doesn't make sense. He was on crutches when the first card arrived. How could he have managed to get the cards in the mailbox? And his printer is in his study, up three flights of stairs. He didn't go up there while the plaster cast was still on. So how could he have even made the card? Unless someone made it for him.

Jessica.

What if it was her who came to the hospital that day and they planned it together? She never did find out who the visitor in the baseball cap was.

She follows him, trying her best to stay a few cars behind. It only takes a few minutes before she realises his destination.

St Christopher's.

He indicates and pulls into the entrance of the school.

Her pulse races, quick and erratic. She trails him, bypassing the main parking area where she usually drops off and picks up the kids, and entering the deserted side car park instead. Slotting into a space behind a low, dense Red Robin hedge, she switches off the engine and watches him.

Madness whirls around her, a fierce cyclone of insanity. What the hell is he up to?

He parks beside a Mercedes. It's the only other vehicle in the parking area. The recognition judders through her. Anne-Marie's car.

Her stomach tightens.

What if it's not Jessica who Michael is having an affair with, but Anne-Marie?

Surely not.

But why not? Anne-Marie has always had a soft spot for him. She's a workaholic, so they could easily have hung out in her office, and no one would've suspected if the lights remained on late at night. It's more than an office. It's got a comfortable sofa and a small kitchen in it.

Is that where he is going now?

She looks to the right of the main school building, where Anne-Marie's office is situated. Sure enough, the lights are on.

And Michael is heading straight there.

SEVENTY

Michael and Anne-Marie! All these years, and she has never suspected a thing.

Christina's mind is in turmoil. Surely, she has got this wrong? She grips the steering wheel. Her knuckles turn white. Anne-Marie was meant to be her friend. You read stories about this kind of thing happening all the time: my husband had a fling with my best friend. But you never think it will happen to you.

That's why Anne-Marie has consistently sided with Michael over the Jessica incident. It's all falling into place. Anne-Marie knew nothing was going on between Michael and Jessica. Because she was the one having the affair with him.

How stupid she has been trusting them all this time. Her mum always used to tell her she was too trusting.

She wants to confront them, yet she can't bring herself to get out of the car. Slumping over the wheel, she rests her forehead against the cold leather and lets out a long, painful cry. She's so tired – and fed up with her choice of men. First Adam with his personal assistant, and now Michael with his boss. It's sickening.

All this time, she has been riddled with guilt for running him over and listening to his lies. Of course he knew where he was going that night of the accident. Anne-Marie must have picked him up from Bridge End, come back here to St Christopher's before dropping him back at the pub.

But somehow, it doesn't quite make sense. Michael felt Anne-Marie let him down over the whole Jessica saga. She led him to believe the deputy head position was his until that Jessica nonsense all kicked off. But was it nonsense? Michael was disappointed in Anne-Marie. She should've fought more for him. At least that's what he told her.

It's no use. She needs to get out there and tackle this situation head on. Lifting her head, she reaches to open the car door but stops. She frowns.

Michael is now standing by his car, holding a folder.

Anne-Marie is standing beside him. Her arms are wrapped around her body, her black hair a wild mess in the relentless wind. She holds an arm out to Michael.

He takes her hand and shakes it. Hardly the actions of two lovers having an extramarital affair. It appears more like the conclusion of a business meeting.

What is going on?

And why are they here at the school on a Sunday? Especially when Michael is meant to be up north.

Anne-Marie turns on her heels and goes back inside without a second glance.

Michael throws the file on the back seat of his car, climbs into the driver's seat and leaves the school grounds.

Christina follows him, careful to stay far enough back for him not to notice her.

He drives a short distance up the road that runs parallel to the right of the school and veers off along the unkept potholed lane adjacent to the school's vast sports fields, pulling into a muddied parking slot.

Taking the bend before the lane, to avoid the possibility of detection, Christina parks behind a transit van. She switches the engine off.

Opening the car door, her face is exposed to the sharp, winter wind. She pulls the hood of her coat over her head and, wrapping her arms around herself, hugs what little warmth she has closer to her body.

Filled with trepidation, she walks back to the bend and peers around the corner to see Michael walking further up the lane. He reaches the footpath on the opposite side of the road that leads onto the sports fields, then heads through the metal gate. The heavy ancient spring catapults as he lets it go. The loud clang echoes around the parked cars and surrounding houses.

He stops.

Christina ducks behind a car and waits. A car door slams shut somewhere in the distance. When she peeps around the wing mirror, Michael has disappeared.

Christina darts after him, crossing the road and heading to the gate, gingerly guiding it back to its closed position to prevent the clank alerting him to her presence. The moon is out, allowing some light to line the dark path. Branches from the trees drip water into her face. Brambles catch on her coat. When she reaches the end of the track, she stops. Which way did he go?

Scanning the fields she spots him, striding along the right edge of the back gardens of the surrounding houses. He is walking with a slight limp, she notices.

Christina follows him. The ground is muddy from the winter's rain, snow and thaw. In better weather, it's a nice walk. She knows the route well. In the summer months, she sometimes brings Wilf up here. But today, it's dark and quiet, intensely foreboding, the only sounds coming from her feet squelching on the sodden path and her heart beating in her ears.

It's as quiet as a graveyard until the sudden barking of a dog startles her as it is let out into the garden of one of the houses backing onto the fields. It heightens her unease. She ducks into the shadows, searching for Michael.

She makes him out, passing the new cricket pavilion, a large white building, now grey in the gloom. Michael was on the fundraising team for this new building and took a great deal of pride as he showed their first visitors around when they hosted the first game of the season after it was built.

She continues following him until he disappears behind a row of outbuildings used by the school's gardening team to store their equipment, hurrying to catch up with him. He enters the school's old cricket pavilion at the end of the row of outbuildings. This old pavilion needed too much money spent on it to get it up to scratch, hence the building of the new one.

Cautiously, she steps closer. A dull light glints from the window. Someone is there already waiting for him.

She tries to convince herself it's kids messing around. Or perhaps Michael has arranged some sort of pupils' Dead Poets' Society.

But who is she trying to kid?

Jessica is in there, waiting for him.

SEVENTY-ONE

Christina approaches the building. Curtains are pulled over the window, but the slightest of gaps enables her to see inside.

She should sense a deep-rooted feeling of dread, but strangely she's not scared. Her inquisitive nature has put pay to that. It's as if all the fear that has engulfed her since the accident has evaporated and left her full of curiosity. The need to know consumes her.

Jessica is in there. Of that she is certain.

She steps onto an old log to allow her to see into the room.

Michael is casually sitting on an old beaten-up leather sofa talking to someone who is out of Christina's line of vision.

She considers walking straight in and confronting them, but she wants to see what she is dealing with first. It could always be another pupil. Not Jessica, but possibly Nina Silver? The thought sickens her.

As quietly and carefully as possible, Christina steals around to the other side of the building, where there's a back entrance. She trips over an obstacle on the ground, a large stone, or another log, stumbling as she tries to right her balance. She steadies herself, catching her breath.

When she gets to the rear door, she climbs the four rickety wooden steps, placing as little weight as possible on each one to prevent them from creaking. She silently prays the door is unlocked. Pulling the handle, she pushes it down. Thankfully, it gives. She gently pushes it. Quietly does it.

She's in.

The door squeaks slightly as it closes. Four rooms lead from the main dimly lit corridor. Christina stops, waiting, hearing muffled voices; although she can't make out what they are saying, she knows exactly where they are coming from. She needs to get closer to see who her husband is talking to and understand what they are discussing.

Her heart is beating uncontrollably, pulsating in her ears. She's never known her senses so heightened. She tiptoes down the corridor towards the room at the far end. The musty smell of damp clogs her throat.

The door is ajar.

Peering through the faintest of cracks, she can see Michael. He has his back to her, talking, but she still can't hear what he is saying.

The other person in the room, who Christina still can't see, appears to be tapping their foot. Tap, tap, tap.

And then Christina hears it.

A sound she unmistakably recognises.

A sound that crushes her.

A baby starts crying as if it has just awoken from their slumber.

Lily is in the room.

SEVENTY-TWO

Christina throws open the door.

It bounces off the adjoining wall and crashes back, fractionally missing her extended arm.

Lily looks around startled, her cheeks red, clinging to Sophia.

Coming face to face with her sister, Christina tries to process the scene being played out before her, but it's too confusing. Sophia and Lily shouldn't be here. It makes no sense.

Michael jumps up from the old sofa and turns around to confront Christina. A floor lamp shines a dull, eerie light across his ashen face. Circles ring his dark, crazed eyes.

'What the fuck are you doing here?' Michael barks, looking from Christina to Sophia.

There's an incredulous pause as everyone digests the enormity of the situation. Who is going to speak first?

Sophia looks her sister in the eye. 'Christina, I c-can explain. We c-can explain,' she says, stuttering her words. 'This is not what we had planned. This is not how it was all meant to come out.' Her nose wrinkles and her eyebrows lower. 'We didn't want it to happen like this. You have to understand.' She starts blubbering, nuzzling her face into her daughter's hair, rocking her child from side to side.

Christina shakes her head in confusion. 'Understand what? Can someone tell me what the hell is going on?' Christina's voice startles them all, including herself. Lily wriggles in Sophia's arms. Tiny sobs escape her shuddering lips. She looks at her sister, then Michael. The harsh realisation penetrates her. 'No. No. No.'

Lily's desperate cries fill the small room.

Sophia scrambles around in her coat pocket for a dummy to pacify her daughter and places it into Lily's mouth.

Placing her hands on her head, Christina tries to digest what lies before her, but it's too repugnant. All she knows is, her life will never be the same. 'How long has this been going on?'

Sophia's cheeks burn as brightly as Lily's. As least she has the decency to show some shame.

Michael stands tall, his expression deadpan.

Christina's shrill voice reverberates around the small room. 'How long?'

Sophia can barely meet her sister's gaze. She shrugs. 'We never meant it to happen. It just did.'

'That's OK, then.' Christina throws her hands in the air and drops them heavily by her sides. She looks from her sister to her husband, unable to decide which one she hates the most at this moment. She points to Michael. 'How did it start?'

His face remains stoic. 'I was going through hell with Jessica James—'

Sophia interrupts. 'He came over one night to chat to Sebastian about it, but he wasn't in, and then—' Sophia stops, unable to bring herself to finish her sordid sentence.

Christina recalls encouraging Michael to go and speak to her brother-in-law. She thought it would be good to get another man's point of view, completely unconnected to the case. Did she unwittingly throw her sister and husband into each other's arms?

'Then what?' Christina screams. 'Say it.'

Lily opens her mouth, a wail of distress forcing the dummy out of her mouth and onto Sophia's chest.

Sophia catches it. She tries to put it back in Lily's mouth, but her daughter's consistent howling won't allow her to.

Michael suddenly covers his ears with his hands, violently shaking his head, as if the noise level has been turned up too loud.

'Can we calm down?' Sophia bounces Lily on her hip, persistently trying to replace the dummy in her mouth.

'You don't even care what this will do to me?' Christina says to her husband, trying to contain her venom.

Pure malice gleams in his bloodshot eyes. 'Like I suppose you didn't give a damn when you ran me over that night and left me for dead?'

SEVENTY-THREE

Dread twists in Christina's stomach. She looks from her sister back to her husband, grateful for the small mercy that her niece is too young to understand what is going on here. 'You knew.' She shakes her head in disbelief. 'All along, you knew.'

'No,' Michael says. 'Not all along.'

'How did you find out?'

'I overheard you and Ted talking about it at Lily's birthday party,' Sophia says. 'How could you have tried to cover it up?'

Christina supresses the urge to slap her sister. And Michael. Only Lily's presence is stopping her. She points a finger at Sophia. 'You?'

'I only told Michael. He's the only other person who knows the truth.'

Christina cries out as the realisation dawns. 'And the blackmail. That was you two as well, wasn't it?'

'We need money to start a new life. I was only taking what was mine,' Michael says.

'What was yours?' she says, incredulous. 'What do you mean, what was yours?'

'I paid out for the conservatory to the house. You're going to get to keep that.'

Christina's loud laugh bellows around the room. 'You paid for the conservatory? You prick.' But deep down, his words are like a knife to her heart. She has been devoted to this man for the past six years. The man she would've done anything for.

Christina rubs her forehead. 'It seems a bit far to go,' she says, addressing them both. 'Was money really that important to you?'

Sophia and Michael exchange a look, answering her question.

Christina sweeps an arm around the room. 'And you've been meeting up here all this time?' She exhales a large breath. 'This is all making sense now.' She points to her sister. 'It was you who visited him that first time at the hospital, wasn't it? Wearing a baseball cap.'

Sophia nods her head and drops it to her chin.

Christina jabs a finger at Michael. 'And this is where you've been coming when you've supposedly been on your Sunday morning bike rides, isn't it?' She turns to her sister. 'While Sebastian was at golf.' She clutches her stomach. 'You disgust me. Both of you. And you were the one who picked him up the night of the accident and dropped him back at the pub, weren't you?'

Her sister slowly nods.

'For fuck's sake, Sophia. You're my sister. My own flesh and blood.'

Sophia can't look at her.

Christina turns to Michael. 'And you. After everything I went through with Adam, how could you?' Her thoughts turn back to earlier. 'And what were you doing here with Anne-Marie today?'

'I've just handed in my notice.'

Christina can't believe what she is hearing. Revelation after sordid revelation, but everything is falling into place. He isn't returning to St Christopher's. And he isn't returning to her.

Lily's wails continue.

Christina stares at her niece and then at Michael, the realisation like a knife tearing through her heart. 'She's yours, isn't she?'

SEVENTY-FOUR

Her world collapses. 'She's yours, isn't she?' she screams again. 'Tell me.'

Michael nods.

Christina glances at her beautiful niece, her anchor in the storms of her life this past year. Lily doesn't deserve a part in this.

Christina crunches over. She can't be sick. Not in front of Lily. She needs time to think. Time to digest the thunderbolt that has struck her life, so she can decide the best way out of the situation. What her sister and her husband have done is beyond comprehension.

And the blackmail. They deserve to go to prison. But by revealing their little enterprise, she would probably end up behind bars as well. What did the DC say? Hit-and-run is a serious business. It would all come out.

She points to Michael while looking at her sister. 'You've really been taken in by him, haven't you? We both have been.'

'Steady on,' Michael snarls.

'He manipulates people. Jessica James, Ellena Masterson, Nina—'

'Stop it,' Michael shouts. He raises a hand, threatening her.

'That's why you were so pissed off with Anne-Marie. She was a woman you couldn't manipulate.'

How come it has taken her so long to see the streak of evil that lives in his eyes?

He strides over to Sophia and kisses Lily's head. 'Take her home while I deal with your sister,' he orders. 'Our baby doesn't need to hear this.'

Her sister's face flushes a deeper red as she suppresses tears.

'Why won't you let her stay?' Christina asks, mockingly. 'Too afraid of her learning the truth about you? That you get your kicks from grooming young girls. Who's Ellena Masterson, Michael?'

'Go!' Michael roars, pushing Sophia past Christina and towards the door. He slams it shut behind them.

Michael's eyes bore into her again. The once gorgeous brown eyes that made his face constantly smile are now full of spite. How could she have fallen for them? Ted always said she had been on the rebound. He stares at her menacingly.

For the first time, alone in his presence, she's truly scared of him. She covertly edges herself nearer the door.

'Conjecture and lies. Nothing was proved, and you know it. All your bitterness won't get you anywhere. She was just another silly teenager. Besides, they were young women, not girls.'

Christina eyes Michael with disdain. 'You encouraged them. I've spoken to Ellena's mother. I've found out the truth, Michael. The photograph of Ellena. The poem from Jessica.' She quotes the first two lines of the poem with sarcasm. '*All that I have I bestow on you. The very fibre of my being is yours.*'

'Jessica didn't write that poem. Sophia did.'

Her sister? How could she? She processes this current revelation. It makes sense. That poem was dated the Christmas before last. Shortly after Lily was born.

'You destroy lives, you sick bastard.'

'Conjecture and lies,' he repeats. 'Nothing was proved with any of them, and you know it.'

'Any of them? So there's more?'

He greets her words with silence.

'I loved you.'

'No! You loved your precious children. Me. I was just a guest in your house who was constantly compared to Adam.'

Christina can't believe what she is hearing. Ever since the accident, she has harboured so much shame for what she did. And every time she pushed him for answers, and disbelieved him, she has been riddled with guilt. Even though deep down, she knew something was amiss. She balls her fists, anger gnawing through her veins. 'That's so unfair. Don't you dare make this about me.'

'All your bitterness won't get you anywhere,' Michael spits.

'Enough!' Christina screams as she launches herself towards him.

Ducking, he instinctively grabs a cricket bat leaning against the wall.

He swings it viciously.

And makes contact with her head with a sickening thud.

SEVENTY-FIVE

When Christina regains consciousness, she is lying in the foetal position on the sofa.

A pounding rhythm beats through her skull, jabbing her sharply behind the eyes. Disorientated, she moves her head, trying to work out where she is. She grabs the edge of the seat, struggling to sit up. Every motion exacerbates the agony.

Wetness has matted her hair. She touches the moist curls stuck to the side of her face and looks in horror at her blood red fingers.

'Lovely bit of willow.' Michael swings the cricket bat. He brandishes it in front of her face. 'Gunn and Moore – good make as well. Have you any idea how much these cost?'

'What are you doing?' Christina says, her voice faint. She needs to get out of here. She tries to stand up. But she can't feel her legs.

He throws the bat at her feet. It catches her toe.

She winces, withdrawing her foot.

Kneeling, he wrenches up a floorboard.

'What are you doing?' Christina repeats, her voice shaking.

'Time for you to disappear. Like you tried to make me

disappear by running me over. What were you thinking, Christina? Murder me and take my life insurance?'

He's insane. 'No! Michael. It wasn't like that. I honestly thought I'd run over an animal.'

He laughs maniacally, his face twisted like the devil. 'An animal. I've heard it all.'

She has never felt such fear in her life. She should never have come here. Not alone anyway.

'You know, you really should've done a better job of killing me when you had the chance.' He stops and holds his head. He sways momentarily before shaking it and continuing. 'Did you know this place is finally being demolished next week? Spectacular timing, don't you think? You're going to go under the floorboards. A keepsake for the school.'

She grabs the side of the sofa again, trying to haul herself up. 'You really don't think you'll get away with this, do you?'

'Oh, come on, Christina, not that old spiel. You can do better than that.'

'You're not thinking this through, Michael.'

'Oh, I have.'

Raw panic races through her. Her voice trembles. 'What about the one hundred thousand pounds? You won't be getting that now.'

'I'll get the house, though. It's in our wills. Remember. What's mine is yours, and what's yours is mine.' He cackles again. 'All mine. Don't worry. We won't chuck the kids out. They'll be happy. They'll get to live with their cousin.'

The guy is deranged.

He's going to kill her.

She can't die here. Abi and Ben's faces flash through her mind. She can't leave her kids. Summoning all her strength, for a second time, Christina attempts to stand. She unsteadily rises to her feet, frozen in place.

Michael steps over to her, a nefarious smile curling on his lips. Laughing, he nudges her shoulder.

Her frail body provides little resistance, collapsing like a ragdoll back on the sofa.

He picks up the cricket bat and raises it above his head.

She screams as she feels herself blacking out again.

He really intends to kill her.

SEVENTY-SIX

Christina stirs as Sophia barges into the room, holding Lily's face into her chest. She doesn't know how long she has been out for.

'Enough, Michael,' Sophia screams.

'Enough?' Michael laughs. 'She tried to kill me.'

'I didn't. What happened that night, Michael, was an accident. And you damn well know it.' Christina's voice is weak with fear. She's lightheaded. It must be concussion. Did he hit her again? She doesn't know. She's confused.

She tentatively places her hand to the wound on her head, willing herself to keep calm. She needs to get through to Sophia, plead with her sister's better nature. It's her only chance of surviving this ordeal.

Blood is far thicker than water. Isn't it?

Christina shuffles her bottom to the edge of the cushion. With all her strength, she leans forward and heaves her body to stand once more. She's unsteady, but succeeding, she faces her sister. 'Don't let him do this to me, Sophia,' she slurs, willing herself to keep strong. 'You don't want this on your conscience.

He's evil. Pure evil. He has manipulated us all. Me, you, Jessica, Ellena, and who knows how many others.'

'I told you to go,' Michael says to Sophia, agitated. His movements are dystonic, lacking control. He struggles to hold the bat above his head. Is this what happens to the insane?

'The blackmail was one thing, Michael,' Sophia says firmly. 'But this is utter madness. Let her go.'

His speech is slurred. 'No. She tried to kill me. She needs to pay.' He cries out as if he is in pain. Swaying, he clutches his head. The cricket bat drops to his side, but he still manages to hold it in one hand.

'Sit down, Michael,' Sophia says. 'You're not well, darling.'

'No!' He attempts to lift the cricket bat again. He stumbles, dropping his weapon. It thuds on the floor.

The door bursts open.

Then everything happens so quickly.

Ted rushes into the room, gasping for breath. How did he know they were here? Sophia must have called him. 'What the hell is going on?' Ted asks, staring directly at Christina.

'Our sister has been having an affair with my husband.' She stumbles over her words. 'And guess what? They are the blackmailers.'

Ted looks around, computing the situation. As the full, horrible, realisation takes hold, he makes for Michael. 'You bastard!' He draws back his heavy, muscular arm like a boxer in a fighting ring, aiming for Michael's jaw.

But Michael stumbles to the side before Ted can land a blow.

Michael's expression is blank. He has turned remarkably pale, as white as the ghostly glow of the floor lamp.

Ted drops his arm as Michael's lifeless form falls forward, faceplanting on the wooden floor.

Lily's sharp shrieks pierce the air.

The three siblings stare at each other in horror.

Sophia lets out a gut-wrenching moan. She closes her eyes tightly, cradling Lily's head, wailing like her daughter.

Ted kneels beside Michael's lifeless form feeling for a pulse.

'What the hell!' Christina cries.

'Please tell me he's going to be OK,' Sophia sobs.

A moment's silence passes before Ted announces, 'He's gone.'

'No. No, no…' Sophia screams. She drops to the floor beside her brother, still cradling her child in her arms.

SEVENTY-SEVEN

'We need to call for an ambulance,' Christina says. The enormity of the situation hits her as hard as that cricket bat did earlier.

Michael is dead.

Did she kill her husband?

Of course she didn't.

But then, indirectly, yes, she can't help thinking she did. If she hadn't run him over that night, he would never have ended up with the injuries. The injuries that surely led to him dropping down dead. How else could they explain this when Ted didn't even touch him?

'And the police,' Sophia sobs. 'We need to call the police.'

'No. Wait,' Ted says. 'We need to think about this.'

'What's there to think about?' Sophia screams. The sound is deafening. 'Look at him.'

'If we call the police, it will all have to come out. Everything. Think about it. We'd all be done for.'

Ted's voice of reason renders his sisters mute. He points at them both. 'If we call the police, they'll get out of us exactly what has happened.' He jabs a finger at Sophia. 'You know you'll have to own up to having an affair with Michael and blackmailing your sister under that pressure.' He points at Christina, his voice softening. 'And you'll end up confessing to the accident and driving off. And you know what that'll mean for both of you?'

Sophia and Christina look at him in horror. Christina knows neither of them would last under questioning. She has been fraying under the pressure of keeping the accident a secret already. This would tip her over the edge.

Ted continues. 'You could get convicted for attempted murder, Chrissy. They'll conclude you tried to run him over because he was having an affair with your sister.'

'But I've only just found out about the affair.'

'They'll still try to pin it on you.'

'I'd get a life sentence,' Christina says, stunned.

Ted points a finger at Sophia. 'And you'll go to prison for extortion. And let me tell you, you won't get off lightly, either.'

After a pause, Ted stands up and continues. 'Think of your kids, both of you. This will destroy our family.'

Christina would argue the family has already been destroyed. The hate she has for her sister at this moment is beyond anything she has ever felt. But her brother is right. She can't go to prison. And however much anger she holds for her sister, she doesn't want to see her suffer. She has done something unspeakable, but Michael fooled them all. 'So what do you suggest we do?' Christina asks, her voice shaking.

Ted takes a deep breath and loudly puffs it out. He eyes his two sisters. 'We take him home and say he collapsed and died there.' He places his hands on his hips. 'I don't want to lose my sisters.' He gives Christina the look. She knows exactly what he is thinking. At this moment, he doesn't care about Sophia, but he'd defend Christina to the end.

'If that's our decision, we need to be quick.' She is shaking so much, Sophia can hardly get her words out. 'Rigor mortis will soon set in. What about this place?'

Christina can't stop the waves of shock convulsing through her. 'Michael told me it's being destroyed next week.'

'Right! You both go home,' Ted says. 'I'll clear up here. I'll take him to his car and drive him back to your house.'

'You can't do that. The kids are at home.' This is crazy. Christina bites her knuckle, distracting the pain in her head from the whack of the cricket bat earlier. 'It won't work. I'm meant to be out getting them food.'

Ted hesitates. 'We have to make it work. All three of us need to act as we usually would.' He looks at Christina. 'Are you OK to drive?'

She nods. Her head is clearing. She knows she needs to keep strong here for her children.

'You go and clean yourself up and sort the kids,' Ted says. 'Eat with them as normal.'

'Are you kidding me?' Christina says. 'We can't drag them into this mess.'

'They'll disappear to their rooms. They always do. Text me, and I'll bring him back in his car. We'll put him in his bed in the lounge. You tell the kids he has come home complaining of a massive headache and gone straight to bed. You find him tomorrow morning and call it in.'

The three siblings stare at each other.

All Christina can think about is Abi and Ben.

'Are we all up for it?' Ted asks.

Christina stares at Michael's body. 'What's the alternative?'

'There isn't one.' Sophia kisses the top of Lily's soft hair. 'Let's just do it.'

It's true.

Blood *is* thicker than water.

SEVENTY-EIGHT

Christina walks away from the old ramshackle cricket pavilion. She doesn't look back. She can't.

Sophia is trundling behind her. 'Christina, wait.'

She ignores her sister, unable to bring herself to even acknowledge the woman who has betrayed her. If she thought the pain she felt after Adam cheated was bad, she was truly mistaken.

'Christina! Listen to me.'

Retracing her steps along the path to her car, Christina stares blankly at the ground. Although her head is pounding, there's also a numbness in her body she can't explain. Is she in shock? She'll need to clean the wound on her head before she gets home. And she needs to get the kids' dinner. She scrunches up her eyes. They will be wondering where she is.

Climbing into her Range Rover, Christina presses the ignition button before turning the heater to the highest setting. She releases a heavy sigh and takes a moment to collect herself. She is shivering uncontrollably.

How could you, Sophia?

Christina thinks back to all the times she has been there for her sister throughout her life. She has so many questions she wants to ask her. But for now, her focus is her kids, and doing what's needed to get them all out of this dire situation.

Her phone chimes in its cradle on the dashboard, alerting her to five missed calls from Abi.

With trembling hands, she locates her daughter's number, trying to regulate her breathing before pressing the call button.

'Where're you, Mum? We're worried sick here.'

'Sorry, I've got held up. The deep fat fryer broke down and I've had to wait. The queue's dreadful,' she lies.

'How long are you going to be? I'm starving.'

Christina winces as she accidentally brushes her hand against the wound from the cricket bat. 'I'll be there as soon as I can.'

'You OK, Mum? You sound... I don't know... odd.'

Christina swallows the tight knot of anguish in her throat. 'I'm absolutely fine.'

'OK. Love you. Hurry up home.'

'Love you, too, darling.'

Tears well in Christina's eyes as she ends the call. She gives herself a talking to. No tears. Not yet. They can come later.

She reaches for a bottle of water and dribbles some of the liquid onto a tissue she finds in her coat pocket. Her head is pounding. Pressing the tissue onto the wound, she waits for the whopper of a headache that is on its way. Checking in the mirror, she presses again, repeating the process until not a trace of blood remains. She tidies her hair and drinks the rest of the water in the bottle. Only then does she put the car into drive and pull away.

She doesn't know how she makes it into the fish and chip shop. She remains remarkably calm. It's as if she has been transported into another world, and she is drugged, watching her life unfold from afar.

A young girl with long dark hair is serving a mum and her

son arguing about what they are going to watch on the telly tonight. She reminds Christina of Jessica James. Now that she has found out about Michael's true character, she wonders even more what really happened with Jessica. Will she ever find out? Perhaps it's better she doesn't.

After collecting her order for three portions of cod and chips, she makes her way home, contemplating anything and everything that could go wrong with Ted's plan. The absurdity of transporting a body across town and putting it to bed in the lounge going unnoticed is pushing the realms of plausibility. But what is the alternative?

Pulling into the drive, Christina steels herself for the evening ahead.

It's do or die. Stay calm. Act normally. Convince the children nothing is wrong.

She falls at the first hurdle.

'Bloody hell, Mum, what've you done?' Ben almost shouts as he opens the front door. 'There's wine all over your coat.' He frowns at her. 'You looked spaced out. What's happened?'

She must be suffering more from the whack of the cricket bat than she thought. 'Oh, I hit my head on the car door. It's nothing, really.' Even now it's all over, the lies keep coming.

Wilf takes more interest in her than usual. Does he sense his mistress is not entirely with it or is he more interested in the smell of the supper she is carrying in a brown paper bag?

The kids set the table, engrossed in a debate about climate change. Christina lets them argue while she tries to control her breaths wanting to come thick and fast. 'Excuse me a minute,' she says and hurries to the lounge where she takes a large swig of Michael's bourbon, and then another.

She can think of nothing more nauseating than having to eat as if nothing has happened – as if her husband never fathered her sister's daughter, groomed however many girls for his own pleasure and is now dead – but she must. She has to remain calm. It's the only way she's going to get through this.

She shuffles a handful of her chips to each of the kids and clandestinely feeds some to Wilf. She just about manages to get through half a portion of the fish. The grease heightens her nausea, but Ted's words drum in her ears. She has to keep things normal.

'When is Michael getting home?' Abi asks when she has finished eating.

'He's not due until later. We'll probably be tucked up in bed by then. Why don't you two go and finish your homework, and I'll clear up here?'

Abi gets up and takes her plate to the dishwasher before leaving the room.

Ben remains in the kitchen, hovering. Something is on his mind. Does he suspect she is lying... about Michael? About the blood on her coat? About there being nothing wrong? About her life being a sham? He drums his fingers on the worktop.

'Is everything all right?' she asks.

He hesitates. He looks so grown up, yet so innocent. She so wishes they could go back in time to when the kids were small. She never realised it at the time, with all of Abi's cancer treatments, but life was so much simpler. 'What?' she asks.

'There's something I have to tell you.'

What now? No more revelations, please, Ben. She really hasn't got time for his drama right now. Ted will be here soon.

'See, the thing is. I kind of had an accident...'

SEVENTY-NINE

A fresh wave of fear rears up within her. Christina grabs the kitchen counter.

'That night you thought I'd gone to London. I came back here as I'd bought something for Maisy and forgot it. On the way up Bridge End, I lost control of the car. No harm was done, but it could've been catastrophic. It really shook me up.'

Where is this leading? 'And? What's the problem?'

'I feel I need to mention it to you.'

'OK.' She is guarded. What's coming next?

'Because it was you I nearly ran off the road.' He holds up his hands, palms facing her. 'Please don't be mad, Mum. I promise it'll never happen again. I was fiddling with my phone and took my eye off the road. When I saw it was you, it totally freaked me out. I learnt my lesson. I won't be so stupid again.'

She had thought someone was trying to kill her. She wants to rant and rave at him. She went through hell that night. But she hasn't got the energy, or the time, for an argument. Not now. Her head is pounding. Keep calm, Chrissy. Just stay focused. 'I remember. Why are you telling me now?'

Ben shrugs. 'I felt so bad about what I did to you.'

She nods. 'As long as you've truly taken something from the incident, we'll leave it there. Now go and get on with your homework.'

He looks at her stunned, scooting away before she can say another word.

When she hears his bedroom door close, she calmly picks up her phone. 'Ted. It's me. They're both in their rooms doing their homework. You can come now.'

EIGHTY

THREE WEEKS LATER

Ted leads her to the kitchen. He takes control and pours two large gins. 'I'm sure as hell glad that's over.' They have just returned from discussing, among other things, the last-minute funeral arrangements with Sophia and Sebastian.

Christina stands by the sink and gulps a mouthful of her drink. 'I still can't get over it.'

'Get over what?'

Her voice falters. 'Whichever way you look at it. I'm responsible for his death. I killed him, Ted. And I'll have to live with that for the rest of my life.' The tremendous guilt that has become part of her morning make-up stings her eyes. The daily reminder that she killed her husband. It's all her fault.

Ted holds up the palm of his hand. 'Stop right there. No you didn't.'

Christina glares at the door. 'Shh. The kids will hear you.'

He lowers his voice. 'I will not hear you say that again. Michael died of a brain haemorrhage. That's what the coroner's report said.'

'Caused by me running him over.'

'Possibly, but it wasn't conclusive. That's what they said. So, indirectly, potentially, yes, but it was an accident. As simple as. Anyway, if he'd taken better care of himself – gone back to hospital when he was suffering those headaches and rested more – it wouldn't have happened. Good riddance is all I can say. The world doesn't need people like him. No one will ever find out what you did. It's time to move on. Your secret is safe with me.'

'What about Sophia? Do you truly think she'll be able to live with what she did?'

'If she exposes you, she exposes herself. I researched it, didn't I? Blackmail is a serious crime. She doesn't want to go to prison any more than you do. She saw what Michael did to you that day. And she knows she's had a narrow escape by him dying. She's lucky she's got Lily, otherwise neither of us would have anything more to do with her.'

'What about the police?'

'What about them? It's over, Chrissy. If they suspected anything, they'd have arrested you, or at least have you down the station for questioning.'

'It still scares me they'll find something out that puts me under the spotlight. And that they'll investigate where he went that Saturday night he spent with Sophia when he was supposedly up north with his friends.'

Ted shrugs. 'Why would they? If they do, they can't tie him to the cricket pavilion. It's gone. All the evidence was demolished. Chill out. Anyway, why would they investigate that now? If they'd suspected foul play, they would've looked into it at the time.'

He places his drink on the side and grabs hold of her shoulders. 'It's over, Chrissy. You heard DS Macintosh. How sorry he was that he was being moved on to another case. That he wouldn't have the opportunity to catch the perpetrator for you. We dodged an almighty bullet there!'

'We sure did. I had a terrible feeling he was on to me.'

He grips her shoulders harder. 'Yes, but now it's over, and it's time for you to move on. That other detective they sent didn't have a clue. Or rather didn't seem overly interested. Box-ticking exercise, that's all he treated it as.'

'They're all too busy,' Christina says, trying to convince herself. 'Overstretched.'

'Michael's dead. They've got much more important cases to focus on.'

His phone buzzes. Letting her shoulders go, he picks it up and glances at the screen, grinning.

'Don't tell me... Mel?' Christina says.

'How do you know?'

'I can tell by your smile. Pick it up. I don't mind.'

Christina wanders over to the window while Ted answers the call. Dusk is on the horizon, but that doesn't obscure the sight that stops her cold. It's the black puffa jacket she notices first. The black attire of Jessica James standing by the post box.

'What the hell is she doing here?'

EIGHTY-ONE

Christina walks into the hallway and purposefully yanks open the front door.

Dashing outside, she strides along the drive towards the ghostly apparition. Drizzly rain mists the air and frizzes her hair. Her heart beats a disjointed rhythm, echoing the thoughts whizzing through her head as she closes the distance between her and the young woman. Christina despised her for so long but soon realised, after speaking to Polly Masterson, that Jessica was just another victim in her late husband's sordid little world.

After Michael's death, she considered reporting what happened at Hillywood School to Anne-Marie. Call her late husband out for his sordid actions. And she wanted to confront Jessica. Tell her she was sorry. But Ted told her both of these actions would do Christina no favours. Confessing to knowing what happened would only raise suspicion around his death.

Christina and Jessica stand face to face. Two wronged women, a body length apart.

Even in the dim light, Jessica looks deathly white, a stark contrast to the darkness of her clothing. Stains of recent tears mark her cheeks. She's wearing a black beanie. So much black, so much darkness around this young woman. But there's something different about her. Her appearance unnerves Christina. What if she is wrong about her? What if she has a weapon? A knife she is concealing beneath the layers of her dark clothing. What if she's carrying a gun?

Christina berates herself for being so paranoid.

'I want to tell you what really happened with Michael,' Jessica says. 'Now that I'm free of him, I think you deserve to know the truth.'

Christina stands numb. She can't quite process seeing Jessica on her driveway. The ghost of her husband creeps out from the dark cavities of her mind.

'I know you think it did, but nothing happened between us. Nothing physical, anyway. He just made me fall in love with him.'

'Why? To what end?'

'He said we would be together when I left school.'

Christina wants to be sick. Sophia and Polly Masterson's words ring like an alarm bell. Michael made Sophia and Ellena, and however many others, fall in love with him. 'Why did you say something did happen when you spoke to your friend?'

'Because I was fantasising. She stepped in and made me wake up.' Jessica's teeth chatter. 'Then he threatened me.'

'What?' Christina asks. 'How?'

Still, after all this time, so many questions.

'He turned evil. Real nasty. He told me that if I didn't deny it, he would start on my sister. He'd make her fall for him. Said he would have all sorts of fun with her. It was disgusting.'

Christina is dumbstruck. Never before did she think she would be standing a breath apart from this young woman, united in their feeling for that despicable man.

'Then he started on another girl. He's so sly, though.'

'Who?'

'Nina Silver.'

Christina wants to throw up. 'I met her at parents' evening.'

'I can't tell you how scared I was of him. You must believe me.'

'I do, Jessica. I do. And I'm truly sorry for what you've been through.' Christina tells her about what happened at Hillywood School with Ellena Masterson.

A look of disgust blankets the young woman's face. 'I know it's a terrible thing to say, but I'm glad he's dead. Now he can't hurt anyone else.'

'Did you ever go and see Michael when he was in hospital?' Christina asks.

Jessica shakes her head. 'No! Why would I have? I hate him.'

'I saw you there one night.'

'That must've been when I was visiting my nan. She broke her hip.'

That makes sense.

'What now, Jessica? What do you want me to do with all this information?' The ramifications of what a full-scale investigation would bring are frightening.

'Nothing,' she says with conviction. Jessica removes her beanie hat and wipes her eyes with the back of her hand 'The whole episode nearly destroyed me, and my parents. My father was so ill after it all happened. What good would it do to bring it all up again? For them, for me, for you. I just want to put it all behind me and move on with my life. He's dead. Good riddance.' She turns to leave.

Christina can't let her walk home along the country roads in the dark. It's too dangerous. She should know. She doesn't want another death on her conscience. 'You can't walk home. I'll drive you.'

'I'm fine. I have my car parked outside the drive. I wasn't sure whether to come in or not. Goodbye, Christina. Take care of yourself.'

Christina watches her leave before heading inside.

Ted is standing at the front door. 'What the hell?' he says, confused.

Christina ushers him inside and closes the door.

'What was all that about?'

'I think we need another drink.' She guides her brother to the kitchen where she necks the remainder of her gin and hands him the glass. 'Make it a large one.'

Ted does as he is ordered as she pours out what Jessica has just told her.

He is silent, digesting the latest revelation about her husband. 'Just bide your time, Chrissy. Keep portraying the grieving widow, traumatised by finding your husband dead in his bed. And all this will pass.'

Will it? Perhaps. But the burden of guilt will never leave her.

He raises his glass. 'To a new start. Just keep away from men.'

She manages a brief laugh. 'Adam kicked my confidence. Michael saw an opportunity when he met me. But don't worry. I've learnt my lesson. When the time comes, you'll be putting me in my coffin a single woman.'

'That's my girl.'

She raises her glass. 'Cheers.'

'Cheers,' he says, clinking his glass against hers. 'Let the truth be buried in the bones of silence.'

EIGHTY-TWO

After the funeral service, Ted drives Christina and the kids to The Black Horse pub.

Paddy and Birdie have arranged a selection of sandwiches, sausage rolls and bowls of crisps, along with cakes and fruit skewers, on a long table in the far corner of the bar area.

For the sake of normality, Sophia drops in. Nancy is with her, but Sebastian has another funeral to attend to. Sophia's face is long and drawn. They are talking to Anne-Marie.

'Drink?' Paddy asks after he has conveyed his condolences.

'A large glass of white, please,' Christina says.

'You look shot,' Ted says after placing his order for a pint of shandy. He always has been able to read her like a book.

'I am,' Christina says. 'I'll be glad when today is over.'

She can't wait for tomorrow. Now that she has buried Michael, she can put all this mess behind her and move on with her life.

Ted nods towards Abi and Ben hunched over their phones. 'It's been a tough time for all of you.'

Christina turns to her children. 'Put them away,' she scolds. 'Respect. What do you want to drink?'

They both order Cokes and tuck their phones in their coat pockets.

Christina is having a quiet moment, standing at a small window by the food table, staring onto the open fields, when Sophia approaches her. She hasn't seen much of her sister in the past few weeks, other than to sort out the funeral arrangements and to discuss the situation with Ted.

'I'm so sorry,' her sister whispers.

Christina doesn't turn around.

'He made me fall in love with him.' Sophia clears her throat before continuing. Her voice is heavy with emotion. 'I knew it was wrong, but I couldn't control it.'

Christina thinks back to the days when she first met Michael, and she had felt like a love-struck teenager again. 'You know, it came back to me last night. I remember you at Lily's birthday party. You were challenging everything I was saying, and I believed you – trusted you – so much.'

'I was trying to deflect the situation from me.'

'And when did you get the opportunity to deliver that second blackmail note on Christmas Day?'

'When you guys were in the snug watching that film.'

Christina shivers. 'That took some guts.'

'I hate myself for what I've done. Really hate myself and—'

Footsteps silence her sister.

Nancy appears. 'We need to get going in case the traffic is bad.'

'I'll be with you in a second.' Sophia pauses, waiting for her mother-in-law to go away before continuing, telling Christina she regrets the choices she has made every day.

But she doesn't regret Lily. None of them can regret baby Lily.

Christina continues looking out of the window, swallowing the tears she can't allow her sister to see.

'We really need to get going,' Nancy calls.

Sophia places a hand on Christina's shoulder. 'I love you very much, Chrissy. I hope you can find it in yourself to forgive me one day.'

Forgive?

She can't reveal what Sophia has done. Christina will hold that part of their truce. She will do everything she has to, to keep her part in all of this from her children, Lily and the police.

But to forgive her sister?

How could that ever happen?

A LETTER FROM AJ CAMPBELL

Dear reader,

I want to say a huge thank you for choosing to read *Did I Kill My Husband?* If you enjoyed it and want to keep up to date with my latest releases, just sign up at the link below. Your email address will never be shared, and you can unsubscribe anytime.

www.bookouture.com/AJ-Campbell

As for all authors, reviews are the key to raising awareness of my work. If you have enjoyed this book, I would be very grateful if you could leave a short review on Amazon, Goodreads and any other reviewing platform you are on. I'd love to hear what you think, and it makes such a difference in helping new readers discover one of my books for the first time.

The question I most often get asked as an author is where I get the ideas for my books from. *Did I Kill My Husband?* began when I read an article about a hit-and-run in our local area. It made me question what could make someone do this. Can they ever be forgiven? From there, I started plotting. I hope you enjoy Christina's story as much as I loved writing it.

All my novels undergo a rigorous editing process, but sometimes mistakes go undetected. If you have spotted an error, please contact me so I can promptly correct it.

I love hearing from my readers – you can get in touch on my Facebook page, Instagram or via my website.

Best wishes,

Amanda X

www.ajcampbellauthor.com

 facebook.com/AJCampbellauthor

 instagram.com/ajcampbellauthor

② ACKNOWLEDGEMENTS

I'm thrilled to be part of the Bookouture team for the publication of *Did I Kill My Husband?* my eighth novel.

Huge thanks to my astute editor, Natalie Edwards, for her vision for this book. Your input has been excellent! It's been such a pleasure to work with you again. And thank you to team Bookouture for everything you've done to help get the finished product into the hands of readers. You are a top team to work with.

To my brilliant beta readers – Mr C, Dawn H, Christine H, Maddie S, John B, Collie L and my sister Sally – thank you for your help structuring this story. Your critique during the early stages is invaluable, helping me to develop the characters and the plot. I always value your opinions. I'm blessed to have you so close by my side.

Thank you to my ARC team and all the book bloggers and media folk who are always in my corner, supporting me and shouting out my books. There are too many of you to mention individually, but please know how much I appreciate your endless support. And Christine Henderson, a special mention for your friendship and your unwavering support.

To my readers. Thanks a million. Writing is a lonely pursuit, but your emails and comments on my social media pages keep me entertained and always make my day. Without you, I couldn't carry on writing.

To my three sons, you make me so proud every day. And

last but always first, thank you, Mr C, for everything: being a brilliant husband, beta reader, pre-ARC reader, accountant, tea maker and excellent chef and for your endless encouragement to keep writing.

PUBLISHING TEAM

Turning a manuscript into a book requires the efforts of many people. The publishing team at Bookouture would like to acknowledge everyone who contributed to this publication.

Audio
Alba Proko
Sinead O'Connor
Melissa Tran

Commercial
Lauren Morrissette
Hannah Richmond
Imogen Allport

Data and analysis
Mark Alder
Mohamed Bussuri

Editorial
Natalie Edwards
Sinead O'Connor

Copyeditor
Deborah Blake

Proofreader
Becca Allen

Marketing
Alex Crow
Melanie Price
Occy Carr
Cíara Rosney
Martyna Młynarska

Operations and distribution
Marina Valles
Stephanie Straub

Production
Hannah Snetsinger
Mandy Kullar
Jen Shannon

Publicity
Kim Nash
Noelle Holten
Jess Readett
Sarah Hardy

Rights and contracts
Peta Nightingale
Richard King
Saidah Graham

Printed in Great Britain
by Amazon

56244933R00192